Outcast

Sakthika Vijay

PUBLISHED BY

SIGMA'S
BOOKSHELF

MINNETONKA, MN 55305
WWW.SIGMASBOOKSHELF.COM

Outcast by Sakthika Vijay

Copyright © 2020 by Sigma's Bookshelf.

Cover design contains public domain imagery from Pixabay.com.

Printed in the United States of America

First Printing 2020

ISBN 978-0-9996577-6-8

Acknowledgments

I want to thank every single reader who gave Mohana a chance (and kudos to you for reading this section that no one remembers). To Namitha Binu, Rhianna Nakrani, Pratistha Praveen Kumar, and Aysa Tarana for being the first readers of Outcast and critiquing it through all of the comma splices and typos.

To my other friends: Gracee Patel, Yashasvi Singh, Nithya Malsetti, and countless more who've encouraged me through every difficult step and dealt with my stressed self during publication. I am ever so grateful for the endless support, praise, and food (maybe the most important) that kept me going.

To my live-in cheerleaders my parents and especially my little sister, Shakana Vijay, who gave me some of the most important ideas for the novel. if you ever write a book, I can guarantee it would be the saddest, most tragic, sobbing-at-four-a.m. story that I'd have ever read. So thank the heavens that you're too restless to write because the world couldn't have handled any of your ideas.

To the wonderful team with Sigma's Bookshelf for being ever-so patient with me and helping me through all the steps.

Most certainly, Lakshmi Aunty: My guru and my music teacher. Without you, the novel would have lost so much of its color. Thank you for teaching me, even through the hours and hours of mistakes and tears.

So, thank you, thank you, and thank you to all of these wonderful people. Without you guys, Outcast would have been hidden away in a remote part of my laptop forever.

Prologue

The Bayend Stadium was the oldest and mustiest facility in town. However, its faded, diminished, crumbling infrastructure had something no other stage I'd ever been on had. It contained about a century and a half's worth of talent, sweat, and tears infused into its worn, wooden boards. Making it to this stage had been a goal for hundreds of entertainers myself included. It was a place of opportunities, especially for me.

"I swear, one day you're gonna become competition to me. I'm gonna have to take you down!" A muscular pair of arms wrapped themselves around my waist. The man set his sharp chin on my shoulder, and stared at my reflection in the stage mirror with those deep, cool eyes of his. I set my lipstick down by my ziplock of sugar cubes and emergency inhaler.

"Take me down? Try me." I gently pushed him away and grabbed my guitar, my best friend that had stayed with me the entire journey.

"One day you're gonna love that guitar more than you love me. I call it."

"Oh, don't be serious," I grinned back at him. "From the day I met you, you've always been second to the guitar."

"Miss Prasad? It's time." The stage manager knocked against the door of my dressing room.

"I'll see you on stage. Break a leg!" He gave me one of those quick kisses that drove me mad.

"Same to you."

We parted. He left for the spot on the stage he was supposed to enter from. I left for the staircase that led to the dead center of the stage. As I neared it, I heard them. My audience, my fans, the people that I'd dreamed about since the second grade.

The people that I'd worked for the past two years; the people who meant the world to me.

Someone tapped me on the shoulder. I turned to face a short man with a headset. My manager.

"All ready?" he asked, but didn't even bother waiting for a reply. He muttered into his walkie-talkie, checking and rechecking. When he was finally satisfied, he gave me a nod and a thumbs up. I nodded back and took a deep breath, a breath that reminded me of the past, of another incident.

Faces, so many blank faces. Confusion and grief mixing into a horrible substance in my stomach. But I couldn't fall, I had to stay strong.

I'd avoided this stadium for a long time because I couldn't bring myself to face the memory again. The tears, confusion, and horror of the last time I'd performed on these very boards. The stadium was a reminder of what my new life had brought and of what I'd lost. Another cheer distracted me from my thoughts.

True, I'd lost many things, but I'd gained one important thing. A thing most people can never find in their life and finish their life void of.

I'd found my purpose.

The time of mourning was past, and with another breath I stepped out into the bright light to play at my first ever concert.

Chapter 1

Oh trust me, I love the spotlight. Maybe it was because I was brought up being hidden, unknown, and always thrust into the corner that did it, that gave me a longing for the stage. I'd been singing in front of an audience since I was seven. Solos, duets, and one weird quartet with a bassoon player (a long story for another time). That was, until my trusted partner, Jamie West, famed pop star and youngest millionaire of the century, became not-so trusted.

But there were some situations involving spotlights that I liked to avoid. Like the floor in the middle of the high school cafeteria with Sage Khand's lunch all over me. The one good thing about that situation was that all the marinara sauce obscured my vision so I could only hear the cackles and not see them.

"Oh, my!" I heard a giggle right above me. "I'm so sorry, you'll have to excuse me. It's just whenever I'm with Johnny I-I don't know what I'm doing."

Classic.

Spills her pasta all over me and then talks about how she was with my three-year crush.

You just gotta love Sage.

"He's just amazing. He's already on his way to get a few tissues." *Wait what?* I quickly tried to rise but to my dismay, slipped and fell again thanks to all the marinara sauce on the ground. It was too late anyway.

"Uhm, here," a deep voice muttered right next to Sage.

"Th-Thank you," I whispered and blindly reached out for the tissues. After a few swipes, I found his hand and grabbed the tissues. Now that I could see, I cautiously rose.

"Thank you, Johnny." I couldn't bring myself to look him in the face so I addressed his basketball shoes.

"'Course! I couldn't just leave you there—I need answers in English." Even though I didn't look up to see it, I knew there was a grin on that happy face of his.

Johnny I. Taylor wasn't all that good looking, I'll admit it without a second thought. And everyone around knew it too, yet every single girl had a crush on him including Sage. Why? I didn't know. In fact no one knew. His face, his eyes, just had a quality about them that instantly made you smile. In every single line of that face, there was happiness etched in. A happiness that chased away your troubles, a happiness that made you feel warm inside, and a happiness that I've fallen in love with. As he was led away by Sage, the devil in pink, I reminded myself of the crucial fact. The one thing that kept me from throwing her out a window. As long as Johnny stayed happy, I was happy too.

"Man, she's such a coconut. Sage? Please, hon, your name's Sanjana," a harsh voice sounded behind me. The nickname, as usual, made me giggle. A coconut: brown outside but white inside.

"Nice timing. Where were you guys when I was slobbering around in pasta?" I turned around and addressed my friends.

"What? And ruin a perfect brewing romance? I don't think so," Shaina nudged me, as everyone else just looked at me, waiting for me to blush red as always. Lucky for me, I was still plenty covered in marinara. None of them could tell if I was blushing, which I'm sure I was.

"And we should get you clean. Your Mom might think you were involved in some gory bus accident," Neela added with her customary smile and guided me to the bathroom where I washed my face.

"You got that on video right?" I looked up to see Kalyani bring out Shruthi's phone. Shruthi snorted.

"Of course! This is how we all become famous!"

"You're not even in the video," I interrupted, wiping marinara off my leggings to the best of my ability.

"No, but we're utilizing you. So let's make a pact. If one bitch gets famous and makes money, then she's taking all us bitches with her!" Shruthi ordered in her usual mother voice. Since she was deemed grandma of the group and kept us all alive, we had to comply with her. We all cheered, but my phone buzzed disturbing us.

"I swear you've been getting way too many suiters lately." Shaina tilted her head questioningly. "Johnny not enough for you anymore?"

"Yeah right, my hot popstar boyfriend Peter Raul's on the phone and we're gonna discuss our engagement in Venice," I jokingly winked at them

"Uhm, excuse me? My hubby Peter Raul?" Shruthi started in a dangerous tone. I answered my phone before she beat me up.

"Hello?" I asked even though I already knew who it was.

"It's Wendy, your trendy, trusty agent. Listen, Jamie's managers really liked that new song you wrote for her. You know what this could mean? Promotion!" she told me in a singsong voice. I snorted. *As if they were going to pay me more money.* "Mh-hm," I nodded, aware of my friends.

"So, they want six more songs by the twentieth." I choked, but played it off as a cough since my friends were watching.

"That," I muttered, "is two weeks away. Too quick of a turn around, don't you think?"

"They really want this Mohana! It could seriously boost your career. I also kinda already said yes." I could virtually see her cringe as she waited for my response. The bell rang, interrupting the string of abuse I was about to give her. Lucky her.

"Fine!" I clenched my teeth and said, "I'll do it for you, not for Jamie!"

"Jamie? Jamie West?" *Crud!* I looked up at Neela,

"No, you know I absolutely hate her. This is Jamie Morrison, someone else," I lied quickly. *Whew*, kudos to Jamie Morrison, saving me since five seconds ago when she was first created. We walked out of the bathroom, a few boys walked past and snickered at me.

"Welp, I guess I'm now pasta girl," I said, sighing.

"It'll die away in a bit," Kalyani tried to reassure me. "Besides, it'll all be forgotten once we all get selected for the Madison Honors Program. Did you get your letter yet?" I pretended I couldn't hear her.

The Madison Honors Program for the Scholar was a little summer camp that looked good on college applications. As you might have guessed already, all of my incredibly smart friends had gotten into the program made for incredibly smart kids.

The problem?

I wasn't incredibly smart.

My friends had made me apply, thinking it might make me feel good to apply for something meant for smart Indian kids like what I was supposed to be—what my friends were. But if you hadn't guessed already, I didn't fall into that category so I never did get a letter.

"Okay, I'll see you all later. I can't meet up after school 'cause I have singing lessons." Kalyani grinned.

"Have fun screaming your internal organs out," she said.

Chapter 2

"Sing louder Mohana," Shalini Aunty told me. I sang louder. A few stanzas later she exclaimed, "Nope louder!" I sang even louder, but that wasn't good enough. "Louder!" Angry, I half shouted the lyrics.

When I was done with the song, Shalini Aunty—What adults are respectfully addressed by in India. I don't know why, I guess everyone's family in India?—smiled and said, "Perfect. You need to sing louder, Mohana, so the audience can feel your passion and connect with you. Are you practicing at home?"

"Yes, Aunty," I responded softly. The kind of music I sang, Carnatic, one of the oldest forms of Indian music, was absolutely lovely with layers upon layers waiting to be peeled and revealed. But, there was one important bit of information that's typically not revealed to a student who starts learning it. *It's damn near impossible to learn it without tearing out all your hair.*

"Shreya?" Aunty turned her head and motioned to Shreya, a fellow student. As usual, she was perfect. It made Aunty smile and me frown and exhale sharply.

"Beautiful as usual. Now gather round I have important news." I moved my legs so they were out of their normal criss cross position and brought them near me and rested my chin on my knees. "We have a big competition coming up, the Raga Carnatic." I heard a few sharp intakes of breath around me. I guess the event was important. That means it's something I'm definitely not going to end up participating in.

"Now, I've already chosen the kids who are going to be representing us there. Please don't feel bad if you aren't chosen. I promise there will be many more opportunities to let your voice shine!"

Not if you suck! My mind muttered in disgust. She looked down at her notepad.

"Shreya, you'll be competing in a month with the thirteen to fifteen division. Sri, you're competing in two weeks so we ought to start practicing right away; and last but certainly not least—" I felt everyone around me lean forward, but I stayed back in my seat. Ever since that heart wrenching day two-and-a-half years ago, I have been telling myself the same thing: *Don't expect it, 'cause when you don't get it, it won't hurt as much.* I know it sounds naturalistic and depressing, but that's the truth. The truth that's been hardwired into me ever since that fateful day. "Vani! You're with Shreya in a month as well."

"But Aunty!" someone interrupted. "Vani had that family emergency. She said she wouldn't be back until June."

"Right! Then we need another singer in the thirteen to fifteen division. *No, she didn't just say that, 'cause there was only one other kid like that. But what if the other kid could hardly sing Carnatic to save her life?*

"Mohana." Aunty turned to face me painfully slow. If it was someone else rather than me I would have laughed. "I guess you're-you're up," she muttered softly as if it might get rid of me if no one heard my name,.

"That's great, Aunty."

"It's a lot of work. I want you to be here early every class day, alright?"

"Yes, Aunty."

"Alright, that's the end of today."

I rose slowly off the ground I was sitting on, deep in thought. A solo, something I hadn't done in a while. It was one of those rare days in February where it wasn't blizzarding or twenty degrees below zero in Minnesota, so I decided to walk home. Enjoying the rare fresh air that actually wasn't trying to freeze your face, I set off at a brisk pace.

"Mohana! Wait up!" *Geeze, just when I was a little bit happy.* With a painfully fake smile, I turned to face Shreya.

"Hey, Shreya!"

"So, we got selected for Raga Carnatic! Isn't that exciting!"

"Yeah, I guess so," I muttered, waiting for her to leave.

"Oh, you're nervous? Don't be! It's never as bad as you think it is. The audience just seems to fade away as you get into the music."

"Well, I know that sweetheart. I've kinda been performing since I was in pigtails. I didn't want to mess with her self-confidence though, so I kept my mouth shut.

"Well, I'll see you next week then?" We'd neared her house. Her Mom stood in her doorway giving shivers to any kid below the age of eighteen. She gave me a smile that somehow conveyed a message to me that said something like—*The toenail of my daughter has more knowledge than your whole family combined*—without even opening her mouth. Indian aunties truly were special in their own way. I hurried home, scared she might invite me inside.

"Hey, sweetie! Aunty texted me the good news." My Mom was working on a slideshow.

My parents were big public speakers. They both were doctors working for the same hospital. They toured the country giving speeches at big conventions. It honestly just made me seem more dumb and stupid standing next to them.

"Meh," I muttered, grabbing myself a banana from the fruit basket. In this household, snacks were equal to the devil. Why eat something jacked up on sodium and chemicals when we have nature's healthy food offered to us at a slightly cheaper rate? Even though they didn't have an Indian accent anymore, their wallets were still very Indian.

"What's the matter?" My Mom turned away from her computer. I recognized her tone instantly. Uh-oh , it was one of those mother-daughter bonding talks.

"I just haven't done a solo in a while, that's all." I turned toward the stairs. Could I make a break for it?

"Well, now that you aren't crying every time Jamie's name comes up, I think it's time to move on. You aren't letting her stop you from the thing you love, right?"

"'Course not."

Well, kinda, the voice inside my head told me. I told it to shut up.

"Where is she anyway? Jamie?"

"On tour in Seattle." Maybe if she wasn't the two-headed snake she was, than maybe I would have been there with her.

"Tour? Wow, I still remember her as the little girl who was obsessed over apple juice."

"Oh yeah, and she always drank all of it, leaving poor Mohana drinking milk and pickle juice." Rolling my eyes, I picked up my phone that had just buzzed from a text. It was from Aunty.

"Mom, wait just one second on the whole good news thing. I think Aunty just got a replacement for me." I opened the text. It wasn't about a replacement.

"Mohana?" My Mom got up.

I was pretty in-check with reality most of the time. You either win a competition, or you don't. You fix your mistake and win next time. There's no time for mourning or thinking so I don't get starstruck or surprised. I just keep working. So it made sense my mother was worried.

"There was a change in the program," I muttered.

"Aww, Aunty doesn't want you to sing anymore?"

"No, I'm still singing." I looked up at her, "But now there's apparently a special guest making an appearance."

"Oh?" My Mom waited on further news. I wasn't planning to give it to her, so she grabbed the phone from me. "Oh," she inhaled.

Yeah, I thought to myself. *This changed things didn't it?*

"So, are you still gonna sing?" My Mom's eyes were, as usual, observing me like a specimen. It was the million-dollar question. A question I didn't know the answer to.

"What do you think?" I asked her.

"You know what I think." My competitive Mom—of course she wanted me to sing. She didn't care that Jamie, the one person I never wanted to see again, was going to be there. That she'd be watching me with her beady little eyes while I messed up Carnatic and embarrassed myself entirely.

My phone buzzed again in my Mom's hand. She shook her head. "Oh yup, you're definitely going now."

"Pardon?" My train of thought disappeared.

"Aunty just paid the fee, and there's no refund." She shrugged and looked at me. "So, you have to go. Have fun."

Chapter 3

"Really! Aww, my baby's all grown up! Soon, she's gonna be singing at concerts and all." Shruthi fake teared up.

"It's just a competition, not some famous music festival," I responded grudgingly. But it didn't work out so I let a smile escape my lips.

"The Raga Carnatic contest is quite popular. Even I know about it. I'm definitely coming."

"You are not coming!"

"I'm definitely coming now! When you're up, I will cheer so loud the building will collapse." Shruthi smiled and tilted her head in a mocking way. She was inviting me to fight her.

"Fine!" I didn't even try. Shruthi always got her way. Why? She's Shruthi. She's really persuasive, and if you stand against her she will hurt you.

My stomach churned as it had been since yesterday. I took another deep breath. You'd honestly think a girl would have control of her own organs. As long as Jamie ignored me when she saw me next week at the competition, like she usually did, I'd be okay.

"I heard Jamie West is going to be there. You have to get me an autograph," Shruthi reminded me of the fact that I was trying so hard to forget.

"Do you know why she's coming?" I asked Shruthi.

"She has never attended a Carnatic event before."

"Does it really matter?" Shruthi picked up another book and read the back. We were in the library as always. Kalyani walked in with a grin on her face,

"I was just in the bathroom. Someone spilled the tea on how Sage broke up with Johnny."

Wait, what?

I bit my lip, forcing my head not to jerk up. I took a shuddery breath, forcing myself to remain calm while inside I was having a party.

"Really? That was really sudden." I tried my best to sound unaffected. But my friends knew me too well. When Kalyani didn't answer, I looked up to see them both staring at me with grins.

"Aww, poor Johnny," I muttered, trying to satisfy them. I felt a blush creep into my cheeks. I quickly picked up a book I'd already read and pretended to read the back, but it was too late.

"Aww, there it is!"

"Ooh, she wants to get with the Johnny!" My friends giggled.

"Yeah, say it a bit louder." I pressed my cold knuckles into my cheeks, hoping it might help hide the blush. It didn't.

"Bro, half the grade already knows. How long has this been going on again?"

"Three years." The blush deepened. Good thing I was brown. I hoped it wouldn't show much. The late bell rang.

"I have to print out my Science paper. See you at lunch," Shruthi said, then hurried away.

"I should probably leave too," Kalyani said.

"Okay, see you! I'll be here for a while. I have to check out a book." I walked away to the non-fiction section to try to find something I hadn't read yet. The task was harder than expected. I made a mental note to maybe go out and actually mingle. Defeated, I walked out of the library, trying to remember if I actually did my English homework. Oh well, didn't matter. I had smart friends I could copy off of. A loud 'ooh' shattered my thoughts.

"Johnny-boy got rejected!" The popular jerk-boys joked. He was standing right there and had a far-away misty look in his eyes that made my heart shudder. I wanted to stick around and listen to the conversation, but I chickened out and put on a burst of speed, trying to walk away as fast as my short legs could carry me. I was almost at the end of the corridor to my class when I stopped and heard more of the conversation from the other side of the lockers.

"He probably learned his lesson. Never gonna date an Indian girl again, are you?" I stood still, waiting to hear what he would say.

"We never were dating. Besides, she's not my type." I wretched my mouth closed. It was a lie, pure as day. The truth was he had liked her. He had liked her very much.

When I got home that day, I went straight to my room to practice. If Jamie was going to see me at the contest, then she was going to see me at my best. *We never were dating. Besides, she's not my type.* His voice kept creeping into the intricate melodies though, disrupting my focus.

I rested my head on my knuckles for one second. I stared down at my music notes. *Stop telling yourself that you're practicing this hard for something you're clearly gonna fail because you wanna impress Jamie. You already know that no matter what you do, she's only gonna view you as a cockroach that helps her get her money. Yes, you're practicing for some other reason entirely.* As usual, my mind was correct.

Johnny clearly valued his popularity. It wasn't the first time he'd lied to make his jerk-friends like him. It made him seem like a horrible person, didn't it? My friends definitely thought so. When I first admitted my crush, they'd laughed and looked at me pitifully, thinking it was infatuation and no more. They knew, even then, that boys like him were not supposed to mingle with girls like us. And even if they did, it was on a dare or something else that was just as equally stupid because that was all they were, stupid boys. They still did think that, no matter how supportive they tried to be. I'd been telling myself that I would change their thinking. That, no, they didn't know the hidden part of him. That he was different.

But was he?

I remembered when I first met him back in seventh grade. He wasn't popular then. No one knew of his basketball prowess. We were paired up to work on a math assignment together. I instantly thought he was funny. We honestly didn't do any work together so the teacher paired me with someone else, but when a few days passed I realized something. I was sitting in my chair, bored out of my mind, listening to my partner drone on. I cast a glance at Johnny on the other side of the room. He was laughing his usual laugh. His eyes were crinkled and his head was thrown back. That's when I realized.

Oh, I like him don't I?

And here I was, three years later.

There is something about singing that relaxes you. Especially with Carnatic, you need all your attention. You have to make sure you sing in Shruthi—in tune— which is nearly impossible to do in Carnatic; and you need to make sure you are doing your Thalam—tapping your right hand on your right thigh (gently if you don't want bruises) in different variations and different amounts of times to keep the beat.

Aunty paid more attention to me. I had gotten used to not getting too much attention. In the four years since Jamie left me, I had gotten used to being in the shadows. At school I'm the girl in the back of the room who no one knows. I am the girl you sit by in Math but don't know the name of. But, when you solo, all eyes are on you. I had forgotten what it felt like to be the center of attention. Aunty made me sing in little shows so I could get used to soloing. It felt great to hear my voice echo through an auditorium again. By the week of the competition, I was feeling good about the song I was performing. It was an easy song, but it would sound good if I sang it loud and bold. As my mom says, play to your strengths.

Before I knew it, the day was here. Competition day. I still remember it vividly. That was the day that my whole life turned around. Or now that I think about it, the day I got my life back on track.

Chapter 4

I was wearing my best half-saree—South Indian clothing teenagers typically wear that is notoriously known for not letting you breathe and falling off randomly. It was green and orange. My mom painted my face with way too much makeup and my dad took way too many pictures. My sister was annoying as usual and almost spilled grape juice all over my clothing, twice. So it was amazing that we somehow made it to the auditorium thirty minutes early.

I got to see the Guru who Aunty practically worships. I did have trouble though believing the legend that he skips eating for two weeks straight before a concert because he spends all of his time awake practicing. He engulfed the already-humongous chair. He had shades on and even though he was in Indian attire he looked more like some punk rock star with his beard.

Shreya was there too, early as always. She smiled slowly at me. She always played it down when she was with her mother. Shreya's mom was wearing a blinding neon pink saree, heels, and scary amounts of makeup. She was one of those Indian moms who thought her daughter was better than everyone and laughed too loudly. She gave my mom an icy stare and sneer that I think was supposed to be a smile. My mom returned her greeting with a head tilt and smirk that I also think was an attempt at a smile. Even my bratty sister sensed the tension and stopped asking for more grape juice.

"Hey! I didn't expect you here. Unlike at your doctor presentations, you don't get anything from coming here. Even if you did, you don't need it 'cause you're already set for life, aren't you?" Shreya's mom asked with such a mocking voice that she deserved a standing ovation.

"Me? I just want to support my daughter in the things she likes to do. You know all about that, don't you?" My mom said with, if possible, even more sass. I know I am a teenager and all, and I'm supposed to hate my parents, but I really loved my mom right then and there. Shreya's mom's leering smile vanished and was replaced with a face of repulsion. My mom gave one of those wolf-like smiles that she reserves for when she wins something.

"How about we go sit over at those empty seats, dear. The competition is about to start. See you later Shreya, good luck!" my dad said with his soft voice. He slowly ushered an angry mom, who was clearly not done with the smack down she was giving, to seats on the other side of the auditorium.

Right along with Shakespeare's black ages and the space time continuum, my parents' relationship was one of the most mysterious and confusing things. They apparently had met at med school. My dad is the kindest, non-competitive person you will ever meet with a kind smile that greets every kid he treats. He faints at the sight of blood or tears. My mom, on the other hand, is like a wolf. Correction, she is a wolf. She's super competitive and will crush you if you challenge her. While my dad is a pediatrician, my mom is a surgeon. It's super fun when my mom talks about the surgeries she did in front of my dad at dinner. Even though he's brown, he turns green and freaks out every time. My mom stopped after a while, but I'm sure she secretly enjoys making my dad sick.

They keep each other in check. My mom makes sure my dad doesn't get taken advantage of, and my dad makes sure my mom doesn't murder anyone. They make it work.

Shalini aunty gestured to me from the side of the stage. My parents smiled and walked away. I took the stairs that lead backstage.

"Hey, Mohana! Not too nervous I hope," Aunty said to me with a nervous smile.

Something had changed. She had a bit of lipstick smeared on her cheek.

I shook my head to show I wasn't scared. "Well, I didn't know this before but it's not a bad thing. If you look there," she pointed to a lady in the back of the auditorium, who was wearing a crisp, white blouse with black dress pants, "she is a voice coach. She recognizes talent and if she likes you tries to boost you to popularity. Also, if you get recognized it's great for college." She was nervous. I could tell she was regretting her decision to send me here. "If someone was spotted it would be wonderful for the school." Oh, she was worried about the future of the music school. I'd have to try not to mess it up for her. More pressure, yay!

There was a swell of noise backstage. All the kids performing started pointing to something. No, they were pointing at someone. I hadn't seen her face-to-face in nearly four years. Needless to say, she had definitely changed. Jamie was wearing a red crop top with really, really short ripped jean shorts. She had an extremely high ponytail and red lipstick that matched her top. She took her seat in the front row, her legs crossed. She had two security officers sitting behind her. At that moment I really did wish it would be like the cheesy movies. Maybe she would be sorry and would walk up and tell me that she had messed up. There would be tears and hugs; but no. She glanced my way, raised her eyebrows ever so slightly, then turned away. She recognized me but didn't care enough to show it. Could it get any worse? I smacked myself right there. I'd said the five cursed words, it could *always* get worse. And yes, it did get worse.

The voice coach lady motioned behind her for a boy wearing a white sweatshirt. He was tall, brown haired, and looked amazing. You guessed it, Johnny.

He looked seriously bored. He cradled a basketball in his arms and plopped down in a seat next to the voice coach. I hid behind the curtains immediately. Shreya was right behind me.

"OMG, Mo! Cute guy! Come look." She pulled my hand and pointed directly at him. Totally ignoring my lack of enthusiasm, she pulled me onto the corner of the stage where you were semi-visible to the audience. Fidgeting with the basketball in his lap, he looked up. Shreya waved her hand enthusiastically. I guess her mom wasn't around. If she was, Shreya would have been dead right now. I pretended I didn't see Johnny and looked away. Out of the corner of my eye, I saw him sit up straighter as he recognized me. That's when a memory hit me from seventh grade, the very first day we met.

"Your mom's a voice coach? Oh that's so cool!"

"Not really. It just means I get random girls wandering my house every day," he told me without looking up from his paper.

"Do you think I can ever meet your mom? You see, I sing. I do Indian classical and—"

"Do you ever shut up?" He looked up at me. Even though his eyebrows were raised sternly, he was smiling.

"Get me a meeting with your mom and I will," I said, jokingly. He smiled and shook his head.

"It doesn't work that way. She has to choose you. You have to get spotted. Maybe one day she'll see you sing."

"Will you be there?" I shamelessly asked.

"Probably not. The contests she goes to are hella boring." He rolled his eyes and focused again on the paper.

"You should come. And when you do, stand up and wave so I can see you. And—"

He remembered too. I watched with amusement as he stood up with his long legs and gave me a short wave. I couldn't help but laugh.

I looked over at Shreya, who was happy because she thought Johnny had waved at her. My smile faded. She looked like a goddess. With her curly hair, her almond shaped eyes bordered with eyeliner, and basically everything else. It made me look down at myself. I looked like an idiot. I hated that Johnny had to see me next to her. From her seat, Jamie looked up at me intriguingly, then she slowly turned around to see who I had waved to. My blood froze.

No, no, no, she is not looking at him.

Her lip twitched, like it always did when she saw someone cute. I couldn't watch anymore. I walked as calmly as I could to the bathroom. As always, Jamie got everything that was supposed to be mine. I clenched the rim of the sink and was grinding my teeth so hard that a mother and a daughter looked over at me with concern.

I looked at myself in the mirror, and I was back in time. I looked exactly like I had four years ago. The night Jamie ruined everything. Makeup, anger, and exhaustion etched into every line of my face. I looked like a mess.

But that was years ago, when you didn't know any better, my mind whispered to me, trying to coax me out back into the auditorium. So I exhaled sharply and looked at myself. I'll be fine. I'll be totally fine. I knew I was going to fail anyway, so I couldn't crash and burn too much right?

How utterly wrong I was.

Chapter 5

Everyone sang perfectly, at least in my opinion. Aunty's favorite guru didn't smile at all, and told everyone they were horrible. He wondered aloud where the fate of Carnatic Music was going. Though, his mouth did twitch slightly when he heard Shreya sing. Of course it did. She was amazing. The sad song she was singing almost brought tears to my eyes. Aunty started fidgeting more when my turn was approaching. She eyed the guru warily and Johnny's mom, the voice coach, in the back.

Johnny's mom didn't do much. She marked some things on her clipboard, but she actually smiled. Johnny looked like he was dead inside. He kept tapping his fingernail on the seat before him, which made an awfully loud tapping noise that echoed around the auditorium. He didn't stop until a mean-looking, bald uncle took a hold of his hand and gave him a killer stare that gave me goosebumps, and I was way backstage.

And finally, it was my turn. Just like I used to all those years ago when I soloed with Jamie, I took out a Ziploc from my bag in the corner. Out of it, I pulled out a sugar cube. No, I wasn't such an Indian that I also casually pulled out a tea cup for chai. The sugar had a different purpose. Back when I was younger and I'd just started performing at the temple, there was one thing that was always available. Chai, and with the chai, sugar cubes. I realized at a very young age that munching on one took your mind off the upcoming performance and calmed your nerves. So diabetes, I'm coming for you.

Some random aunty pushed me toward the stage. I brushed the sugar off the sides of my mouth and took my time walking to the center of the stage. Jamie's eyes were like lasers as I walked. I ignored her. I plopped down on the little podium that was set up in the middle of the stage. I turned on the Shruti Box, and hummed with it to make sure I started in Shruthi. Johnny had perked up in his seat, his mom smiled at me.

I started singing.

I'd observed from backstage. Every girl that had sung did great, but they all sounded absolutely *same*. Quiet and restrained. So I did the exact opposite.

I gave it my all and made sure Johnny could hear me from all the way in the back. I let myself get lost in the music, I let myself forget everything. I swam in the music. I made some words short and sharp, others long and melodious. It felt great to sing like that. It felt as if nothing was holding you down, that you could fly.

When I finished, Johnny enthusiastically started clapping and his mom joined. They were oblivious to the fact that you weren't supposed to clap at these types of events. His mom smiled warmly at me. My mom's smile engulfed her face. She gave me two thumbs up. Jamie looked confused. She kept looking outside and to me. It was the face she gave while doing math, and when she made plans.

The Guru picked up the microphone. He looked at me directly and said with the straightest face I've ever seen, "Dreadful and totally off Shruthi. It didn't even look like you were paying attention to the Shruti box in the first place. You're too focused on making your voice sound good. You definitely need more practice. Stop wasting everyone's time."

That took me by surprise. After the shock, I felt the tears in my eyes. I blinked a bit and walked off stage as quickly as I could. I didn't want to look at Johnny or Jamie. Aunty tried to catch my eye but I stared right on ahead. I walked straight to the bathroom and locked myself in a stall.

I mean, you came here to fail, right? my mind asked, trying to make the situation better. It didn't. True, I had come to fail. But for just a second, I'd let myself stray away from my saying: D*on't expect it, 'cause when you don't get it, it won't hurt as much*. A tear streaked down my cheek and made a dark circle on my half-saree.

A wave of hate washed over me at that moment. I hated my smart friends who were all going to Harvard without even putting much work into it. I hated the pretty blonde girls at school who had Johnny wrapped around their fingers. I hated Johnny himself. I hated Shreya and her perfection. I hated Aunty for actually letting me go to this event, even if it was against her will. I hated myself. I hated everyone. I hated everything. When I stepped out, I was a seething ball of anger and self pity. But when I saw my mom leaning her back against the sink, the anger was instantly replaced by tears.

"Mohana Devi Prasad, are those tears I see?" My mom's words confused me. I looked up to see her raised eyebrows. "Why are you crying?" she asked me. "It doesn't do a thing. Do you know what will for certain make you feel better?"

She walked forward and looked into my eyes.

"When you come back here one day, more famous than that guru. He pissed me off, as if he can sing as well as he expects everyone else to, but, today you truly were amazing! I don't know about the whole Shruthi thing but your voice today was exemplary. I got goosebumps."

Her words made me smile. Other people looking in on the scene might call my mother harsh for her words, but

I knew better. They provided exactly what I needed: a goal.

She fixed my hair and we walked out. I was ready to leave that building and stuff my face with ice cream and binge watch something.

"Mohana, wait!" My heart skipped a beat. That voice hasn't called my name in, well, four years. I turned and saw Jamie walking toward me. Reporters rushing behind her. She put an arm around me and turned to the reporters. "This—everyone—is Mohana. One of my prized songwriters and a very close friend of mine." I was too surprised to throw her arm off me. The last time I encountered her in front of the paps she pretended not to know me, but now she is acting like my best friend. Why?

"Ms. West, we've never heard you mention her name. Why not?" a reporter asked quickly.

"She doesn't like attention, but I have felt so guilty these past few weeks. She's been doing all the hard work and I've been getting credit for it." She put on a face that was so fake I thought someone had to recognize it. I saw what she was doing. How low can she get? She was using me to make herself look sweet and get more attention. It was disgusting.

"Are you planning to have a career in music?" a reporter asked me. I got myself together, took Jamie's arm off me and looked at the reporter. I opened my mouth to answer, but Jamie didn't let me.

"As I said, she doesn't like attention, and she doesn't sing anything except Indian classical. Besides, she wouldn't compete against me for fans. We're best friends. She wouldn't betray me." Her fingers held my arm tight. She laughed a tinkling laugh that made me look at her. Any inkling that I had of the old Jamie coming back shattered right then. Her security started chasing the paps away. When no one was looking, she looked straight in my eyes and repeated, "She wouldn't betray me." Then she walked away. My family could finally make their way to me across the sea of paps. My dad smiled.

"If you thought you couldn't sing, this just proved that wrong."

"What do you mean?"

"She thought you sang so good you might become her competition later."

"And you are going to do just that, aren't you?" a voice said. I looked behind me and saw Johnny's mom, still holding her clipboard. "My name is Melody Taylor and I couldn't help noticing your daughter's voice. Bold and loud. Maybe it wasn't right in Carnatic, but if we trained you right up I think we could have you perform in the Wainscott Show."

Well, she doesn't like to waste time.

The Wainscott show was a competition for rising singers. It was televised and everything with famous celebrities acting as judges. This year Minnesota was hosting it, and Jamie would be there.

"Sorry, Ms. Taylor, but I can't sing." I smiled as genuinely as I could. One, coaches don't just *select people* for the upcoming Wainscott. You practice with them for years and years. Second, even if her offer was genuine there was no way she was going to do this for an affordable price no matter whose mother she was, there was no way.

"But, I just heard you," Melody Taylor said taken aback. She clearly wasn't used to rejections.

"I can sing Carnatic, not anything else though." I internally was dying with laughter. *Good? Carnatic?* Shaliny Aunty would have dropped dead at the words.

"Are you sure? This is huge sweetie. It could help with college."

"Maybe you'd want to reconsider?" My mom butted in. Of course she did. Whenever someone mentions college scholarships, that gets her attention.

I looked at her. She wasn't dumb. She knew her way around the world. So, she didn't think this was a scam?

Is that why you are rejecting? 'Cause you think it's a scam. Or is something else stopping you? I asked myself.

I looked down for a second, and it came back, my wish. Paps taking photos from every angle, their cameras flashing everywhere. Fans craning against each other, just to get a look. But most of all, a name for myself. For people to know me as not Jamie's songwriter, not that girl seen around the hallways of the school, a random face in a yearbook. But, *Mohana Prasad.*

It had always been a daydream of mine, until Jamie came around and ruined it.

"I'll give you time to think about it."

She turned to leave when I called out,

"Wait!" I think my face said it all. She smiled and ripped out a piece of paper from her clipboard. It was her address.

"Meet me here, say tomorrow evening at five?" While my parents figured out the date, Johnny walked toward me from the shadows. He leaned against a wall. The setting sun outside made his white sweatshirt look pinkish orange.

Poser.

It worked though, a shiver extended from my heart to the tips of my fingers.

"You never told me," he said with his grin, and we were suddenly transported back in time three years ago to math class. When I first met him.

"Told you what?"

"That you knew Jamie West."

"You never asked."

He chuckled. "Do your friends know about this?"

I perked up from my permanent slouch.

Oh no! With everything that just happened I totally forgot. "My friends are going to kill me."

"We're gonna do what?" a voice called out behind me. *Shoot! My* eyes widened. I'd totally forgotten.

Shruthi.

Chapter 6

All I saw was a blue blur before I was slammed against a wall.

"You're dead!" The hands gripping the front of my hoodie tightened.

"Shruthi let her go!" When my eyes refocused I saw an angry Shruthi inches away from my face. Neela was behind her, looking amused and scared at the same time.

I had run away too quickly at the competition to tell her anything about Jamie.

"Explanation, now!" Shruthi shook me.

"You better explain before she commits her first murder—or second. We never did hear from Emma Thompson again, did we?" Neela was next to me now, slowly coaxing Shruthi's hands away from my neck.

"Look, I'm sorry! You never would have believed me anyway," I told Shruthi, my voice slightly hoarse.

"You at least should have tried!" Shaina's angry voice told me from behind. She and Kalyani were walking toward me holding pencils like daggers. "Sorry we're late. Kalyani takes forever."

"Sorry if I'm the only one here who actually cares what they look like," Kalyani retorted back.

"Wait, you guys planned this out?" I asked.

"Yeah, we were gonna torture you for information," Shruthi said with a smile. "It was my idea."

"Of course it was. Let's sit down. I promise I'll tell you everything."

I smiled and steered them toward a table. I had mentally prepared for this situation last night, and I had imagined us sitting.

I took a deep breath then said, "Ever since I was little I had a way for words. I wrote a lot of poetry at like the age of six. I started writing songs at ten, just for fun. My parents thought they were good, really good. So, they entered my songs in some competition. The winner would get their song sung by Jamie. She was just starting out so no one knew her. Anyway, there really wasn't much in the way of competition from other songwriters at the time, so I won easily. Jamie's managers really liked it my song, and since then I have been writing most of her songs for her," I finished.

Simple, just like I had planned. True, I had left a major part of the story, but I really didn't think it was relevant.

"But yesterday Jamie said you were one of her best friends. How did that happen?" Neela asked. I didn't fret. I had planned for this.

"We met while I was at the studio one day, and we became friends," I responded as calmly as I could. Either I couldn't lie or my friends knew me too well because they figured out I was lying pretty quickly. Shaina slowly brought the pencil to my face.

"Shaina that's not gonna work," Shruthi said as she put her hand down into her backpack and picked up her phone. "Johnny and I were in the same group for the chem project last month. I still have his number. I should text him about your feelings for him. About how you looove him!"

"No stop! Fine! I hate you though!" I took her phone and kept it in my hand just to be safe before I took a deep breath. I had to go unscripted now. I didn't think this would be brought up last night when I was deciding what to say.

"Mo, you don't have to tell us if you don't want to," Neela said just when I opened my mouth. I thought about not telling them for a second, but I had to. They were my best friends and they needed to know.

"Thing is, Jamie and I have known each other since we were five. We were always close and we both had a dream of becoming famous together. We performed my songs at little competitions and talent shows. We got recommended for this one talent show in L.A. We were going to go on the same flight and stay in L.A. with Jamie's aunt." I took a breath. I couldn't start crying now.

"The flight left at nine in the morning, so to be safe, me and my family got to the airport two hours early. We waited and waited for Jamie, but she never came. I couldn't go without Jamie. I wouldn't ever ditch her like that. We kept calling her, but she never picked up. We went back home around four in the evening. When my dad went to the computer to send an e-mail to the flight company, he found a message saying that the flight had been rescheduled to the day before. We shared an account with Jamie's family."

I had tears in my eyes now. "That was the show where she was spotted by an agent. I confronted her in front of her managers when she got back. She pretended to not know me and had me removed by security."

I wiped my eyes with my sleeves. That was the day my dreams and hopes crashed to the ground. That was the day I created my saying, *Don't expect it, 'cause when you don't get it, it won't hurt as much.* "Two weeks later my songs were chosen through the contest I told you about." My friends were silent. I guess I would be too if my idol ended up being a jerk. Shaina was the first to break the silence. "Wow, and I thought she was my role model." She put her hand on my shoulder and hugged me. All my friends joined in. "Also, if you are her writer why isn't your name anywhere?"

"It's on every album cover in small print in some corner," I said. Two of the most important people on every singer's team are the songwriter and the person who sets the tune of the song, but their names are always the smallest.

"That's not fair," Neela retorted. I smiled. When had the music industry ever been fair?

"Oh, and I got spotted by a voice coach." They all released me at once. "And it's Johnny's mom. I'm going to their house tomorrow morning." They all looked stunned for a bit. Shaina was the quickest to recover.

"People say he sleeps in his boxer shorts. You better send a picture if you see him in them." Shaina winked at me.

"No, he's mine! Back off!"

* * *

Saturday morning came quick. I wore makeup that morning, which was rarer than me being athletic. I never cared much about makeup, cause why was anyone going to stare at my face for more then a few seconds? Anyway, now my dream was back on track I felt like anything was possible. I knew it was dangerous straying from my saying, but I couldn't help it.

Arriving at Melody Taylor's home that morning was surreal. Every single window was open and there were flowers on every sill. Inside, family pictures hung everywhere. I frowned and looked closer at a few.

Johnny looked so happy and *different*. It was a side he hadn't exposed in ages. Johnny, himself, was nowhere to be seen.

"That was taken two years ago," his mom said as she walked up to me, pointing to a picture where Johnny and his dad were on a boat. "I take it you know Johnny?"

"Yes, Ms. Taylor. We go to the same school."

"Call me Melody," she said, extending her hand to me. I shook it. She then led me into a bright yellow room with a keyboard and a guitar in the corner. We sat down in two chairs in the middle of the room, facing each other. I awkwardly placed my hands on my knees.

"I heard a uniqueness in your voice at that contest," Melody said. "You have a boldness that would be amazing on a big stage. I understand you also write songs, yes?" I nodded. "That's even better because record companies prefer it if you can write. They don't have to hire a writer for you. Now, sing the first thing that comes into your mind."

I sang the beginning of a Peter Raul song. There never is a time his songs haven't been on my mind. Ms. Taylor, *Melody*, stopped me after a few lines. "Hey, where did the energy go? At that contest your voice was so loud and amazing. It carried so well. Try to sing like that. Johnny's still asleep upstairs. Try to wake him up."

She picked up a guitar and counted off. I took a breath and imagined myself in an auditorium, just like the old times. I envisioned Jamie next to me giving me an encouraging smile. I had never soloed without her. I sang loud. I took deep gasps of breath and it felt great as I let everything go. Melody played along with me. When I opened my eyes, I realized there were tears in them. Melody looked at me sympathetically.

"I've taught for years and years," she said, "The singers who go the farthest are those who get most involved with the music they are performing. I see a lot of potential in you, Mohana Prasad." She smiled warmly at me and I felt something simmer in my stomach. The moment was rudely interrupted by a deep voice at the door.

"We are out of cereal and bread. Just thought you should know." I jumped in my chair and whipped around to see a tousled Johnny leaning against the doorframe.

Aww, he's not wearing boxers. The voice in my head made me blush. He gave a little nod to me and faced his mom again.

"I got bagels yesterday. They're in the pantry," Melody told him. He nodded and left.

We moved on to little singing exercises for the remainder of the session. It helped me remember how to use my voice like that again. It also helped me reach a conclusion.

I loved Carnatic. I really did, but some things just weren't meant for everyone. For some people, Carnatic came naturally, like Shreya. For others, like myself, Carnatic was just too high to reach. It just didn't come, no matter how much I practiced.

As soon as I got home, I found my parents. The first thing I said to them was, "Mom, Dad, I'm not going back to Carnatic lessons ever again."

Chapter 7

"Come on, take a deep breath and try again."

"I need a break!" I shook my head and said out of breath.

Time didn't just fly when you were having fun, but when you were struggling as well. The Wainscott audition was exactly a week away and I still couldn't do it. I leaned my head on the back of my chair and stared up at the ceiling. I was going to sing a song I had written for Jamie a long time ago. She'd gotten at least a dozen awards for it. If I sang it, it would guarantee me first. The song was just really, *really* high pitched.

"You just need more power behind the notes, Mohana. I know you can do it," Melody told me. Her voice grew more and more anxious each time I tried to sing and failed. She handed me a glass of water, but I didn't drink it.

I had done it though. I had sung the song that I was supposed to sing right now. I didn't set the tunes to my songs. Most of my songs just had a tune after I wrote them. I'd sing it to Finn, Jamie's tune setter, and then he'd use it. I had set the tune for this song. I had sung it with ease in the past, so what was wrong now?

"Everything is amazing, except the high part. For that part you could reduce your voice, but it will sound more nasal. Obviously not appealing. All you can do is keep practicing at home." Melody stood up and looked at the clock. We'd gone twenty minutes over the time the lesson was supposed to end. I looked out the window to saw my dad's head lolled against the window as if he was sleeping.

"Sorry Melody. I guess we lost track of time. Did you miss anything?" I asked her.

"No, at least I sure hope not. Now you go home and practice. You have a week to nail the song." She gave me an encouraging smile and showed me out. It turned out that my dad had fallen asleep against the window. I had to knock at least eight times before he woke up. Smiling an apologetic smile, he unlocked the doors.

"You look stressed. Want me to drop you off at the library or something?" he asked. I smiled and thought about it. A few hours of Charles Dickens would probably get rid of my headache, but a better place to go popped into my head.

"Actually, could you drop me off at Kalyani's?"

"Sure, anything for my little pop star!" Dad grinned and pulled away from the curb.

I usually went to Kalyani's whenever I was bored. Shruthi had left for Nevada yesterday, Neela was probably at some math camp, and Shaina was probably at the temple. She always had been the most religious out of us all. Kalyani was the one I could trust to be home. As expected, when I rang the doorbell she was the one who opened the door.

"Hey! You came at the right time. My parents aren't home. Bet I can lip sync to Peter Raul better than you!" I waved to my dad and entered her house. Taking off my coat, I let the warm air of her house warm me. It was April, and it was cold and snowing again. Just a normal day in blistery Minnesota.

We played our favorites on her speaker and lip synced along. We used hair brushes as microphones and ran around the house. We both danced to our heart's content. I got a break from all that stress haunting me for the past week. Out of breath, we sank down on her bed.

"One day soon we'll be dancing to one of your songs," said Kalyani as she sat up, still gasping for air.

"I'm not so sure about that." I smiled and rolled my eyes.

"I'm so pissed at what Jamie did to you. I unfollowed her on Insta if that makes you feel any better," she told me proudly. "You know what would make me feel better? If you would become as famous as her." She nodded sternly at me. It made me laugh. It would make me feel better too, but I can't even sing a song of hers that I set the tune for.

"Could I see what she posts?" I asked her, changing the topic.

Social Media seemed like too much work, so I never got involved in it. Kalyani showed me Jamie's Instagram. It mostly consisted of selfies and red carpet pictures of her.

"She shows a lot of skin," I concluded after a bit. " She used to hate girls wearing crop tops and booty shorts." In all the pictures, she was wearing clothes with strategically placed rips and holes that made her clothing look airy.

"Really?" Kalyani said sarcastically and laughed.

There was a picture of me from the Carnatic competition. Jamie had her arm around me while I looked disheveled and confused. People commented on the photo, saying things such as how Jamie was such a nice person. There was one that even said she was so loyal to her friends and supported them. Kalyani and I burst out laughing at that one.

After that, we stalked a few hot guys cause, why not? "Hey, I follow Johnny on Insta." Kalyani pulled him up and we scrolled for a bit. They were mostly pictures of him playing basketball or some other sport. There was one picture though of him at a mathlete competition. While the others got like millions of likes, this picture only had two. "Neela was at that competition. She told me he beat her and won first."

"Of course he did. I've never seen him get a question

wrong in math." No one knew he was that good at school. He got straight A's (yes, I know his grades. No, I'm not creepy, just dedicated). But in school he's Johnny, the tall basketball kid. The one who the team counts on to help win the games for us. I smiled. I never understood boys. If I was as smart as him, I would make sure the whole school knew, but not Johnny. He was too cool to brag.

"Wait, don't you have Carnatic today?" Kalyani asked.

"I quit," I said simply. Ha! I wouldn't have to be lectured on my Shruthi anymore. Find someone else to pick on Shalini Aunty!

"Aw, why?" Kalyani asked.

"I figured out that I could never do it. No matter how much I tried I could never sing as well as my peers."

"So you gave up?" Uh oh, I know that voice. Kalyani's mom voice.

"I tried my hardest. I've been singing Carnatic for four years. Wouldn't I know by now if I can sing it or not?"

"Remember in second grade when you just couldn't read. The teacher said you were a slow learner, but you picked it up pretty quickly. Now everyone thinks you came out of the womb holding *Pride and Prejudice.* If you'd have given up, then a big chunk of your personality would have been lost. You're 'the Carnatic girl'. Neela's the math one, Shaina's the religious one, and Shruti's the one obsessed with boy bands. If you stop singing Carnatic, you won't be you!" The doorbell rang.

"That would be my dad. Thanks mom for the advice, but I'm not going back. I've shed enough tears over Carnatic and it feels great not practicing it every evening. I have so much free time now."

"What about Wainscott? Aren't you practicing for that?" Kalyani grabbed my coat for me.

"Thanks." I slipped into it. " I go to Melody's house every

evening now. My throat is sore. I can't practice at home too!" I had been drinking herbal tea since I started singing for Melody. I normally hate tea, but it's the only thing that makes me feel my throat again. Kalyani gave me a look.

"Sweetie, it's *The Wainscott.* Of course it's gonna hurt." She opened the door for me. "I'll see you."

"Okay, bye!" I stepped out into the blustering wind and waved back to Kalyani. I took my time walking on the slippery sidewalk and getting into the car. My mom was the one driving this time. She handed me the phone she was talking on and mouthed, *"Aunty."* I violently shook my head as if to say "No," but my mom pressed the phone into my hand.

"Aunty!" I said it with as much enthusiasm as I would have had if I joined the basketball team, which was not that much.

"Mohana, sweetie, we miss you here. Why'd you stop coming?"

"Miss me? Ha! And Peter Raul is my boyfriend," my mind muttered.

"Sorry Aunty. I've just been so busy lately," I lied to her.

"I understand, high school and all that. I heard you're participating in the Wainscott show. I'll see you on television. What are you singing for it?"

"A song I wrote for Jamie West, Aunty."

"Is it *The Mask?*"

"It is, Aunty! How did you know?" Was it witchcraft? I wouldn't be surprised if it was.

"I know I'm old, but not that old yet! That song had hints of Carnatic in it, the chorus especially. I knew you set the tune to it immediately after I heard it."

"Really, Aunty?" I paused. Should I ask her for help? In a quick second, I concluded that I needed all the help I could get. "Aunty, I have been having some trouble over the song. I just can't sing the part where it's higher."

"As I've always said, Mohana, sing louder. If your voice is stuck in your throat, it isn't going to help at all. Try singing the upper sthayi varsays in your loudest voice, at least every day."

"Alright, thanks Aunty!"

"Of course." Would it work though? Carnatic never does stop chasing me, does it?

Chapter 8

"*D*on't *you ever get nervous?" Jamie asked me. The lights backstage made her look paler than ever. She was clutching her guitar to her chest.*

"No, we worked hard for this. I know we will do great. Being nervous is for people who think they might mess up on stage. We won't. I know so," I responded bravely, being the cocky middle schooler I was. She smiled and her fingers loosened on her guitar. But her face was still pale. I pressed a sugar cube into her hand and hugged her. She hugged me back. The organizers called us up as the person on stage introduced us to the crowd. I let her go and made my way to the stage with Jamie following me. When I stepped on stage and felt the light's warm glow on my face, I realized something.

This is what I wanted to do for the rest of my life.

It felt so right. When I positioned myself in front of the microphone, I didn't see the crowd. They didn't matter. Right there, it was only Jamie, me, the stage, and the music.

There was always one performance in a performer's life that marks something important. The beginning of their independence on stage, which then leads to their love and respect for the stage.

When they *want* to be on stage more than anything. When they give everything up just for that adrenaline rush as the lights hit their face. That performance for me had been held here, the very stage that held the Wainscott show's audition.

I'd already sent a recording of my voice, and they apparently only choose a few of those recordings, but it definitely didn't seem like it. The vast auditorium was brimming with people. Adults, teens, and even kids who could barely walk. There never was an age restriction. They only cared about talent. I even saw a lot of familiar faces, people I had seen around Jamie's recording studio. Some nodded at me, others ignored me as usual. I shrugged it off as usual. Even though I was always somewhere in her studio no one ever noticed me. I was just the girl who was always there, like a part of the wall.

Melody and I had gotten a spot at the back of the auditorium. We were so far behind that we had to squint to see the organizers up on the stage.

"Hello, hello, hello! My name is Vanessa, and this is Hugh." The lady on the stage with a bright pinkish red blazer motioned to the man next to her. He wore a suit with matching pinkish red stripes.

"We are the main organizers of this show and we mean it when we say we can't wait to hear all of the talent today!" The man had an unnaturally high voice. I heard a familiar laugh come right below me. I looked down to see Finn sitting in the row in front of me. I hadn't noticed him with all the chaos happening around me. His curly, black hair bounced slightly as he tried to contain his laughter while the man on stage continued talking.

Finn was Jamie's tune setter. He was two years older than me and had a messed up sense of humor. We were the only teenagers who worked for Jamie, so we naturally became friends. When the crowd stopped talking and the first few people who were performing got up, I called to him. He turned and raised his eyebrows.

"I knew I'd see you here. Finally going to give Jamie a run for her money?" The people next to him left. He moved to sit directly below me.

"I'm not going to remain in Jamie's shadows forever. Anyway, how come you're here? This is a singing competition," I said with a smile. He rested his head on the back of his chair and looked up at me. His familiar smile tugged at his lips as he pulled a fake frowny face.

"Are you saying I can't sing? Please, I'm like a better looking version of Peter Raul." As usual, he knew exactly how to make me smile.

"You and the god Peter Raul? Yeah, no way." I pushed his head off the back of his seat as he grinned up at me. Melody tapped me on the knee with her pen and motioned to the stage with her head. *Focus.* I rested my chin on my knuckles and looked at the stage.

The contestants were all really, really, good. There were four year olds who could probably beat some of the top artists of the day in a singing competition. I felt myself, for the first time in a very long time, get nervous.

I had sung a lot, so the fear of the stage slowly vanished. I was always prepared to the fullest, but not this time though. I did what Aunty said, and it actually kinda worked. But, there was still a decent chance that I might mess up. And if the rest of the contestants sang like the first few had, only one mistake was all there was between success and failure. I quivered at the thought of it. I wasn't the only one nervous though.

Finn's legs kept bouncing up and down. Melody was getting paler by the second. I was one of the last people to go, so I thought everyone would have left. But, that was not the case. People who had already gone stayed to watch the others. And they weren't the easiest audience to please. Their eye rolls and judging stares made that obvious. Finn was performing two spots before me, so we waited backstage together. His dirty jokes and usual smile were replaced with nervousness. He was trembling. Sweat beaded his forehead.

Muttering something about a bathroom, he left a bit before he had to go on. I waited for a while but he never came back.

When I turned to search for him, I felt a hand on my shoulder. "Mohana, you're on in a few minutes." Melody made her words seem like a small reminder, but the way she was looking at me made me realize it was something way larger.

"I need to go after a friend," I responded.

"You're gonna miss your only chance, Mohana. Everything you worked for is going to be lost. We're beating Jamie, remember? Is it him, or your fame?"

Well, that was quite intense.

Just like Johnny, Melody was quite dramatic. But, I could be dramatic too. I didn't hesitate for one second. I looked her in the eye and mustered all the strength I had.

"If my dream costs my friends, I don't want it." I took her hand off my shoulder and ran after Finn. I called his name as loud as I dared in the hushed wings of the stage. I even looked in the men's bathroom. He better be grateful. Backstage was filled with all types of props. I saw Finn's curly hair next to a bridge.

"Finn?" He looked blank, just staring ahead of him. He was breathing heavily though like I sometimes did with my asthma.

"Don't bother, I'm not coming."

"Huh?" I was scared. I'd never seen him like this.

"Social anxiety. I love to sing you know? It gives me a wonderful feeling. I just can't do it in front of anyone. I thought maybe today I could—" Finn smiled. "I wish."

My dad talks about social anxiety all the time. I racked my brain, trying to remember how to make it better. There wasn't a cure so what was I to do? Of course I wasn't listening to my dad at that moment!

I looked at Finn. The poor thing looked miserable. I never

thought happy, always-laughing Finn would have something like this. But, when I thought about it, I saw it. How he never liked looking anyone in the eye, how he always walked with his head down, how he always avoided meeting new people; and when he had to—how he stuttered and blushed. It took awhile for him to actually talk to me without stuttering.

I just never noticed.

"Hey," I didn't know how to stop this, but having a friend helps everything, "I know I can never feel what you're going through right now. I can never know how hard it is, but I'll try. I'm here for you, and I always will be. I will be here, backstage, when you sing on stage today."

"I'm not singing."

"Yes you are. The feeling you said you got, I get it too. And the feeling only grows on stage. You need to feel that feeling. Finn we need to go." He looked at me with a pained expression. "I have something that'll help," I said with a reassuring smile and pulled out my sugar cube Ziploc. His eyes widened.

"You are amazing Mohana, really, you are. But I am not doing anything illegal—"

"Finn! They're not drugs. They're sugar cubes and they are just as effective." I slowly managed to coax him out of his spot by the bridge and we made it just in time. The singer before me was almost finished. When Melody realized I was back, she gasped so loud the organizers threw her a look. It looked like she hadn't breathed all the time I was gone.

"Aww, you missed your chance, Finn," I said with a frown as I checked my sheet of paper.

"Doesn't matter," he grunted. He looked angry at himself and sad that he missed his chance. His curly hair covered his sad dark eyes. You never could take him seriously when he was sad. He looked like a puppy who had lost his bone.

I couldn't help it, I quietly laughed. I walked to the manager, Vanessa.

"Excuse me? I was wondering whether I could change my performance from a solo to a duet?"

"Sure, Sweetie!" She changed some things on the clipboard as the singer on stage sang the last few notes. Finn looked over at me as I tapped him on the shoulder.

"*The Mask.* I set the tune for it. It was supposed to be a duet, but Jamie wanted to sing all of it. Remember it?"

"Of course. It was one of your best ones. Never forgot one of your songs." He smiled.

"Then let's do it." I grabbed his arm before he could back out.

"Mo—" Melody started but stopped herself. I had shot her a killer look.

I couldn't believe it. I had just given the killer stare to an adult. And I surprisingly wasn't shot down by lightning on the spot or carried off by killer fairies as I'd always imagined.

I felt myself shrink back, but to my relief nothing happened. She smiled. "Do me a favor, please never *ever* change." She motioned for us to wipe the sugar crumbs off the sides of our mouths. When she was satisfied, she nodded and said, "Good luck!"

I looked around, where was it? I just saw one. There!

"Can I please borrow this for my performance?" I asked the owner of a guitar, a little girl who looked about eleven. The guitar was smaller than I would've liked, but I guessed it would have to do. But that wasn't my main problem. The girl raised her eyebrows.

"Where's yours?" she asked defensively.

"I forgot it. Now please. I promise I'll return it." Hugh was on stage. He introduced us.

"Pinkie promise?" The girl held out her pinkie. I almost tore her pinkie with the harsh promise I made. But even that wasn't enough. "Do you really mean it?" She narrowed her eyes at me as if I'd bolt as soon as I got my hands on her small guitar. I mentally swore. I quickly promised her again and yanked the guitar out her hands. With my other hand I grabbed Finn and dragged him onstage with me.

Chapter 9

Once I was up on stage, all of the nervousness I had forgotten about came crashing back. It was enough to almost knock me off my feet. *Almost.* I couldn't blank out now because it wouldn't just affect me.

I looked over at Finn. He was blushing hard now. Could he sing? I didn't know. He looked blank too. Would he even remember the lyrics? I tripped over my feet while I walked on stage, almost taking Finn down with me. A few people in the front row smiled. They looked at me with pity and amusement.

I felt my blood instantly turn from normal to boiling. All of the anger I had at Jamie, at Shreya's perfectness, at all my friends' intellectual superiority, and at myself combined. I found it to be stronger than my nerves, and as the intro began I sang with more passion than I'd ever had.

Soon Finn took over. His voice, I had to admit, was actually decent. I had positioned him facing me so he couldn't see the crowd, and the blush on his cheeks slowly vanished. After a while his voice grew stronger and he even began to look at the audience.

Like mine, his voice was pretty loud and strong, like a rock star. In the chorus our voices blended perfectly. It surprised us both. We didn't mind though. He actually remembered the lyrics and everything went surprisingly smooth. The audience started clapping along and we started having fun. We bopped along, Finn even twirled me. The end came pretty quick. It ended on a high note held for about six beats. That was what I was nervous about, what I had been practicing for, but at that moment I totally forgot about it. Everything was actually going good until I did the thing every singer dreads. On the last beat my voice cracked.

* * *

"Mo, you have to come out."

"No! I sounded like a little boy going through puberty."

"But, the rest was great."

"I don't care, Finn!" I was crying in a bathroom, again. Good thing there was always one conveniently located near the stage for me.

"Please Mo!"

I felt like an idiot. No matter how much I got hurt, I never learned. I had wandered away from my saying, *Don't expect it, 'cause when you don't get it it won't hurt as much.* And it cost me as usual. Hope is a dangerous thing. It's like a drug, or sugar cubes for that matter. It makes you happy when you have it, but you feel just awful when it is gone.

"They're going to announce the people who qualified, Mohana, you should come out." Melody's voice joined Finn's.

"I can hear them fine from here," I responded. That was true, no matter how much I tried to ignore Hugh's abnormal voice.

"At least let us in."

"Ugh, fine." I wiped the tears off my face and opened the door for them so they'd stop pestering me. I was engulfed with a hug as soon as I opened the door. The comforting smell of Melody's perfume engulfed me. Finn stepped in, looking uncomfortable. He looked around, making sure no one was around the women's bathroom. I would have felt bad for him if I wasn't so busy feeling bad for myself.

"That was amazing. Seriously, you guys looked so comfortable up there. And your voices are perfect together. It looked like it was planned and as if you guys practiced for months. No matter what happens, Mohana, I'm proud of you. I don't care if you get in or not. Always keep singing!" Melody smiled such a warm smile, it was contagious. Even Finn, who was pretending to vomit behind Melody's back, had the right corner of his mouth turned upward. Are all voice coaches like Melody? Every kid should have someone like her. Finn was leaning against the door.

"You can actually sing, huh Finn?" I asked with a smile. He was now wearing the gray knitted hat that he always wore.

"You're not the only one who sings. I'm better though." He winked purely to annoy me.

"Are not!"

"Really, are you sure about that?" Finn asked with fake voice cracks. I rolled my eyes.

We stayed in the bathroom, Melody and me sitting against the door, Finn playing with the stall doors. He managed to hit himself in the face with one, which even cracked Melody up. We finally heard Vanessa from the stage.

"And now, what you all have been waiting for, the qualifiers!" Finn stopped messing around and Melody perked up. "But, first we would like to thank our sponsors—" Finn groaned and Melody started checking her phone. There were at least eighty sponsors, so that took forever. Then Hugh came back, which made Finn start giggling again.

"Before we announce the qualifiers, we have to say it was a really hard choice." All three of us, including Melody, groaned and rolled our eyes. "Every single one of you has so much talent, I couldn't believe my eyes watching a lot of the performers today."

"If you keep talking, Hugh, I think our contestants will roast you alive!" They both laughed for like two hours at their corny joke.

"And, now, for real, the qualifiers are—" Hugh paused for dramatic effect, which really only just made me hate him even more.

Ten people were chosen out of the big crowd. Needless to say, it was basically impossible to get chosen. With my voice crack, there was no point in listening. But, I still felt the tension in my stomach, no matter how much I repeated my saying to myself, *Don't expect it, 'cause when you don't get it it won't hurt as much.* Even Finn sat down, which I was pretty sure I've never seen him do.

Vanessa and Hugh both started listing names and the reason why they were chosen. The audience started off cheering loudly for each chosen person, but the enthusiasm slowly went down as the spots left decreased. By the ninth person chosen, there was a weak applause that lasted for about two seconds. Even though we weren't in the auditorium, we still felt the tension. I kept listening for Vanessa or Hugh's voice for the last contestant, but I couldn't hear them. I heard a murmur ripple through the audience.

"I'm going to go see what's up." Melody left. As soon as she left, something in me snapped. A giggle escaped me, making Finn look over at me with a frown.

"And I'm the weird one? What are you laughing for?"

"I hate tension," I replied to him. I had always laughed when things got to be too much for me. It was something I created when I was little. A little laugh solved most problems back then. Not anymore though. I still do it though, probably because it makes me remember the time when everything was simple.

"Sorry for the confusion." It was Vanessa's voice, "But, we decided to do something we've never done before. I'll

explain later after I announce the tenth contestant." I put
my head against the door and closed my eyes. I sucked in
a deep breath. No one in the audience was talking, which
didn't happen very often. It was so quiet I could hear the
furnace running.

"The tenth contestant in this year's Wainscott show is a
wonderful duo." There were a lot of duets, including us.
"They had so much energy and enthusiasm that could be
heard in their voices. Their love for music is unquestionable,
making them this year's tenth contestant. And they are—"
I honestly thought my stomach was trying to rip out of my
skin at that moment. It could be us, or not.

"The wonderful duo of Lavender and Ryan Sink are part
of this year's Wainscott Show!"

Lavender and Ryan Sink

Oh

The let down you feel is something I can't explain with
words. Only people who have felt it know. I couldn't bring
myself to look at Finn as my eyes glazed since the shock had
now worn down. But I knew I wasn't the only one. I didn't
need to see it to know there were tears out in the auditorium.
Tears, hugs, and vile looks at the ones who got in.

"But this year, we had two duos that matched Vanessa's
description didn't we?" I listened to Hugh but my mind
was far away. "For the first time in Wainscott history, we
are going to have an eleventh place, a duo that just needs
to participate in this year's show."

Well that's not really fair, the voice in my mind remarked.
I told it to shut up. It could be us. I perked up, but it wasn't
like before. I had been let down already. I couldn't get back
up again. I wanted to know who it was, that was all. "The
last participants of the Wainscott are—" Finn stood up
and took his hat off, he was ready to go. And frankly, so
was I. He ruffled his hair with a sigh. He looked tired,

I probably looked worse. "Congratulations to the talented duo of Mohana Prasad and Finn Winston!"

Well, anyway—wait what? Who?

Finn, who was putting his hat back on, froze. The feeling I felt right there, again, I can't explain. It was more than feeling surprised, more than feeling happy, more than feeling accomplished.

I felt invincible.

Only when Melody ran in and almost lifted me off the ground with the hug she gave me could I digest what was happening. I felt myself jump and felt the tears slide down my cheek. I ran over and hugged Finn whose tears were sliding down his long nose.

"We did it, Finn, we did it!" I needed to say it out loud. Finn looked like he still didn't register what was happening. Only after a bit did he give a whoop and hug me tight. After he let me go I got a clean look at his face. "You're actually crying, huh?"

"Shut up!" He pretended to itch his eyes while he wiped his tears. I laughed at him while I continued to jump around. After that it gets kinda hazy. I think I hugged Melody again, maybe had a few more sugar cubes? Everything was covered by the happiness at that moment. I wanted to live in that moment forever.

I was going to be in the Wainscott show.

The good-for-nothing, has-no-talent me was going to sing on television. Even Jamie never got in. Jamie was going to be at the Wainscott, and she was going to see me sing. I would get to show her that she should have never left me. I would get to show Shreya that she's not the only one who can sing.

Carnatic had helped me. Because of Shalini Aunty I had been able to do what I had. If the only thing that is going to help me keep doing that is Carnatic, then I guess I have to go back to Shalini Aunty again.

Chapter 10

"Man, Shalini Aunty is gonna be so pissed!"

"You only skipped a day."

"Yeah, a whole hour of devotion according to her." I rubbed my fingers against my leg. It was freezing in the hockey arena and holding a cold metal flute wasn't helping matters.

"Oh, here they come." Morni, a fellow flute player, motioned to the hockey players and picked up her own flute to play the peppy school song. I jolted my hands off my thighs and to their position on my chin. The cold mouthpiece felt as if it burned my skin. There really was no point in us being there. No one could hear the flutes over the blasting trumpets behind us, but we did get extra credit though for giving up our Saturdays to play in a cold rink. Morni gave a dirty glare at the trumpets behind us, but it turned into a smile quick.

"Your bae's coming." I saw Johnny's back as he and his friends moved to stand behind the glass. They cheered and booed the players. "Jerks," Morni muttered. Her eyes suddenly widened as she realized her mistake, "Oh, not Johnny. No he's great—"

"You're fine," I distractedly waved her off. Johnny glanced my way as he tried to find another friend of his. My stomach sent a wave of emotion. Morni was casually grinning at me while she pressed random keys on her flute. "Watch this—Hey Johnny!" I jerked in my seat. Morni was pretty close to Johnny, closer than I ever was anyway. He hopped up the stairs to her. I stared determinedly at his big, boat-like, red Adidas shoes.

"Yeah?"

"Can we borrow five bucks?"

"What for?"

"Mohana wanted something." Morni leaned on to me.

"Popcorn," I determinedly grunted still looking at his shoes.

"Fine, you can pay me back Monday in English." I looked up at his hands to get the money. He was holding it in such a way that only a little bit of the money showed.

I'd have to touch his hands.

I found the thought strangely exhilarating. I'm pretty sure he felt my hand shake as I grabbed the bill, the tops of my fingers touched his outer palm.

Look up, Mo, just once. You can do it—right..now!

I jerked my head up, maybe a bit too forcefully. The back of my head hit a trumpet. Morni burst out laughing next to me while Johnny bit his lip with a grin.

"Thanks for the money," I whimpered at him while massaging my throbbing head. He nodded, his mouth still quirked upwards, and walked back down the stairs to his friends.

"That was really painful to watch, and not just the trumpet part." I gave her a glare and watched the game timer.

"*Thirteen, Twelve.*" At exactly 11:11 I closed my eyes and made my wish. "*I really want Johnny Taylor to truly, from the bottom of his heart, somehow show me that he likes me.*" It was what I wished for every 11:11, or basically any eleven I saw anywhere. Better safe than sorry. I opened my eyes and they flicked to Johnny on their own accord.

I found him looking back at me.

Our school had made a goal, the stands erupted. It didn't matter, it was like the movies. The sound faded, everything was darker, except for Johnny and his glittering eyes. Except for that little smile on the side of his mouth, except for that curious look.

I could tell he knew exactly what I'd wished for.

* * *

"Mohana, focus!" Melody patted my thigh with a pen. The light coming in from the windows in our normal practice room at Melody's house made her hair look like it was glowing. I shoved Johnny away into a hidden corner in my brain to take out later. "Alright, Wainscott is exactly a month away. I know that seems like we have a lot of time, but that's not the case. It runs quickly." She spoke like an army general preparing for war. I guess in a way, we somewhat were. "Mohana, you need to finish writing the new song quickly. Try to finish it by this weekend. Finn, the song has to be challenging. Really challenging! It's the only way we can win. Make the song have lots of crescendos and decrescendos."

"Yes, ma'am!" Finn nodded with a salute. He was smiling.

"And, no more cold drinks. Hurts your throat." Melody grabbed Finn's Mountain Dew and threw it in the trash. Finn's smile vanished

"Actually, I have another idea," I said with a soft voice. I just remembered that Jamie and I had always planned to sing a particular song if we ever got in the Wainscott. It was the song that my parents entered into the competition Jamie was holding to find her songwriter. "Instead of singing a totally new song, I wanted to sing a song called *Painful Bliss*. It was Jamie's first song, but no one knew it existed. I wanted to change the tune and maybe sing it as a duet."

"Oh, I remember that one! That's when I first met you," Finn said with a smile. It was true, he'd spilled his coffee all over me and the machinery of the recording room. It had to be replaced. I smiled at the thought.

"Okay. As long as it's a challenging song that you can sing, I'm fine with it. Now, I wanted to talk about something else as well." She pulled out her laptop and got a picture. "Everyone who got chosen is mighty talented, you guys know that, but there's one group we have to be especially aware of. The people who were in tenth." She pulled up a picture of Lavender and Ryan Sink.

"Oh." I had just realized.

"Oh indeed," Melody responded. Lavender and Ryan were the Internet famous siblings who made covers for songs. Lavender was also very known for her work on Broadway. I hadn't realized who they were on the audition day because of all the tension.

"Their voices are just like yours, loud. They are the only other duet in the show. These people are the real competition."

"They're famous too. They'll have the audience's heart," Finn added softly.

"But isn't it the judges who choose the winner?" I asked.

"Yes, but the judges are celebrities. In the past they've chosen the audience's favorite performer so they get a better fan base, and so their fans don't turn against them." Finn looked at his shoes

"They wouldn't would they?" I asked.

"Fans? They probably would," Melody said with a smile, "but we have something that they don't have. Lavender and Ryan never sing together. Not even in the chorus. Their voices don't blend at all. Your voices blend perfectly. When you sang, it sent shivers down everyone's spine, I saw it. The organizers definitely noticed. We're using that to our advantage. I want you guys to sing together for most of the song.

Got it?" Melody looked at us. We nodded systematically. She looked at us a bit softer, "And, the passion you guys have, it's amazing! You guys are naturals. Just imagine, if you did that amazing without even practicing, how awesome would you two be with practice? Sing with that much energy and passion, and the trophy is yours."

She kept talking about all the other contestants, about their strengths and weaknesses, and how to beat them. It all felt surreal. Everyone Melody talked about seemed so amazing. Were they talking about Finn and I like we were about them? The thought made my head spin. "Oh, I almost forgot, we need to discuss clothing."

"Clothing?" Finn turned around. We were just leaving.

"Wainscott doesn't give us a designer so we have to find one for ourselves. I have a friend who does this type of thing. You two are gonna need matching costumes," Melody said, and Finn groaned. "Trust me, it'll be fun. I'll email your parents when I know what time you guys can get dropped at her studio to get fitted."

"*Fitted?*" Like a celebrity?" I asked. My smile stretched across my face as if it were a part of a toothpaste commercial. Melody laughed.

"Yes, fitted. Then we can try some different styles for you two."

"We get the final say, right? Not some lady?" Finn asked.

"Trust me, you two will be the ones picking everything out."

"Ugh, I have to wear something Mohana thinks looks good?"

"Excuse me?" I butted in.

"I mean, look at what your wearing." Finn pointed at my shirt. True, it was old and was starting to look worn out, but it was the weekend, or in other words, a day for me to just relax. I rolled my eyes. But my heart was thumping in my chest. I was going to get fitted!

Chapter 11

The building Melody's fashion designer friend worked in was huge. It was really close too, I had just never noticed it before. Melody was waiting at the entrance. Finn was there too, on his phone. My mom came with me.

"Mrs. Prasad! Wonderful to see you again!" They talked for about an hour. My mom just doesn't know how to stop talking. I rolled my eyes.

"You're lucky that your parents didn't come with you," I muttered to Finn. He looked up from his phone for a second then went back to text someone. I thought he hadn't heard me but then he responded with a whisper. "Am I though?" Before I could question him, the door opened. Johnny walked in, smelling his hands.

"They have fancy soap," he responded to my questioning look.

"What are you doing here though?"

"My dad is out of town. My mom doesn't trust me home alone, ever since I broke her imported china vase." I didn't ask how he broke the vase. It probably involved a basketball and his stupidity. My mom finally stopped talking and Melody took us to her friend's workplace. It was a very small, crowded, and quite messy room in the very back of the building. Papers with sketches of beautiful dresses and outfits covered the walls, leaving not a single speck of the wall visible. The designer, herself, was quite young. She looked only nineteen or twenty.

"My name is Brianna. Melody has told me all about you two. I have some ideas, come on, I'll show you." She had such a quiet voice that Finn and I had to lean in so we could hear what she said. She led us to another room filled to the ceiling with racks and racks of clothing. They all had the Adidas logo on them.

"You work for Adidas?" I asked her.

"It's a side job to pay rent. I study at the university." I hadn't realized it before, but up close I saw her eyes looked tired. She led us to the corner of a room and pulled down a few hangers with plastic wrappers over the clothing on them. "We'll try on some stuff first. It won't fit very well. Once we've chosen what we're going to wear, I'll get your measurements and fix them up." Brianna took the plastic wrapping off the first two hangers to reveal a black dress on one and a tuxedo on the other hanger.

"Yeah, no." My mom had beat me to it. The dress was quite short with a lot of rips and holes. It looked quite airy. Johnny sniggered. Finn was too busy inspecting his own outfit to see mine. I was glad.

"Melody told me the song you were singing, and I thought this would suit the mood of it," Brianna replied to my mom. True, it would fit the mood of the song perfectly, but I'd rather hang out with Shreya for an hour than wear that. My mom sighed.

"Your choice, Mohana." I could see the Indian in her struggling when she said that. I looked at the dress. It was quite pretty. Looked like something the popular girls at school would sell their mothers on, but my dignity came first.

"Sorry, I can't."

"No problem, I have more." Brianna brought out more outfits, mixing certain hangers with others.

Finn and I tried out all sorts of things. There were more dresses, there were some less fancy things, and there were heels. Being the doctors they were, my parents never bought me high heels. Every time I asked for some, my parents would start ranting about how half the patients who come to them came because they fell due to their heels or the problems wearing them caused your body in the long term. Being the clumsy thing I was didn't help either. With lots of persuasion, my mom finally let me try walking on heels, and it actually wasn't that hard once I got used to it.

"See Mom, nothing to worry about. I think I just grew out of my clumsy phase." I took a step but slipped on an Adidas shirt on the ground. Finn was behind me so he caught me in a quick fluid motion. We started laughing.

"Graceful, not clumsy at all," Finn said with a grin. I heard a cough. I looked over at Johnny, who was giving Finn a killer stare. It looked like he wanted to pin Finn to the wall with his eyes, but it vanished in a second and Johnny joined in on the laughter. I sighed to myself. I was imagining things now. Finn placed me on the ground, and that's when something caught my eye. On the very bottom rack, I saw faint sparkles underneath the plastic cover on a hanger. It was poking out slightly, as if it was calling my name. I pulled it out and took off the plastic to find a stunning blue leather jacket with a bit of sparkles on the collar. Badass and childish, I loved it. It was a kind of blue that couldn't be missed in a crowd, a richly vibrant, yet soft blue that warmed my eyes when I looked at it.

"Oh," Brianna took the jacket from my hands, "I thought I'd lost it."

"Who'd you make it for? It's marvelous," Melody said while she marvelled at it. Brianna smiled.

"This is the jacket I submitted to get a scholarship for

my college. I also had my first kiss in that. I've considered it lucky ever since."

"I have an idea," I muttered. I never had a good fashion sense and I just didn't care enough about what I looked like, but sometimes I get an occasional good idea. I got a tank top from another outfit I had tried and went into the bathroom to change. I wore the jacket over the tank and black leggings that I was already wearing and let my hair out of the braid I had it in. I was still wearing black ankle boots with heels on them from the last outfit. The jacket fit like a glove. It was meant to be. And the last outfit Finn tried would match perfectly with mine.

I looked in the mirror, and was taken back. I felt invincible, like I could do anything I wanted in that thing.

With my hair that beautifully curled over my jacket, I knew this was what I had to wear. I stepped out, and everyone loved it.

"Perfect! As long as I get it back, you should wear it. It fits perfectly as well. I don't think I have to make many changes," Brianna said with a smile that quickly turned into a frown. "I don't know much about hair, but from what I do know your hair is too long for that outfit."

"Aww, but I liked the jacket," I responded with a frown.

"Then cut your hair," Finn scoffed. "Problem solved."

"Yeah, not too much. Just a bit would do, right Brianna?" Melody said with a smile.

"Wait—" I tried to stop them.

"Yeah, just a bit. And lucky for you I know the hair stylist here. I think she's still working."

"No wa—" I tried to interrupt, this was going way to fast.

"Let's go. It's time you got a haircut anyway." My mom turned to the door.

"Stop," I said it loud and clear this time.

My hair was waist long and I loved it that way. It made

me feel less exposed. It gave me more room to hide. Did I really want to chop it off? There was a full body mirror I stepped in front of. I held the end of my hair just below my shoulders to see how it would look cut to that length. I saw what they meant; the shorter hair would look better with the jacket.

"Mohana, it's just hair," Johnny said with a smile.

"No, it's not," I responded quietly. I hadn't cut my hair in six years. I loved my long hair. It was familiar to me. No matter what changed my hair will always be there. It was with me through all the tough times. Sounds stupid, I know, but my hair was like my best friend. I looked in the mirror one more time and reached a painful conclusion. I couldn't hide underneath my hair now. I couldn't hide from Jamie and Shreya and all the people I hated anymore. I had to show them I wasn't the shy girl who couldn't do anything anymore.

That meant my hair had to go.

"Fine let's do it," I told them.

"The building manager's daughter is a hair stylist so she has her studio here. Except for her, all of us work for Adidas," Brianna explained to all of us. I wasn't listening, I was too nervous. The hair stylist, whose name was Becky, had a room more spacious than Brianna's. It was neat and filled with wigs of all shapes. There was a stage mirror in a corner of a room with a big chair in front. That was where I had to sit. Becky was a short lady who talked way too fast for comprehension. In seconds, I had a sheet over me and I was leaning back in my chair. I closed my eyes and felt my fingers twist themselves into the sheet on me. My dread grew larger and larger as I heard the scissors snip. It was over really quick. The first thing I saw was all the hair that littered the floor around my chair. My heart wilted at the sight.

Becky took the sheet of me. I looked up to see myself

in the mirror. My hair, which now ended just below my shoulders, curled beautifully around my shirt. My back tingled. I felt so exposed, but it looked so pretty it didn't matter. I saw Finn looking at me with his eyes scrunched. He smiled when he realized I was looking at him. I swear he was blushing.

"It looks great, not as good as my hair, but good," he said, fluffing his curly hair. Johnny looked over at Finn. He looked sad and confused.

Wait, sad and confused? But why? But he didn't look as confused as I was feeling at that moment. God, I hated feelings.

Chapter 12

"Welcome!" said Hugh, the Wainscott organizer with the high voice, as he motioned for us to sit in the front row of the auditorium. I felt Finn shake next to me, trying to control his laughter. I rolled my eyes at him. The eleven other Wainscott competitors were already seated. Melody, Finn, and I squeezed in next to them.

Melody was right, time had flown. The Wainscott was now only two weeks away. All the competitors and voice coaches were called today to the humongous auditorium that held the actual show for a trial run. Finn and I were singing a song that I wrote years ago to see how our voices would sound in the new setting.

I could feel the tension come off the competitors in waves. While Hugh was talking, I felt eyes drilling into my head. I saw furtive glances thrown around. With my new haircut, I felt as exposed as ever. The only nice person I saw was Lavender Sink who gave me a smile when I sat down.

Finn glanced at me, again.

Ever since the day we had been fitted, Finn was different. He was silent for most of that day. Every time I saw him after that he was still his annoying childish self, but whenever he looked at me his eyes were distant. It wasn't romantic. He didn't *like* me. That was certain. The glance he gives me now is more brotherly, as if he's trying to protect me. It's sweet and all, but just because he was two years older than me, didn't mean he had to keep me safe. I could protect myself thank you very much.

"Our first performer is lovely Miss Ellen Winters." When Hugh finally left the stage, he was replaced by a stunning lady in a dress. All the performers, no doubt, were spectacular. I was expecting it, but it still took my breath away. There were rappers, jazz artists, and so many different varieties of singers. It was hard to believe that the songs they sang today were just for a trial. I couldn't imagine what the actual songs for the show were going to sound like. My heart sank with each contestant, as if Finn and I had already lost the competition. Nope, I shut my eyes hard and opened them again. No negativity, not right now. So I smiled and enjoyed the music. There was a guy who looked like Peter Raul and sang a Peter Raul song. I made sure to note his name for future reference.

Finally, we were up next. Lavender and Ryan were climbing up stage and we moved closer to sit next to the stairs that lead to the stage. I had always envied Lavender's hair. It was as black as the night with little ringlet curls. She reminded me of a black-haired Hermione. She looked down from the stage at me. I froze, but then I realized she wasn't looking at me, but at Finn. I smirked and elbowed oblivious Finn who was playing with his hands. But, by then, she had looked away.

"That hurt," Finn hoarsely whispered as he elbowed me back.

"Even my little sister thinks I'm weak," I said, smiling as he frowned at me. Melody gave us both a glare. She had her clipboard out and was noting down everything about the other contestants. She mouthed for us to focus as Ryan, on stage, strummed his guitar. I don't need to tell you how great they were. They were like the sun, powerful enough to power the world. My envy for both of them only grew. As the song came to a close, I saw Finn's legs start bouncing.

I had kept a close eye on him, making sure he was okay. Another panic attack might just kick us out of the competition. It also might just ruin his confidence. I pressed my hand down on his knee to make his legs stop and looked at him. My eyes conveying a message: *It's gonna be okay. We're in this together.*

He smiled at me gratefully as the last few notes were played out of Ryan's guitar. I got up quickly and made for the stage. Act quick so your mind doesn't start thinking, thus panicking. That was only theory though. I felt my heart shudder. I looked over at Finn who looked worse. I had to be brave, for Finn. I didn't look down at the audience. Pretended not to hear the pencils scratching on paper. I let myself imagine I was alone and opened a part of my brain I'd never known I had and when I did felt myself move unconsciously, sing unconsciously, and act unconsciously. It was so natural that it surprised me. I consciously smiled though.

The performance ended as soon as it started. None of the other participants clapped. I didn't really care. They didn't clap for anyone. We were last so everyone left with us.

The auditorium was close to where I lived so I had biked there. With a quick goodbye to Finn and Melody, I biked over to the nearby bookstore I always visited. The other contestants looked at my bike with amusement. They all were riding in fancy cars. I even saw a limo, but I was still feeling the happy effect that singing gives you. It was too bright for anger.

Once I got to the bookstore, I parked my bike and took the leather jacket I was supposed to wear at the Wainscott from my backpack and slipped it on. Brianna had told me not to wear it until the day of the show, so nothing would happen to it, but I wore it all the time. It gave a nice warmth, as if someone was hugging you. I brought out a ripped book as well. It was something kids my age dreaded, poetry. It explains why I got it for free from a librarian. I smiled, remembering how her face lit up once she realized I would actually take it. As soon as I entered the store, I moved my hair forward so it obscured my face.

Every Friday from six to eight Johnny worked at the café inside the bookstore. So you could probably guess what I spent my Friday nights doing. Hiding behind the shelves watching Johnny in a button-down shirt and an apron making lattes; but that particular evening I forgot something. My once long hair normally obscured my face so I could usually pass by him without being noticed, but did I have that long hair anymore? No I didn't.

"Oh, hey Mohana. Could you hand me that rag on the floor?" I flinched, and the hair in front of my face didn't help matters. I walked head first into a column and ended up falling, but I played it off as if I'd bent down to get the rag. I don't think it looked as cool as I wanted it to. "Thanks," he said with his eyebrows raised as he reached to grab it. Our fingers brushed each other's. His fingers froze.

The key to Johnny was his eyes. His body could be doing something totally different, but his eyes would give him away. Right now there was something in them. Was it hesitation? Confusion? I couldn't tell. I dropped my hand and gave him a smile and a nod of welcome. I felt his eyes bore into my skull as I turned and walked off, or tried to at least. I spotted a little spiral notebook with Johnny's messy handwriting on one of the tables. I squinted. It couldn't be. "Poetry, Johnny?" The words were out of my mouth before the usual fear Johnny brought with him hit me. But the words on the page that were organized perfectly into stanzas and numbered lines had gotten my attention.

"Oh, it's probably nothing compared to what you're used

to, being a writer and all. It's just that it gets really boring here. No one spends their Friday evenings in a bookstore. Well , except you of course."

"Oh, you've seen me here before?" My voice cracked and I could feel my cheeks burning.

"Oh, yeah. Every Friday, am I right?" I quickly scanned the room trying to change the subject. My eyes landed on the notebook. His long arms shot out to try to get the notebook instantly, but I wasn't done yet.

"Oh trust me, constructive criticism is all I have to offer. No judging, I promise." With a laugh I dodged behind a table and opened the little book. I was astonished at what I saw. Pages and pages of beautiful similes and comparisons describing nature, things, people.

"Johnny—" I looked up at him. "Companies kill for stuff like this. You could make triple what you get wiping tables if you show them these, especially this one. Is it—" I opened to the last page to show him, but I found myself suddenly dragged forward. Johnny held my free arm with his right hand and reached for his book with his left. I cradled it to my chest with a smile and shook my head.

"I don't think I can keep up with all those deadlines," he said in the low rumble of a voice that I'd fallen in love with over the years. I took a breath so wouldn't didn't collapse right there in his arms. *In his arms.* How did that happen? He had his arm around my waist and was trying to get the notebook I was dangling away from him. I felt his breath tickle my forehead."Trust me, it's not too bad, not too bad at all." I felt my voice trail off. My what a great hard chest he had.

"But you're Mohana Prasad, the teacher's pet, the goody two-shoes. If anyone can handle deadlines, it's you." He'd given up trying to get the book, but he hadn't let go of me either. I frowned at him."Goody Two-shoes? Well, I shall have you know, I missed two assignments last week."

"But you made them up?"

"Of course. I'm not a common criminal." In the time that we were speaking his hand had slid down my forearm and now clutched my wrists. They slid down farther, to my hands. My hands instinctively met his halfway and gripped his hand tight. His dark eyes had found mine. I felt myself drown in them.

"Huh," he murmured.

"Pardon?" I cursed in my weak sounding voice.

"You literally haven't grown an inch since seventh grade." I gave him my best attempt at a glare in my weakened state.

"Do you have something against short people?"

"No, of course not. Sage was short." Her name spurred something deep inside me. I stiffened against him and handed him his notebook back.

"Was the last one about her? The last poem?" I found my voice had been reduced to a whisper. He let go of my waist, but he still held my hand. "Sherlock Holmes you are," he muttered.

"You liked her a lot didn't you? It broke your heart when she called it off." I expected him to hide his feelings as all boys did, but he didn't.

He looked at his feet, still maintaining his smile. "She wasn't the first girl I liked, but definitely the first girl that asked me out. I said yes so she wouldn't get hurt, but I guess I did start liking her after a while. I definitely started trusting her more, but it was clear we weren't meant to last. I mean, she's smart and she has to focus on all her AP classes and all her extracurriculars. I was never that important to her."

"I think that's a lie in its purest form. I'm pretty sure you meant a lot to her. It probably broke her heart to break it off with you, but not as much as it hurt her to see that she couldn't give you the attention you deserved. She knew you deserved someone who could stay dedicated to you."

I winced in my head. Sage was not a nice person. And maybe it hadn't reached his ears that she was now dating Levi Jones, but as my Mom said, lying for a good cause was always right.

"Well, you seem to know a lot about these matters." He took a step closer to me.

"Maybe I'm not all that much of a Goody Two-shoes." I laughed as he raised his eyebrows disbelievingly. "Fine, I've read a lot on the matter. Besides, I probably know more than you, anyway."

"What makes you say that." He'd taken another step, I knew he was tall but never this tall. He towered over me, which made me realize his cheekbones were way sharper up close. I looked up to meet his eyes, resting my chin on his upper chest.

"Well, I mean, you being an ignorant little poet and all." His deep, deep eyes. He raised our entwined hands and pressed them against his rock-hard chest.

"Well, you'd be surprised," he murmured and plunged down to close the little gap between our lips.

Chapter 13

"I've never seen you this peppy. It's kinda scary." My mom scrunched her eyes at me. It's really scary when she does that. It's like she's x-raying your soul.

"Can't I just be happy for a day?" I responded.

"I had the impression you teenagers don't become happy over nothing."

"That was a rhetorical question. Besides, you just kinda have to be happy on bright sunny days like this when the birds are singing, and the trees are dancing in the breeze." *And when you finally actually have a love life.*

I'd been peppy all weekend. It was exhausting. You know what else is exhausting? Johnny never gave me his number, and I was too preoccupied to ask for it. I didn't talk to him all weekend, and it drove me nuts. The butterflies in my stomach erupted at the thought that I would see him tomorrow. My mom skeptically looked out the mall window at the rainy day we were having.

"Birds are singing, trees are dancing?"

"Let's go here." I led her into a clothing store to distract her.

"Oh, these look good. Cheap too. Since you've been working hard for Wainscott, which is just two days away, I guess you deserve a treat. What do you want?" She picked up a green t-shirt from the rack.

"Gross, mom. Can I have that please?" I asked, motioning towards a yellow sweatshirt that I really liked.

"But, that's not on sale."

"Maybe not, but I really want it," I said. Times like these were rare. My sister was too impatient for shopping and my dad just didn't get the point. I had my mom all to myself. It took a while, but I eventually convinced her to buy the sweatshirt for me. By the time we left the store, the rain had finally stopped. It smelled like grass when we stepped outside. It was an aroma I loved. I closed my eyes and I was in mid breath when I felt a tap on my shoulder.

"Is that one of your secrets Ms. Prasad? Taking a breath? Do you do it before performances as a stress reliever?" a tall woman asked me quickly. My mom was there in the blink of an eye.

"Maybe, and you'll be?" She had a protective arm around my shoulder.

"Darla Hamilton with the press," she said, extending a hand to my mother which she reluctantly shook. "Your daughter is singing in the Wainscott I believe? I want to ask her a few questions for an article. I'm sure everyone will love it."

Ms. Hamilton had a strong Jersey accent. My mom looked down at me and I shrugged. The interview began right then and there. "Alrighty, Wainscott is exactly eight days away, and you're the youngest contestant, yeah? You nervous?" She took out a notepad and was already writing things down.

This was my first interview. Yes, it wasn't fancy, true that the interviewer was wearing a t-shirt and shorts instead of formal wear, but it was still my first interview. I closed my eyes and decided what to say.

"Yes I'm nervous, but I'm trying not to think about it. Nervousness usually cau—"

"So you're confident? Think you can beat everyone?"

"Me? Uhm, I don't think winning is the problem. I believe it's more about having fun."

"Fun? So you haven't been practicing? How about your partner, is he practicing?"

"Uhm, yeah, yes. We've both been practicing really hard."

"Yeah, I'm sure you are," she muttered to herself. "Alright, thanks for your time." She left as quickly as she had come. I turned to my mom with a thunderstruck face.

"Mom, tell me it didn't go as bad as it seemed."

"No, sweetie. It went worse. Did you catch what company she was working for?"

"No, should I have?"

"No, hey it's fine. She probably didn't mention what newspaper because it was some small company that no one knows." My mom put her arm around my shoulders reassuringly and led me to our car. She had to be right, right? I mean, what professional journalist would wear t-shirts and shorts and interview in mall entrances?

I figured out the next morning that a lot of them apparently do. As I entered school, heads turned to look at me. I was used to it now, with the whole Wainscott thing and all, but this was different. Everyone's eyes where x-raying me up and down. Some eyes were even filled with hatred. I felt a jerk on my hand and Neela pulled me aside.

"Hey, so—" She was cut off by Shaina.

"Do you know what's happening?" Shaina asked quickly. All my friends were here, including Morni so I knew it was serious. Morni wasn't exactly part of our group but she was one of my close friends, nonetheless. She'd usually be in the cafeteria being the life of the party as usual.

"No, what's up?" I asked, even though deep down I knew.

"Hamilton," Morni said, as if it would solve all my doubts. At my raised eyebrows Morni took out her phone and showed me a picture of the interviewer from yesterday. "She's one of the more famous journalists. I don't know how you didn't recognize her. Anyway, she's like the meanest person there is. Writes trash articles about basically everyone who existed."

"She's like the Rita Skeeter of the muggle world," Shruthi butted in. Andie, a fellow freshman, who was usually friendly scoffed in my direction and kept talking to her friends.

"Can I see the article?" My voice cracked. I choked back the tears as Morni scrolled on her phone. Shruthi and Kalyani both hugged me as Morni started reading.

"Today, one of the most known ways to fame is winning the Wainscott Voice Competition, and this year's competition is especially special. Instead of the usual ten contestants that are chosen, this year a duo changed the minds of the judges and won their way onto an eleventh spot on the show. The duo of Finn Winston and Mohana Prasad—"

She stopped talking but continued to scroll. Why? Was it bad? Did I really want to hear this? Before I could answer that, Morni continued reading out loud.

"I got a chance to speak with Mohana Prasad, a short girl whose ego is taller than herself. Bright-eyed Ms. Prasad strutted out of the mall yesterday with her mom trailing her laden with shopping bags. As I was talking to her, one thing was certain, she really needs to tone her ego down.

'Me? Uhm I don't think winning is the problem,' Ms. Prasad told me with her eyebrows raised."

"That's not what I meant," I whispered.

"I don't think she cares. Let me read the rest," said Morni, continuing. *"So I hope I have helped clear your doubts on which duo to support. Famous Ryan and Lavender Sink, who have worked hard and won their way to their spot, or Finn Winston and Mohana Prasad, who god-knows-how cheated their way into the competition. Bitch, I hope Karma beats her up good."*

Morni shoved her phone back into her backpack and looked at me. Everyone was—they all looked scared.

"Mohana, you okay?" Shaina asked. How was I feeling? I didn't know. It wasn't sadness, I felt kinda hollow. My phone rang, disturbing my thoughts.

"Yes?"

"Wendy," a sad-sounding voice murmured. This wasn't going to be good. Wendy doesn't just say one word. She usually makes sure no one else can talk except her. "I saw you've been busy. Congrats, by the way on the Wainscott thing."

"Thanks." The bell rang so I waved to my friends and headed to class. They looked surprised, just cause I was dead inside doesn't mean I would be mean.

"So bad news. It was just a rumor for a while that they were gonna kick you off Jamie's team. You know, with the whole Wainscott thing, they thought you would become competition later. I never believed a word of it 'cause they need you,' but now with Hamilton's article the—"

"I'm fired? That's great!"

"Mo, I'm sorry. I tried to stop them."

"I know you did. Thanks Wendy, really." That settled it for me. Now I had to win Wainscott.

Chapter 14

All the kids who were in boys' basketball were not here all day, which was kind of good because I didn't have the mental willpower to deal with Johnny at the moment. That reporter debacle, and the fact that Wainscott was tomorrow, had left me drained. All I wanted was for school to end so I could rant to Finn. From what I saw, he'd been having a bad day too. I'd gotten a single text consisting of three words.

They fired me. I could feel the waves of anger coming from the message.

"Ms. Prasad!" I jumped at the raspy voice of old Mr. Abernathy who just wouldn't retire.

"Yes, Mr. Abernathy?"

"For the third time, what is the value of x in this problem?" I did some quick mental math.

"Four."

"Wrong. Mr. Taylor, I recommend you look here and focus. What's the value of x?" I looked around. I guess the basketball team did make it to school from their tournament after all. I then realized that Johnny had been staring at me, my cheeks instantly warmed up.

"Twelve."

"Correct, but I would like it if you'd make eye contact with me next time." Mr. Abernathy droned on as usual but my mind was far, far away. I never thought he could look better, but in that basketball jersey Johnny looked angelic. His eyes flickered to me and he shifted uncomfortably in his chair. He messed up his hair in some weird unnatural way.

Oh, oh wow. He was self conscious.

He looked even cuter when he was unsure. It made me smile. I looked away and out the window, but my eyes wouldn't stay put. They flicked back to Johnny of their own accord. In all, I had no idea what Mr. Abernathy had said.

Johnny approached me after class. He motioned with his head and we started walking toward the buses. "Hey Mohana," he muttered, looking basically anywhere but at me.

"Hey," I said back as I looked around too, but in awe. People literally made way for Johnny, like he was some prince. And at that moment, I was the princess. The thought made me nervously giggle.

"You alright? You're looking around everywhere," he said.

"Oh no, I'm totally fine!" My mental mind started think-ing. I needed to say something, "W-What'd you have for lunch?"

Shit, shit, shit. Mo, you complete idiot! Johnny ignored my question, I didn't blame him. He softly chuckled. "Lis-ten, Mohana, our friendship i-is important to me. More important than anything—"

"Me too!" I smiled as I interrupted him.

Oh my god Mo, you cut him off! Could you at least try not to scare him away? I listened to the voice in my head and shut up. Johnny seemed grateful for it.

"I know I can always talk to you and feel better. And I don't want anything to change that, especially not some dumb thing I did—" He abruptly stopped in his tracks. I saw recognition dawn on his face. I saw his eyes widen at his mistake, but I was too hurt to care. "Oh-wait, I—"

"Yeah, I agree. Don't worry, some worthless evening isn't

gonna change anything. I'll see you tomorrow." It broke my heart, those words. But at that moment, I couldn't care less.

"Wai—" I walked sideways and out the door to the buses, ignoring him. When I was a safe distance away I looked back. I saw the tall, slightly bent shadow of Johnny still in front of the glass doors.

He looked as if he hadn't moved an inch since I left.

I couldn't think of anything else during the bus ride. I couldn't think of anything else during dinner. I just couldn't think. I had to get this out of my mind, so I quickly picked up my phone after dinner.

"I was just about to call you!"

"He said it didn't matter."

"What, wh—"

"He said our kiss didn't matter." Finn was silent for a second, then I heard his voice again seething with anger.

"Do I need to beat Johnny up?" It brought a smile to my face. Finn and I were spending so much time together recently, we'd almost become the same person. And seeing toothpick-Finn trying to tackle a towering Johnny may have contributed to that smile.

"Don't Finn, he would have you pinned in seconds. He didn't mean it, I saw. But it still came out of his mouth. He must have been thinking it to have said it. Ugh, Finn I'm so confused."

"Uhm, I dunno."

"Finn!"

"Well, you don't ask the one with social anxiety for social advice, smart one. Look, try to get some sleep. We have Wainscott tomorrow. Don't wear yourself out."

Oh wow, I'd almost forgotten. The thing I'd been anticipating for about my whole life was tomorrow. "Oh yeah, how you feeling Finn?"

"Me?" I heard a chuckle. "I feel as if I'm slowly dying inside. But, it's all good."

"Hey—" Before I could finish my sister entered my room and before I knew it she had my phone.

"Ooh who's this?" She put my phone up to her ear. "Hey, Mo's secret boyfriend, talk to her later cause she's spending time with her awesome little sister now." I swiped for the phone, but she easily dodged me and cut on Finn.

"Ria, I need my phone. Give it back!"

"Not right now, you need to help me with my homework."

"I'm telling mom!"

"I'm telling mom," She mocked me, then she stopped. "Something's wrong. Why are you sad? You miss school tomorrow." My sister was like that. She could go from a yipping small dog to an actually kinda compassionate person. Her eyes were filled with concern. It made me smile. I sighed and gave her a small hug. I buried my face in her hair.

"I have a performance tomorrow, Ria, a big one."

"I know you do. I'm gonna come, remember? But you know what you should do right now? Take a deep breath and let it out. It always solves everything."

Aw, if only a big breath would solve things. I did it to humor her, and it actually made me feel better. I chuckled and said, "Huh, I guess your Disney Princesses give good advice."

Chapter 15

I was up at five that morning, and not just because I couldn't sleep. We had to be at the auditorium at seven. My mom was going to drop me there, then come back when I was supposed to perform later on that evening.

How was I feeling? Weightless, I felt weightless. It was such a weird feeling. I was too preoccupied to have weight. Finn looked the same. We met him inside. He was with Melody. They both had red eyes from lack of sleep. Were my eyes red too?

Probably.

Melody gave a small smile. "Mo, you guys are the last performance. So you're up at 8:05 tonight. The show itself starts at four."

"Then why were they asked to be here at seven?" my mom asked.

"Would they have focused in school?" Melody responded. Both of them looked at me.

"Probably not," I said and shrugged.

"Plus, we have a lot to do. I have to leave you guys right now, but make sure you align yourselves with the stage." Melody hesitated for one second, and motioned for us to come closer. "You can speak to the other competitors, but don't reveal what you're singing, or anything about your performance, really. There have been accidents in the past."

Finn and I nodded. After Melody left and my mom left for work, I got a good look at Finn.

He actually seemed, well, fine.

Better than at the Wainscott auditions. He caught me staring at him.

"Don't worry, I'll be fine. This is a duet now. I won't let you down." Before I could respond, he walked up to the foot of the stage where other competitors were milling around and knocked on the wooden floor. The sound vibrated through the auditorium.

"Isn't it cool? The acoustics I mean. You really don't need a microphone." Lavender Sink sat down on the edge of the stage. Finn immediately looked down and stared down at her boots. Lavender didn't seem to notice. She extended her arm out toward us. "I'm Lavender."

"Mohana, I'm a huge fan of your work. I loved your newest cover of Jamie's song."

"*The Mask*? That was inspired by you guys at the auditions." I felt myself go giddy inside. I had always admired her. She was such a nice person, but could be total badass when she wanted to be. Even now, when she was sitting, she looked like she was supposed to be in some rock concert with her over-the-knee boots and red leather jacket. And we weren't even in costume yet.

"And I really liked your part," she said as she looked at Finn. "At the bridge, you handled those high notes very well. If you two ever wanted to collab, me and you, I'm always here." She was blushing again. This time, Finn actually noticed. I saw his eyebrows quiver.

"You and I."

"Hmm?"

"You said 'me and you' you don't put yourself first so it would be 'you and I,'" Finn softly corrected.

"Oh yeah. I don't like English. I suck at it. Okay, I'll see you guys later." She walked away with still a red tinge on her cheeks.

"Really? Correcting her grammar? Even I can do better."

"What? She needed to know she was doing something wrong. Besides, we're here to win, not see me try to flirt."

"Aw, but it's fun." I hopped on stage and walked to the middle to face the empty seats. The auditorium was bigger than any room I'd ever been in. I could hardly see the back row. They were testing the lighting. I closed my eyes as the light person increased the light. I felt it penetrate my sweater and warm my skin. Like a warm bath on a cold, sub-zero Minnesotan morning, it soothed me in the perfect way. I felt something brush my shoulder. Finn stood next to me. We silently looked out into the imaginary crowd.

"My mom still has a video of me from when I was three. We were watching the Wainscott and I said, 'Mommy, I wanna be that girl,' I can't believe I'm finally here, Finn." I felt a sudden rush of adrenaline.

"Yeah?" He hesitated as he always did when I shared something personal. "I've wanted to be here ever since I saw Jamie perform. I was with the agent who recognized her. And I don't know, seeing the happiness on her face when she was recognized made me want that too."

"Huh, I never thought I'd hear you say anything deep like that." I laughed. Finn sighed.

"I didn't either. I'm spending way too much time with you."

The rest of the day went kind of like that. The place had practice rooms where Finn and I practiced for most of the morning. We had lunch in a conference room as well so we didn't really get to meet any other contestants until the evening. I could tell Melody disliked the idea of us mingling. She had tried to keep us separated for the whole day, but she had to talk to the organizers so she left.

The contestants themselves were mostly nice. They were

in their twenties and thirties with the exception of Lavender who was eighteen, her brother, and one girl who was the same age as me.

"Hello! I'm Maxine Brown, but call me Max." She had a strong British accent. "I moved from Manchester about two months ago, and when I heard about Wainscott I just had to try. Back in Britain I have quite a lot of YouTube followers. Have you heard any of my songs?" She talked very fast, her shoulder-length hair bobbing.

"Uhm not really, sorry. I'm more of a Peter Raul person."

"Peter Raul! I love him so much, what do you like?"

"Uhh, my favorite would have to be *Pictures*. What do you like?"

"Never heard of that. I only listen to the singles."

You know love at first sight? I don't really believe in that. What I do believe in is hate at first sight. And Max definitely fell into that category. She rubbed me the wrong way and I could tell I wasn't the only one. Lavender's eyebrow literally went a mile up when she met Max.

"S-Sweetie, okay let me throw this away and I'll be back," Lavender interrupted Max's monologue and walked out the door, ignoring the trash can near the exit.

"Ooh snap, I wanna see this girl-fight. Are they gonna start insulting each other's pants?" Finn muttered next to me.

"I'm pretty sure Lavender's not that type. She'd probably take her heeled boots and throw 'em at her." That's when the doors opened and Melody walked in. She was followed by two ladies and a man holding suitcases. Turns out they were the makeup artists and their cases were humongous. They did all of our makeup according to the lists they had. I recognized Melody's handwriting on my makeup artist's list.

"Alright, sweetheart, keep your face still," Finn giggled. I gave him a stare.

"Right Shistar, breathe in that aroma of the foundation."

He snorted and walked away. The guy was too focused on his makeup to realize. He finished efficiently and moved on to Finn quickly, and Karma got him good. I had to say, watching Finn whimper and grip the seat handles as the makeup guy applied highlight to his cheeks was the best moment of my life.

"I swear the guy put too much on. I look like I collided with a fairy." He touched his cheekbones in front of the big stage mirror backstage. We'd changed into our costumes and last minute mic-checks were being performed.

"Well, he is gonna go a bit overboard so you can be seen from the back row," I told Finn.

"I literally can help fishermen at sea. My cheeks can be used as a lighthouse." I scoffed at him while I crunched on my sugar cube, careful not to mess up my lipstick. After I finished, I walked up behind him to see myself in the mirror.

Huh, you actually look decent for once. But this time the voice in my head didn't matter because I was too occupied with something else. I felt my heart blossom at the young girl I saw in the mirror. She was wearing a leather jacket with pretty heels and bright red lips. Her jet black eyeliner matched her black curled hair.

In other words, she looked as if she belonged here perfectly.

So, when the backstage managers motioned for silence, when I heard the mutterings of an audience instead of nervousness, I felt calm. I knew this was what I was supposed to do, and I wasn't about to let anyone take it from me.

Chapter 16

We had to stay pretty deep backstage. But from a certain viewpoint I could see a little bit of the audience, and the judge table. They all arrived thirty minutes before the start of the show. Jamie was first. She was in a stunning, navy blue, knee-length dress. She caught my eye, and huffed. She rolled her eyes and continued talking to the organizers. At least she acknowledged me now.

There were seven judges total, all music artists. They all give a score out of five for each performance, the top three performances perform again. Then the judges vote for the best performance. Finn and I were singing Jamie's, now that I think about it my *Painful Bliss* for the first round, then Peter Raul for the second. That is if we got to go again.

Why Peter Raul you ask? People traditionally sing one of the judge's songs because they're the only one who actually knows how hard the song is. Which means, yes, Peter Raul was a judge. He was the last to arrive. I felt a tap on my shoulder.

"Sorry, mind if I squeeze past you for a moment?" He was going kinda fast so I couldn't see his face. It took me a second to recognize his voice with me being anxious and all. But, when the gasp escaped my mouth he was already on stage apologizing for his delay. I only saw part of his arm and a bit of his outfit as he was talking to the organizers.

He was wearing a classic suit. Too bad I could only see part of it. The audience went wild when he arrived. I saw his arm give a wave. He then walked across to the other side of the stage and entered a room.

"Alright, alright." A bald man in a suit motioned for silence. He waved to the people far, far, up in the light box. The lights increased, the cameras that hung from the ceiling moved, and the people backstage counted off until the cameras would start rolling.

"Three-two-one—"

Music blasted from the speakers as the man gave a smile with incredible white teeth.

"Good evening folks watching at home, I'm your host Bleeker White here to help you through this year's forty-seventh Wainscott Show." He raised his arms and the crowd took its cue and cheered. I saw my parents in the front row holding signs with my face on them. The cameras zoomed in on them. I couldn't help but laugh as my dad went red. "I'm pretty sure you didn't come to see me though, let me introduce you to our wonderful judges—" The host left the stage.

Every year, the judges all made like a little show together to start the show. The music started, it was Finn's. He was entering from the opposite side of the stage when it was our turn. I saw him across the wide stage, eyes closed and foot tapping to the music. His fingers counted along. I moved back a bit and saw Jamie. She was standing behind the curtain, beautiful in her blue dress. She took a deep breath, and moved the break in the middle of the curtain. She was greeted with a wild cheer. A familiar song flooded the speakers. I closed my eyes and smiled big as she sang my lyrics. Then all of a sudden the music changed. Finn opened his eyes from across the stage. The music turned jazzy, the total opposite of Finn's style of alternate rock or pop. His mouth was hanging open. She'd started out with my lyrics, but now she was singing something different. I guess Jamie found her new tune setter and songwriter. Her eyes flicked toward backstage at me. The corners of her mouth turned up and she continued singing the alien lyrics.

This was her way of telling us she had waged war, showing us that we weren't needed anymore. I think she was trying to tell us to back off. But that's just the opposite of what I wanted to do now. I saw Finn agreed with me. As the other judges joined her on stage, his eyes remained glued on her. He had a fierce look of hatred, any sign of him being nervous was gone, which was good for me as well. The judges all linked hands, gave a big bow and took their seats at the judge's table below the stage. The host took the spotlight again and started thanking the sponsors and tried to be funny. It was over pretty quick and the performers were out.

I really don't need to tell you how great they were. I'm pretty sure you can guess. Max rapped so perfectly that the rapper who she was singing to, herself, came down and gave her a hug. Lavender and Ryan sang some Broadway musical with a matching dance routine which left the audience cheering for hours. It was clear they both were going to make the finals, which only left one spot open.

"—And now, put your hands together for the duo who changed the tradition of ten performances, the duo who changed the minds of everyone, the duo of Finn Winston and Mohana Prasad. Me and Finn made eye contact from across the stage. He still looked angry over his mutilated music.

He gave me a look that said, *Let's annihilate this,* as the light decreased and turned a little bit blue. My sister in the crowd started dancing with the sign. I squinted even farther and saw another sign with my face on it. *"Don't mess this up,"* it said. I saw my friends waving it around. Melody was standing on the other side with Finn. She counted off as the music started, the familiar Finn-made music.

I took my cue.

The crowd's cheer wasn't as loud, but it didn't matter. All the contestants were already famous in some other way, all except us. Woah, Peter Raul looked so good. A man in the front spilled his fries on an elderly woman. She looked pissed. A toddler was crying in the arms of a sleep-deprived-looking mom. The host in the wings was picking his nose.

Focus Mohana, my mind told me.

All of this ran through my head while I was singing. It was normal when performing. Your mind always thought of every single detail that wasn't what you were performing. The hard part was to make your mind focus on the one thing you were performing.

Pretty soon Finn came in.

Uh-Oh, Finn looked determined. He sounded determined too. Maybe a bit too determined. His loud voice quickly took over mine. In order to make it perfectly blend you needed my voice too. But, if I was to sing as loud as Finn it would sound like we were yelling the lyrics.

The crowd or the judges didn't figure it out yet, but Melody could tell. She had moved to the bottom of the right side of the stage with a horrified expression. I had to do something.

I grabbed Finn's hands and did a little spin in the center of the stage so he could look into my terrified eyes. I stopped singing so he could hear himself. His eyes opened wide and he lowered his voice, maybe a bit too much. We stopped twirling and faced the crowd. I continued singing again, but now I was in control and kinda taking over Finn's voice. But that's the thing, the crowd liked it. It did sound pretty cool. Jamie's eyebrows raised and she tilted her head. When your enemy approves, you know you didn't mess up. Finn got his confidence back and we were in sync again. Melody breathed again.

"Mo-Mohana Prasad? Did I say that right?" We straightened from our bows and faced the judges. The cheers died down. Did Peter Raul just say my name? I think he did! Oh he looked better in real life than in pictures. I didn't think it was possible.

"Mh-hm," I nodded. I felt myself take raspier breaths. I took a big calming breath. I couldn't have an asthma attack now.

"I loved it. It was spectacular, the crescendos between you guys. Whose idea was that?"

"That'd be Finn's." I tried to not whisper.

"It was great! It was a twist on the loved song, Jamie?" Traditionally only two or three judges comment on your song. Just my luck, Jamie got the mic.

"Uhm, is this working?" She tapped the perfectly working microphone with a tinkling laugh. Of course, you have to milk it for all it's worth, you know? "Okay, Mo, bestie, I've always loved your voice."

Besties bitch? Since when?

Oh yeah we were besties now, since the Carnatic contest. I forgot about that.

"And I don't need to talk about Finn Wins-Wo's-Wonderful abilities. I think those crescendos Peter mentioned should have proved it." The crowd cheered for Jamie. Honestly did no one notice she didn't even know her ex tune setter's name? "I do think, though, that you guys didn't incorporate the song's meaning as much as you should have. Do you get what I mean? I think you should focus on not only the power of your voice, but also the meaning."

But, sweetheart, you didn't write the song did you? How would you know the meaning? I asked her in my head. But on the outside I was forced to smile and nod. I felt like I was playing chess with makeup and hair extensions.

Chapter 17

"*Eeek!*" I looked behind me, mortified. We'd just gotten off the stage when I heard it, the excited clique girl scream.

"Finn?" I asked, aghast.

"Yes?" He pretended to have recovered, but he couldn't keep a straight face.

"Oh, I'm so proud of you all!" Finn and I were in a hug as soon as we stepped into the little corridor backstage. I was soon tugged out of that one and was in an even tighter hug.

"Sweetie you did it! You got your dream, you're one of the Wainscott finalists!" I blinked my mom's black hair out of my eyes.

"Mom, you're gonna ruin my makeup." I looked over and saw Finn standing a bit farther off with his dad. I've only seen him through his car when he'd occasionally pick Finn up from Jamie's studio. He gave Finn a pat on the back and left.

"Where'd your dad go?" I asked.

"Not all parents are like yours, Mohana. My dad is a film producer. He has to go to the set."

"It's 8:30."

"That's actually quite early."

"Alright, the show will start back up in three minutes, you guys know what you're singing, you'll do perfectly. Peter

Raul is gonna love you guys."

"I think it's more Mo liking Peter don't you think?" Finn looked at me. Melody smiled.

"I have to talk to the other voice coaches. You guys will wait right where Mohana was waiting backstage. I'll meet you guys again just before you go on."

We parted ways for round two.

"Aren't we like famous enough now?" Finn asked me when we were back in my spot. I was holding the polished electric guitar I was using for the performance. I heard a loud cheer as Max walked on stage. It would be her, then us, then Lavender and her brother performing in that order.

"No, not to me. Yeah, we can probably get a lot of You-Tube likes right now, or maybe some back-of-the-alley record studio but none of the big studios will accept us. And that's where I need to go."

"But, it can be done," Finn said, "Jamie did it."

"Do you remember the finalists from last year, Finn?" I asked him. He shook his head. "Exactly, I don't either. I do remember that Evangeline Winchester won though. Finn, I'm not in the mood to be forgotten." I'd planned everything out in bed last night. I would win, write an album, publish it, maybe collab with some famous artist and do a concert. It's a quick and foolproof way to getting famous, I've seen it multiple times.

The music came on for Max's performance. I sighed to the soft guitar music, then I stopped mid-breath. That was supposed to be what I was going to play on my guitar.

On stage, Peter smiled and nodded to the music. No, no, no he was supposed to nod and smile to my, wait-*his*, music. The people around me looked at their clipboards confused, but did nothing to stop it. They couldn't because this was live. And that's when I saw Jamie. She was smiling like the Joker, staring right at me from that one angle you could see her from backstage. She had something to do with this. I was not in the mood. I flipped her off.

I heard a wheeze behind me. Melody shoved an aghast Finn out of her way.

"I heard her talking. West knew you were gonna sing this. Someone told her."

"How?"

"Half the human population knows you obsess over Peter Raul. And your 'bestie' probably knew your favorite song," Finn spoke softly. We listened to Max sing. She absolutely nailed it. The crowd cheered again when Max had finished her song.

"Max, absolutely perfect." Peter's angelic voice was supposed to say that to me not her!

"Uhhhm." Melody's finger's started moving in the air as if she was playing an imaginary piano. Finn started trembling.

"What are we gonna do?" He looked as if he could be knocked down with a simple breeze. I took a deep breath, desperate times called for desperate measures. I walked to a corner and reached into my backpack that I had set down earlier. I brought out my sugar cubes and took two out of the ziplock instead of my usual one. I needed all of the help I could get.

There's one guaranteed way to win this, I said to myself. I always knew deep down I was absolutely crazy. This just proved it. I reached down again into my backpack. Past the water bottle and the food there was a notepad with a pen clipped on to it—my writing notepad I carried everywhere. I grabbed a chair from deeper backstage and handed my guitar to Finn just as the managers motioned to me. I walked along with Finn trailing me. I closed my eyes and tried so hard not to shrink from the bright lights as I put the chair to the side and motioned for Finn to sit in it. I walked up to the microphone and cast a sideways glance.

The host was speaking quickly into his headset. The managers looked mortified.

"Hey Folks, I'm Mohana." I gave a wave. There were just so, so many people. All of them had confused faces as they munched away on their popcorn. My voice sounded so squeaky and awkward. I heard myself wheeze. I didn't have my inhaler with me. I blinked and told myself to focus. I motioned to Finn. "This is Finn. Now what we've done for most of our lives is make songs. I write 'em, then give them to Finn and he comes up with a tune for it in no time. What I wanted to do today was to demonstrate how well we can do this." A few oohs came from the crowd. "Alright I need a subject, a main idea, something I can write about." I raised my hands to que the people. A few hands went up timidly. And Jamie raised her hand. Guess who I called on.

"Betrayal, you gave your heart to someone, friend or a boy, and they broke it." She told me softly. I saw where this was going. I jotted down four lines while keeping an eye on my watch. One performance was ten minutes. I only had seven left.

"What genre? Pop, rock, or something else?" I picked on a bald man in the front row.

"'70s music," he yelled out. Finn nodded with a smile. That was his favorite. His old soul loved that kind of thing. His foot started tapping. This might just not crash and burn.

"Alright." I looked over at Finn. If he did this right, his guitar work would help me know the tune and he would change also to accommodate the tune I'd use. He held up his fingers to show how many beats per measure, my parameters. I'd have to keep my song in those. I looked back at the crowd and gulped. Everyone was looking at me with interest, even the judges. I nodded at Finn and gave four clicks with my boot so he knew the tempo. He had two measures of intro music.

"When I look into your eyes, I see every evil plan you'll knit. And I need to let you know one thing, I'm not sorry not one bit." I looked down at my four bullet points I had written. I had used them all and I wasn't even close to finishing. I looked up at Jamie for inspiration. *"You smile, you wave, you smooth down that dress all neat, but I know, I know, you're not all that sweet."* I looked down at my watch, I'd better move into the chorus. I sang a few more and casually wrote the chorus down on my notepad and gave it to Finn. I looked at him and made sure he knew to join me. *"You broke my heart, you threw it in the gutter now I'm gonna toast, toast your fun with butter, it's the end yo-ou."* I cringed, I hadn't eaten too much today and I guess it started to show but Finn's heavy and complex guitar work made up for it. It made the audience happy. They whooped and cheered me on. I continued singing. Soon I had only a minute left. I'd better finish it. I motioned for Finn to quiet down. *"And yes, maybe a bit of my conscience hurts, but I gotta ignore now that my heart's in the gutter."* I held the last beat out long, fixing the mistake I made at the Wainscott auditions.

"Th-thank you." I had to wait for the cheers to fade. I might have even gotten more cheers than Max. The judges stood up and gave me a standing ovation. My heart melted. Peter Raul was applauding me. Shruthi was going to be so jealous. I saw her far off. I saw all my friends, waving and hollering, waving their sign. Shruthi yelled, or I saw her lips move.

"That's my daughter!"

I had to sit. My legs were like jelly. As soon as I got off stage, I walked to my corner and took out the brownies I had baked last night. I normally am not allowed to touch the kitchen after a certain time, but I think my parents felt sorry for me 'cause they didn't stop me when I started baking at two in the morning.

"Can I have one?" I gave Finn a brownie. "We're lucky we have you around. I'd have probably just stood there on stage and waited until someone dragged me off."

"Same. Good thing you kept your head Mohana." Melody joined us in our corner. Lavender and Ryan had already started their performance. Before I could dust my pants to get rid of brownie crumbs, I was on stage. I guess they were running late since the guy didn't even re-announce the sponsors.

"The winner of the forty-seventh Wainscott show is—"

The auditorium held its breath. The judges already knew though. With the way Jamie was looking at me it wasn't that big of a surprise when the host opened the envelope and said, "Mohana Prasad and Finn Winston."

Chapter 18

"**A**ww, it all works out! You'll see him a lot too since his mom is your voice coach." Morni popped a sour patch kid into her mouth. I remembered yesterday night with a pang of emotion.

"This is it, your dream achieved huh?" Melody picked up my backpack from the ground and handed it to me. I blinked hair out of my eyes. After a hurricane of hugs from my friends everything was in my eyes. "You proved yourself to that mean reporter. You won everyone's hearts." She leaned onto the wall and crossed her ankles like Johnny always did. My heart hurt at the thought of him.

"Not yet. I've always wanted an album out."

"Album? I'll be first in line to buy it."

"Mo!" my mom called out. I turned and saw my dad waiting in the car behind the glass doors.

"Well, I'll see you tomorrow," I told Melody.

She raised her eyebrows and said, "Oh, this is where I leave you, Mohana. You don't need me anymore." She smiled and pulled me into a hug. "I'll keep my ears out for you. I know I'll hear great things about you Mohana Prasad." She gave her kind smile and turned to walk out the other door.

"Melody!" She turned around. "Th-Thank you. Thank you so much!"

"Just doing my job." With a tart wave, she was out the door.

"She's not my voice coach anymore. Apparently I don't need one."

"Well, you'll still see Johnny at school," Morni sighed. "Remind me to never third wheel with you guys again. I have so much homework to do." You heard right, Morni was third wheeling with me and Johnny. I took out my phone to look at the texts again. My arm ached as I reached into my pocket. Everything ached since yesterday.

> Hey Mohana, it's Johnny. Morni gave me your number. I just wanted to congratulate you on Wainscott.

> Thanks!

> Look, I'm sorry about what I said on Thursday, I didn't mean it.

> I know you didn't mean it. it's not what you said that counts. You're right. Maybe we should be just friends for now.

> Mohana, I've been thinking of this all weekend. I think it's worth another shot.

> I don't want you to feel uncomfortable because of me.

> I don't! It's the total opposite actually. I feel so happy when I'm with you. Meet me at the SK Theater at five.

> Johnny I have homework.

> Please!

"Bro!" Morni nudged me. I looked through the glass doors to see Johnny in a red sweatshirt and khakis. His sweatshirt matched the red tones in his cheek. I felt Morni shiver next to me. "Damn, I bet Sage Khand would be so jealous," she said.

"You came." He walked up to me with his hands clasped behind his back. I took a step back from him. He didn't think this would be easy now did he? Without saying a word, I stared back at him with my head tilted. He closed his mouth and stared back.

It was a long silence.

A very long silence.

A very, *very* long silence. His dark chocolate eyes glimmered from the lights and I succumbed. I sighed. How did I think I could pull off being just his friend?

"I hate you so much!" I walked forward and it seemed natural he gave me a hug. I closed my eyes as my head came to rest perfectly in the ridge of his chest. I felt his arms as they tightened their grip.

"Bet."

"Awww, you cute couples make me sick. I'm never coming with you on a date again Mo."

"It's not a date." We both responded in unison. Johnny awkwardly looked at me.

"It's more of a peace treaty," I softly told her.

He'd apparently wanted to take me to the ice cream shop across the theater. But, Morni made him buy us tickets to the new Avengers movie. He didn't complain. I think he was looking forward to sitting next to me in the dark, but we forgot an important detail. I was famous now.

Wainscott itself was heavily watched. Nine out of ten houses had their televisions prepped and ready to go on Wainscott night. So, more than half the people there knew who I was. I always wondered what would happen next.

Would no one still know who I was or would everyone instantly know? The latter was correct, and it was startling. Just yesterday no one knew who I was.

Here's the thing. I didn't hate it—all the attention I mean. It was just different from what I knew. But, I could tell Johnny hated it, which surprised me considering his popularity at school. I thought it might get better once we were in the dark, but people were starting to go nocturnal and see in the dark. I held Johnny back from lunging into an older couple that was pointing at us.

"I have an idea," he whispered to me. "You wanna go on an adventure?" Duh, I nodded affirmatively. We looked to Morni.

"I'm not leaving my superheroes. Just don't get pregnant Mo," she whispered back. I slapped her arm with an annoyed look. We were good kids, for now. Johnny led me out into the lobby and waited next to the sliding doors meant for employees only.

"Johnny?" I motioned to the sign.

"Aww come on! Let's keep the Goody Two-shoes act in school." As someone came out the door, he grabbed my hand and we slipped in. There was a flight of stairs on the immediate right that Johnny dragged me up. It led to the roof.

"Oh." The sun was setting. I swear this guy was too perfect. He probably had everything timed and ready to go. I walked up to the ledge, and saw the orange sun just in the middle of the budding trees. I felt his arms slip around my waist. They shook a bit. He was hesitant. I leaned back onto his chest to show it was okay.

"I used to come here all the time two years ago," he said. I sighed as I felt his voice rumble through his chest. "Back then, my mom worked here, and ever since then I've wanted to bring you up here."

"Your mom worked here?"

"When she was just starting out. It was tight back then, until she started getting some people into the music industry. We've been good ever since. Even better now that she got you all famous." He ruffled my hair.

Melody? Poor? She seemed too happy to be like that. We stayed like that for a while, just enjoying each other's presence, or in my case getting over the fact that I was leaning on my crush's chest. "We ought to get going," Johnny sighed. "The movie should be over by now." I turned around and looked up into his face.

"'Ought' Johnny Taylor you are the first basketball head I've ever heard say that."

"Yeah? I also like kittens. They warm my soul." Getting back down was a bit trickier. But, what's to fear when you got Johnny the Spy as he called himself? He waited at the top of the stairs until the footsteps faded. His long legs then dragged me down the stairs and out the door in a second. Morni was waiting at one of the tall tables there. She smiled at our clasped hands.

"Well, my mom would get suspicious if I don't leave now." Johnny gave me a smile. " I-I'll see you around Mo." Our hands fell to our sides. My hand felt cold without Johnny's touch. I pulled them under my sleeve as I smiled and gave him a wave. He left with an awkward smile.

"Aww, I think you're blushing!" Morni pinched my cheeks when he was out the door. I didn't know if it was a figment of my imagination when I saw him give a little skip when he was a foot out the door. I squirmed away from Morni's grip. "I never would have guessed you would have been the first to get a boyfriend."

"What do you mean?" I was still processing everything that just went down. Then I realized and said, "Wait, actually don't respond to that."

Chapter 19

"A wwwww." All of my friends said in unison. I blushed and looked down.

"Yeah, and we texted until like midnight."

"Mohana Prasad, awake after 9:30?"

"Shut up Kalyani. What did you guys talk about? Wait! Let me guess, books?" Shaina asked while adding like her twentieth pickle onto her sandwich.

"And poetry. If you're puking up those pickles later you better not touch my boots!" I stopped Shaina's hands from adding another pickle.

"Mohana?" Shruthi started when the laughter faltered out. Uh-oh, I sensed something brewing. She was using her mom-voice. Not the joking around Indian accent mom-voice, but her higher pitched questioning voice that meant advice was coming your way. I already knew what she was going to ask.

"Shruthi, I don't know. Will I tell my parents? I don't know. Will people know? I don't know. We'll just have to see." I bit my lip and shrugged.

"No, not that." She gave me complete eye-contact like some counselor. "Have you ever considered whether he's just with you because you're famous now?" All my other friends elbowed and gave her disapproving looks.

"Bro, don't ruin it for her. No guy is ever gonna do all that for popularity, and he's popular enough!"

"But, like, he waited until you won Wainscott, a whole day after she had her 'argument' thing. I mean—"

"I know what you mean." I stopped her. I hadn't thought of it. I didn't want to think of it, but it sounded right. But, his eyes. His soulful eyes and his soft touch. No one could fake like that, could they? "I just don't know, Shruthi. We'll see where this goes. I guess I just don't know." I gave my friends an apologetic smile.

"Anyway, I forgot, what's with the clothing? You looking for a job?" I looked down at my black dress pants and white blouse.

"Well, I am attending an interview. Wendy, my agent, set up an interview with a record company." A collective 'ooh' came from the table. "Yeah, I want to release an album. I get to leave early." I looked at the clock, "And I have to go in ten minutes. But my mom's always early so make that five." And, I was right, when I got to class the teacher had already gotten the phone call.

"Nervous?" My mom looked sideways at me in the passenger seat. I smiled and shook my head. "No, Wendy and I agree it's likely they'll accept me because I can write as well as sing."

"That's good. No daughter of mine gets nervous. No Prasad does. It's in our blood to stay strong." She parked in front of a normal looking office building next to Wendy's car. It was pretty easy to spot. It was hot pink.

The inside of the building smelled like wood, and the people there all had dead faces, except Wendy with her gigawatt smile.

"Aww! I could just squish you! You look like a little cocoa bean!" She gave me a tight hug. "You guys are a bit early, so we're gonna have to wait a bit. But, we need the time 'cause you need to know some things." She led us into a reception room with bland looking couches.

I blinked. It couldn't be.

Occupying those couches were girls about my age dressed in exactly the same slacks and blouse as me. They were all sitting and talking to what I presumed were their agents or voice coaches in low murmurs. "Manager's kinda strict, likes things in a certain order. I'm happy mom got the outfit I wanted." She nodded at my mom. We took a seat in a corner, the other girls glaring at us the entire time. "Okay, Mohana when you're in there I need you to be an airhead." As usual, Wendy got right down to business. "Ask him to repeat each question. That way he knows you won't be too smart to cheat the contract and will probably hire you. He likes attitude. Be rude. Look out the window when he's talking. And, most importantly, read the contract thoroughly. I've already looked through it, but it has happened before where they change some things after I look. Pretend not to read it, but do." I batted my eyelashes. Was she serious? She was—dead serious.

"You want me to act like a rude idiot who doesn't want to be here?"

"You heard me. Act like you don't care, but care. Being famous isn't all makeup and waves. It's a poisonous environment. You need to make sure no one hurts you."

"And, have fun," my mom interjected. She looked over at Wendy. "Wendy, there isn't any way for her to be herself and get an album out?" my mom asked.

"She could try. I just don't think it would be as effective." She shrugged.

"Mohana Prasad?" A tired looking lady opened a door in the front and motioned for me.

"Huh, they're calling you early. That's good." We rose from our plump couch. "I'll just be in the corner. I won't talk. Remember what we talked about, say uh-huh."

"Uh-huh." I nodded.

But I really wasn't going to follow her rules, was I?

The manager was a plump little man. He was eating banana bread when I walked in. He licked his fingers clean and moved a few papers around then said, "Mohana Prasad, please take a seat." He pointed to the chair in front of his desk. I sat down, trying not to cringe. "Ah my dear, winner of Wainscott, worked with Jamie West, a *writer*. I see why you think we will accept you. You have talent *ma chérie*." He had a raspy voice that chilled me to the bone. "But, so does everyone here. Tell us in your own words, why should we take you?"

"Mr—" I looked at his nameplate. "Mr. Nelson, the first thing I remember, sir, is sitting on the ground in preschool writing words with my crayon instead of drawing. Writing and music has been my passion for a very long time and it always will be. I believe it lets you escape troubles into a loving and caring world." I spoke with my hand on my heart. It didn't have the effect I desired. Mr. Nelson seemed unchanged. Wendy had her eyebrows raised.

"What did I tell you?" she mouthed.

"Mh-hm, and what's normally the main theme in your songs?" he asked while moving a few more papers on his desk

"My songs?" I sighed. There wasn't a choice. I reached out and took a piece of gum from his desk. I popped it in my mouth. I chewed loudly while I looked out the window. "Boys." I tried to imitate all those popular girls at school who annoyed me so much. I shriveled inside.

"Boys?" I'd caught his attention. He looked up from his desk.

"Yeah, bad ones." He seemed to like it. I put my legs on his desk, trying so hard not to wince. I felt a part of me die inside.

"Alright." I took his smile as a good sign. "What about

the young man you sang with, Finn Winston? What are you gonna do with him?"

"Finn? I dunno. We might collab for a song if I feel like it."

"So no dual career. Not gonna sing every song with him?" he asked. Good question, was that an option? I looked over at Wendy. She shook her head. I guess not.

"Nah." I blew a bubble.

"Okay, next question. I've heard your voice, *ma chérie*, strong. How do you get your voice out?"

"Excuse me?" I stepped out of my act for a bit and took my legs off his desk. The question caught me by surprise.

"Your voice, how do you get it out? I was a singer too, apparently used my throat too much and had to get surgery. Now, I sound like an eighty year old smoker, not that I'm lying about the smoking part!" He laughed a croaky laugh.

"I use my stomach," I answered after he stopped laughing. I put my legs back up. "It's something I found. Project with your stomach and you can reach higher and sound better." I quoted Shalini Aunty's words.

"Different approach, but works nonetheless! Now lets be real. I'll probably choose you. I don't even know why I have other girls here, so let me get you a copy of the contract." He licked his fingers again and took out a few sheets of paper. He handed me a pen which I took with a wince.

"It's all for your dream. A few extra germs won't kill you." Well, actually they might. I told my mind to shut up.

"We need to get a few things ironed out. My assistant can help with that. We need to get you social media accounts, you need to start getting in touch with other celebrities—" I looked over the contract being inconspicuous as possible. It looked about right. It even said I can resign whenever. So why did I get a bad feeling about all this? Wendy gave me a nod from the corner. I sighed, put down the signature quick, and left in a heartbeat.

Chapter 20

"Up and away! David Nelson, I've heard my mom mention him. Soon you'll be out doing concerts all over the U.S., meeting all types of guys." I put my hand out in front of Johnny to slow him down. I couldn't keep up with his long legs.

"I will, but none could ever match up to you." I smiled up into his face. Now that I had a guy I could spit out all the cheesiest fluff I wanted.

"You can't like me forever."

"Then, I'll love you forever." Being a writer has its perks. I knew a ton of cheesy things. We'd started climbing the stairs to get to the fourth floor where we both had English. I was already winded and we were only on the second floor.

"You okay?" Johnny asked with a mocking smile. Johnny, himself, hadn't broken a sweat. I gave him my classic annoyed look that I'm known for.

"We get it, you're athletic." We reached the top, I waited for it. I'd always seen it happen. Johnny gave a casual hop and touched the top of the door that led out of the staircase. It must be a tall basketball player thing, trying to reach everything higher than your head.

I couldn't relate.

He looked back and smiled, the lack of concentration causing him to lose control of his legs. He tripped and fell against the wall.

"Smooth. You alright?" I smiled as I offered my hand. Must be boy code not to accept help. He got up himself in a weird way with his legs crossed. He wobbled a bit when he was up.

"That's like the eighth time this week. What are you doing to me Prasad?"

"It's a little magic spell my friend Dumbledore taught me. You sure you okay?" I was actually kinda worried. He took two steps and he seemed fine.

"I've been practicing a lot this week. My legs are tired. But, we were talking about you. What are you doing next?"

"I'm working on an album with the title *Blessing.* The main theme is gonna be love. We'll save the breakup songs for later." We entered the classroom, and I put my stuff down.

"Any songs about—" There was no need for him to finish the sentence.

"I'm pretty sure the whole album is gonna be about you." I laughed at him. "Bro, half of Jamie's were about you."

"But they were sad or angry breakup songs."

"Sage was annoying." I answered with a shrug. It was true.

"Fair enough." He set his stuff down and looked back at me with a playful grin. We were the first ones there, even the teacher hadn't arrived yet. I raised my questioning eyebrows, but his grin was contagious, damn.

This is how I wanted to remember him.

"It used to scare the shit out of me when you did that," he remarked.

"The eyebrows?"

"Yeah, back then you would catch me staring at you, you'd raise your eyebrows."

"Hu—" I was interrupted by a high-pitched scream.

"Oh, I haven't seen you in ages!" Something resembling a blonde tornado crashed into me. It grabbed me around the waist and squeezed me until I couldn't breathe. But I didn't need to see her face to know who it was. I knew who she was. Cassie, the cliquiest girl in our grade.

I looked at Morni, who had just entered and was standing next to Johnny, for help. She shrugged with pure amusement. Johnny caught on quick and started smiling with her. "Oh, Mohana I always knew you could do it. You go girl!"

"T-thank you, uhm, what's your name again?" I asked even though I already knew, trying to emphasize the point that I hardly knew her.

"Cassie Langston, of course! You were with me in Math League."

"I'm pretty sure that's Neela—"

"My uncle owns the company you work for. Told me how nice of a person you were. He forgot to tell you something. He gave me this last night at dinner to give to you. He thought it would reach you faster than if he told your agent."

It also means you can get information through without an agent knowing, my mind muttered to me. She handed me a letter. "And, uhm, can you do me a favor?" She smiled and took out a piece of paper and a pen. She handed them to me.

"W-what do you want me to do?" I asked, staring at the blank piece of paper. Cassie and Morni gave me a look like it was obvious, but it wasn't.

"Autograph, wise one."

"Oh." *Oh my.* It took me ages to learn my name in cursive. I had failed handwriting in third grade 'cause I didn't even have time to finish writing my name. Every time I had to sign something it took like eight minutes. I set the paper down on the table and sat down. I took a deep breath and started slowly drawing my signature on the paper trying not to shake. Cassie looked surprised. The end result looked fine though. She seemed over enjoyed with it.

"Probably gonna go show it off. What does the letter say?" Morni asked. Johnny took the letter out of my hands.

"Hm, blah, blah *ma chérie*, blah blah. Ooh you're doing an interview."

"Wait, what?"

"Yeah, on the thirty-first."

"Johnny that's tomorrow!"

"I know, there's more. He wants you to be backup for someone for a while. Says it'll get your name into the music industry and you'll get introduced to the equipment." He gave me the letter.

"Oh, fudge," I muttered.

"What?" Morni looked at the letter.

"At the moment there's probably only one artist who would take me for backup."

Chapter 21

"Yep, Jamie's the only one who'll take you for sure." Wendy moved to let someone stick another microphone on my waist. "I agree with Mr. Nelson. It would help a lot. Singing backup requires a lot of skills. Vocal and social. It requires patience; we'll see how you do." The makeup lady finally finished with an eighteenth layer of lip gloss. "Alright, let's go." Wendy walked me down the short corridor that led to the recording room.

The room was set up to look like a cozy living room, well most of it. It had a fake fireplace and a red sofa with matching red mugs on the coffee table. I was disappointed that there was nothing in them.

The top half though, had all sorts of un-living-roomy things. They had at least eight microphones dangling from wires. Oh and wires, so many wires. It looked like one of my sister's drawings when she used black crayons, so basically a mess.

"Coming up, a short interview with Wainscott winners Mohana Prasad and Finn Winston—" The anchors on the technician's computer finished their report that was broadcast from a different room. Another lady was going to interview us. I saw her in the distance in a blue bandage dress talking to the cameraman.

I heard a familiar gag. I looked around and saw Finn's back. The same makeup lady that worked on me was lip glossing

109

him too. He turned back with his face scrunched like a baby, spitting out lip gloss. I took a photo for blackmail purposes.

"Alright my dears. I'm Paige Wilson." The anchor had sneaked up behind us. She spoke with perfect crescendos and articulation. Must be a side effect from speaking on camera 24/7. Finn shook her hand instead of just gaping at it like he normally did. I gave him a surprised look. Fame was already affecting him. "Not too nervous I hope."

"I'm trying my best to ignore it," I said, which was very true, 'cause this was very different from what I was used to, the stage.

Yes, it was weird. I felt more exposed in front of a single camera than in front of thousands of people.

"Oh, I promise it's not that bad. There's really nothing to worry about. See, you have cue cards." She sat us down in the red couch and pointed just above the big camera. A big note card with big print was held up by a stand. "We know you guys never had any Social Media or Screen training, so we made it easy. Just say what's on the card, if you will, and the show will be over in a jiffy. Red's you Miss Prasad and blue corresponds to you Mr. Winston." She said it like it was our choice whether or not to follow the cards, but her tone said otherwise. It was clear we had to say what was on the cards. Eh, I wasn't surprised. They didn't let Jamie say her own words until two years into her career. "Any questions?" Anchor lady sat herself in her seat and tilted her head so her curled hair fell in front of her.

"Th-this is live isn't it?" Finn asked. Ms. Wilson nodded her head. His legs instantly started bouncing. I pressed my hand gently on his knee.

"You'll be fine, I promise," I muttered sideways to him. He gave me a disbelieving look. "This is nothing compared to what we did in Wainscott."

He snorted, "Yeah, I'm never following you on stage again."

"Hey, my crazy idea made us win." *Ungrateful bastard.* The lights suddenly increased, making me squint. And I thought stage lights were bad. I clenched my stomach. I felt even more exposed now.

"Alright." The entire recording crew was now silent and staring at us. The cameraman raised both his hands and gave us a countdown. I felt Finn's legs start to jog again. I didn't stop them this time.

"Today I'm here with the wonderful duo of Finn Winston and Mohana Prasad who, as you all probably know, spectacularly won this year's Wainscott. I'd first like to express how grateful I am to have you guys here!" I looked at the cards and read my part with the best smile I could muster.

"Oh, and we are just as excited to be here, Paige!" I winced at how fake it sounded. Oh, and hundreds, no thousands of people were watching this all over America. I clamped my hands. I couldn't psych out, not now.

"You are just a darling, aren't you Mohana? Let's start with you. I believe you are a Sophomore in high school. How's school life?" There was a guy who changed the cards.

"School is wonderful. I have so many supportive friends there, and without them I wouldn't be here."

"You must be popular."

"Not before all this, no. I was more in the background so everything really is a dream come true! When I was little, I'd stand in front of the mirror and wave to fake crowds. I just can't believe how far I've come." Finn nodded next to me.

I heard the rustling of paper and I turned to see the card person frantically turn to a card in the stack. He got to the blue words so quick it seemed natural when Finn spoke.

"Yeah, when I was young I stole my mom's curler so I could pretend it was a microphone."

"Oh, ha, that's adorable you two! So Finn, you must have been more of a rebellious child."

"When I was younger, yeah. Now I think it's safe to say I've calmed down." Finn said it perfectly. He was a natural, which was surprising because he couldn't even talk to anyone without stuttering.

"Tame now?" the reporter asked.

"Tame? I sure hope so!"

"Okay, Finn, let me ask you one thing. If you've been on the Internet you must have seen fans rave about your hair."

"My hair?"

"Yes, your hair. Now tell me was it always this curly?"

"No, it curled when I turned twelve."

"When he had his little growth spurt," I added. See, it wasn't on the cards but it had to be said. I patted his head.

"At least I had one Miss 'I'm so short I need my bestie Finn to get me everything,'" Finn retorted.

"You guys are friends outside of your career as well huh?" reporter lady asked with a smile.

"No, we hate each other," I responded quickly. The cue cards guy seemed lost. I guess our interviewer was going unscripted.

"Any chance your friendship could be, could more than friendship?"

"Oh, uhm." Finn and I stopped laughing and awkwardly looked at each other. "No, we've always just been friends. We've known each other for so long."

"Besides I don't think I'd last a full day with Mo. There was this one time—" Finn casually steered the conversation away. I owed him one.

The interview ended normally, and I got to leave, but something was amiss. Finn treated me normally, but we both knew there was a problem.

No person has ever paired Finn and I as a couple, ever. Which was surprising because we spent most of our time together, but maybe that was why. We spent so much time together everyone thought we were practically siblings. So, when our lovely interviewer asked us if we were together it had changed something. Finn had shifted in his seat so his legs wouldn't brush mine. I'd looked at him for the first time in a way different than just friends. And, yes, if you were wondering, he did look good. Not hot looking, but curly haired cute looking good. What did he think I looked like? One thing was clear though through all this, we were on the precipice of problems.

Chapter 22

"Of all the things to do on a Sunday," I muttered to myself.

"Try to show a little gratitude," Wendy muttered back. We walked down the familiar halls of Jamie's recording studio. But instead of going to the manager's room where I normally went to submit my written songs, me and Wendy walked to the main recording room. She opened the door with her keys and let me in.

I'd come here once or twice with Finn. But his normal seat behind a glass window was now taken by a gaunt old-looking man. He looked bored and bland. Actually, I could use that description for the whole room, boring and bland. The walls were the color of dust and there was nothing on the walls themselves. I made a mental note that if I ever had a recording studio of my own I would make sure the walls were a nice yellow and were laden with pictures and paintings.

There were five rooms with glass windows that all looked into one room with a big microphone. That's where Jamie would be. It had a nice big microphone with a comfy looking chair. The room I was in had no chairs. I took my spot, standing in front of the window next to some of the other backup singers. They all were jittery girls who nervously congratulated me on Wainscott. Jamie, herself, was conveniently thirty minutes late. And since phones weren't allowed in the recording room to keep the songs private, I spent that time staring at my nails.

If you are a details person, my nails were a mess.

Jamie brought with her some scary looking dudes in suits and a lady in a pantsuit. They took the room across from us and stared at her through the window. I recognized the lady. She was one of the people in charge that actually knew music.

"Alright everyone, let's take it from the top until measure eighty or how far we actually get. Backup singers, be aware of measure twenty five and it's decrescendos, and let's get started." The lady in the pantsuit talked to us through her headset.

We were all given headsets, though I did have to say ours did look a tad shabbier than Jamie's. They worked nonetheless. I heard the intro music through mine and mimicked the backup singers by leaning toward our shared microphone.

I heard Jamie's voice, soft with a lot of variations. It wasn't the best in a group. She never was heard, but in solos I had always admired her soulful voice. I sang my part with ease. It was just going "*Wa-oh*," like one hundred times in different ways. I looked down at my music to see if we did anything else, and yes we did. Backup singer-two was the only one who sang a line with Jamie after the chorus. Guess who was Backup singer-two, me.

This was going to be interesting.

The chorus ended pretty quickly and the other backup singers eyed me with envy as I took a breath.

It was a blast from the past. I remembered all those times when me and Jamie used to perform. Our voices blended nice as usual, meaning they sounded as one voice, meaning one voice could be heard a bit more than the other. Guess whose voice that was! I heard pantsuit lady's voice through my headphones. "And we'll stop there. Backup number two, darling, I need you to reduce your voice. Let's start back up at the chorus." Meanie lady, I did have a name. I tried my duet with Jamie again in a softer voice. I hated it. It sounded nasal and weird, and even that apparently took over Jamie's soft voice. "Girl, loud isn't the only thing you need in music!" Jamie gave me a glare through the window. I was taken back, but I remembered there weren't any reporters in the room. She could say whatever to me, but that also worked vice versa.

"Sorry, Janaki," I softly said into my headset. The use of her old name made her wince. She nervously glanced at the mean looking men in suits who were ferociously writing on their papers and closed her mouth, which was sure going to give me a smackdown. She huffed and we started at the chorus again. This time I sang in the softest possible voice I could muster without my voice cracking.

We stayed there for two hours after that, us not Jamie. She got to leave while we had to finish the backup. The end result was well, disappointing. In my duet with Jamie they'd reduced my voice even more electronically making my voice a mere whisper in the song. It could've been any of the other backup singers.

As soon as they let us go, I quickly ran to the nearest bathroom and changed into my Indian attire. My whole Carnatic class was performing thirty minutes away. I ran out and climbed into my dad's car and we zoomed away. Even if we didn't stop at any stop lights we'd get there five minutes late. But you see, my dad would probably stop somewhere to help an old lady or something, being the annoyingly compassionate thing he was so we would be about ten minutes late. I didn't really mind, I mean, it's an Indian-ran thing so they must be running late by at least twenty minutes.

"Let's go, let's go. Your mom will have my head if you're late." My dad opened my door and yanked me out.

"Wait!" I tried to stop but it was in vain, I was too late.

My sugar cubes lay forgotten in the passenger's seat.

I rushed up the stairs of the temple we were performing in. Well, I rushed as fast as I could in a floor length skirt, which wasn't that fast, but I still made it.

There was actually a big turnout. The people who show up to these events are normally the parents of the kids singing and older people who don't have anything else to do. But today, there were a lot of people. A lot of people who ignored the 'no phones' sign and started filming me as soon as I was up those stairs. I smoothed down my hair with an awkward smile as I made my way toward Shalini Aunty and the rest of my class.

"What's with the crowd?" I asked Shalini Aunty once I sat down.

"Well, one of us has quite the fan base now, don't we?" She smiled, happy with all the attention we were getting.

"How'd did they know I'd be here?" I asked. Aunty gave me a copy of the schedule. Our class would perform next. I looked down to see all the names. There was my name in bold, underlined and in twice the font size. And, the best part, it was right next to Shreya's name. They'd decreased the font size to make her name fit next to mine. I sneaked a glance at her as I rose to take my seat on stage, and boy did she look pissed!

As we sang I noticed a lot of cameras. Normally, everyone looks dead or stares at their watches while we perform. But, today everyone had a big camera on a tripod and filmed us, but they didn't film anyone else. And I had the sneaking suspicion that whenever they zoomed in, they zoomed in on my face. Well, I hope they got the attention they were seeking 'cause it's really scary having Shreya's mom glare at you the whole time you were on stage. She didn't blink, not once.

Chapter 23

"Opening for him just at his Minnesota concert? Like, you're gonna sing before him, before his fans, oh Mo!" Shruthi picked up my notepad that I'd dropped and grabbed my phone. She read Wendy's texts again. "You get to bring a friend backstage with you! Mohana Devi Prasad, I know Peter Raul better than he knows himself, take me!"

"Mh-hm," I nodded absentmindedly.

"I'm gonna meet my Peter, what would I say? 'Hi, I'm Shruthi and I have obsessed over you since I was in pigtails.' You think they'd let me stay backstage while he's performing? To support you, of course." Shruthi looked out the big window of our school to see if her dad had come yet to pick us up.

Yes, we had stayed after school, on the last day, to help teachers take stuff down.

No, we are obviously not the cool kids.

The light from the window suddenly seemed too bright. I felt the room spin.

"Woah, we can't have you faint on the first day of summer break." Shruthi touched my shoulder. "And you are my chance to see my man so we need you to stay alive." I sat down. My asthma kicked in and I started breathing hard. Shruthi eyed the inhaler I took out.

"It's harder to sing with asthma, isn't it?" she asked after a bit.

"It requires more effort. I have to give an extra push to get my voice out, and I get tired easier. But, that's not an excuse." I took deeper breaths, trying to bring my breath under control.

"And that is why Peter called you instead of Jamie," she said with a hint of pride. I looked up at her. "Shruthi, I-I'm-my—" *My dream was going to be achieved.* I would have a whole stadium downtown cheering me. "I ought to keep writing." I picked up my notepad and finished up the line I was working on.

"You have all summer."

"No, I have three weeks until the concert. I gotta finish at least all the singles by then." I checked my phone, "One week. They're due in a week." I crossed out a word. "Plus I'm going to faint if I don't keep myself busy."

"Suit yourself." Shruthi took out her yearbook and started drawing faces on the people she didn't like. "You think my Harry Potter sweater didn't look good? Well—" She drew a goatee and devil horns on some girl. I took out my own yearbook for inspiration and flipped to the T's. Johnny had really outdone himself with his smile this year. It's warmth radiated to me from the page. I guess I knew what I was going to be doing for the rest of summer, staring at my yearbook.

Eh, I've done it before.

"Look at what Sage Khand wrote in my yearbook, 'I totally can't wait to know more about you.' She looked so pissed when I sat next to Johnny at lunch today." I raised my eyebrows at Sage's picture.

"She has liked him for like six years, and you came along and ruined it."

"Oops," I muttered, without an ounce of regret. "Can

you draw a clown wig on her? You're way better at this than me." I handed Shruthi my yearbook and continued writing my song.

"Oh, and Mo, what are you doing for you birthday? I'm pretty sure it's in three weeks," Shruthi asked.

" Yeah, it's a day before Peter's concert. I'm having two parties, one for Mr. Nelson at the roller park and the other one for myself at home."

"Mr. Nelson's making you host his birthday party?"

"Yup, I get no say in it either. I have to invite Jamie, and I have to take a minimum of twenty pictures for all my social media accounts. Speaking of that." I got off my chair and onto the floor while I put my pen on my notepad that I'd left laying on the bench. I also took out my earbuds and spread them out next to the notepad while I chose a filter on my phone. "I have to post at least once a day. They even made me take a class on how to post correctly," I muttered as I angled my phone so the sun made my pen glitter aesthetically.

"Watch this." Shruthi took out a red tulip from my backpack and laid it next to my pen. "I'm pretty sure Johnny will be happy to see his prized tulip on your Insta. You're welcome. Where'd he get it anyway?"

"No idea." Johnny Taylor had, yet again, outdone himself by giving me a tulip at lunch. I guess reading a lot of poetry did have its benefits. He knew how to treat a girl.

I put the flower in my hair and took a picture. I sent it to Johnny and put it on my Snap story.

"You inviting Mr. Klutz to one of your parties?" Shruthi finished drawing a clown wig on Sage Khand.

"You can call him Johnny now." After an eventful lunch a few months ago where Johnny tripped and spilled his lunch all over the new math teacher, we'd given him the nickname, Mr. Klutz. He caught on pretty quick because he'd look over whenever we used it. "I'm gonna invite him to the roller park one, as long as he doesn't get in any of the pictures it'll be fine," I wrote another line down on paper.

Would I sing this in front of a crowd? I checked my phone to see the texts once again. The Bayend Stadium.

"Yo! Have you been to Bayend Stadium?" I asked Shruthi.

"When I was younger, to watch a circus."

"How big is it?"

Shruthi smiled. "It's one of the older ones. You can't see the other end of the crowd. I remember I was scared I was going to fall from my seat and get trampled by the elephants. I hugged my mom the whole time."

I sighed.

"But I was young, I haven't been there in a while. I'm probably exaggerating. It won't be that big," Shruthi added on hastily.

"I hope not." I smiled. She'd misread my content sigh. "It needs to be big enough so Jamie can see me from across the country." *My dream was going to be achieved.*

"Let's go." Shruthi picked up her bag. Her dad's big red car was parked right outside the entrance.

"Good riddance," I muttered back at the school.

Despite how my mom's wallet had quivered when she'd heard the news, I was going to be homeschooled next year. Mr. Nelson had insisted on it, saying that I wouldn't be able to go to a public school with all the fame I was going to get.

I still hadn't told anyone.

"What are you writing anyway?" Shruthi tried to grab my notepad once we were in the car, I yanked it away from her.

"I have strict rules from Mr. Nelson, can't risk my lyrics being leaked."

"You don't trust me?" She shrugged then said, "Makes sense. Can you at least tell me the name of it?"

"Nope." I scratched out a word and replaced it with

another. Shruthi pointed to my phone that was buzzing. I picked it up to answer, but it wasn't a call.

"Twenty three messages in about a minute, now that's talent," Shruthi remarked.

"Well, it is her job." I scrolled through Wendy's texts. "Huh, they told me once school was over, I'd get busy. I have an interview tomorrow, I'm in two commercials and they're both shooting Sunday, I'm singing backup for some other artists, and I'm going to be on a radio show next Tuesday."

Wendy had told me we were running out of time. My singles were all coming out three days before I opened for Peter Raul, and I apparently needed to be more famous before that. Right now, when people passed me, they just kinda give me a second glance with a squint. My Instagram had two hundred thousand followers and was growing every day, which I thought was pretty amazing, but it wasn't enough according to Nelson.

Made sense, Jamie had fifteen million.

I scrolled through Peter's Insta. Me and Shruthi both sighed at the pictures. I saw his newest post.

"Don't miss out. Come to the Bayend Stadium on the thirtieth for merch and more! Minnesota's own legendary Miss Mohana Prasad, winner of the Wainscott, will also be there signing autographs and will sing her singles from her album 'Blessing'. Can't wait to see you all there!"

"*Legendary Miss Mohana Prasad.* Damn!" I only heard Shruthi's lips move. I could only hear my heart. *My dream was going to be achieved.*

Chapter 24

I smiled and faced the green screen.

"Cut!" I flinched. Someone applied more highlight to my cheeks as a short guy walked up to me. "Ms. Prasad, we really need a bigger smile at the end. It's really the point of the commercial," he said quickly and ran back behind the camera again. I got back into position. Someone shouted,

"Twenty-sixth take! Three, two, one, action!"

"For some people, smiling is a big part of their everyday life, and that spinach ravioli from lunch doesn't really help." My mouth started cramping from smiling too much. I moved with the humongous camera like I had all morning and picked up a tube of toothpaste from a table that couldn't be seen. "That's why I use Allclean toothpaste to keep my teeth white and clean for all my performances." I held the toothpaste up to the huge camera and smiled as wide as I could then said, "Allclean, for those whose career is smiling."

"And scene!" I sighed and rubbed my mouth. *Finally!* I literally felt twenty pounds lighter as the makeup lady took all the foundation off my face and I could breathe again. My hair still felt like some black helmet though with all the gel and product in it. I checked my phone as I walked into the lobby. I had told my parents to pick me up later, giving me two hours until they'd come. I smiled and looked up from my phone to see Johnny, exactly where he said he would be. He was staring out the window with one earbud in while carrying two Starbucks Frappuccinos. He was looking at two little toddlers playing in the grass outside and smiled as one of them fell.

"They're so innocent. I feel like I grew up too fast," he softly told me as he handed me a Frappuccino. Quiet, serene. I closed my eyes and said thanks to the gods that had helped me meet him.

"Can you imagine you were like that too sometime ago?" I leaned onto his arm and held his hand, tracing his knuckles with my thumb. I took a sip of my coffee, "Caramel, my favorite."

"Caramel."

"No, Caramel." I raised my eyebrows inviting him to fight me. He smiled and sipped his coffee.

"Fine, Caramel." He opened the door for me. I stepped out. It was perfectly sunny. There wasn't a cloud out and the wind blew my hair back. It made me smile. "Grew up too fast huh? Lucky for you I'm immature enough for both of us combined." I ran forward and picked up a dandelion, then blew its seeds into his face.

"Oh, it's on." Johnny grabbed two dandelions and started to blow. I took off running. We probably looked nuts, me running and screaming with him chasing me. The toddlers playing outside had stopped and were watching us. We didn't care.

"Whoa!" Johnny's long legs caught up to me pretty quick. He caught me around my waist and we fell to the grass in a bundle. We laughed until we felt like our stomachs would burst. Johnny blew the dandelions into my hair. "I win," he shouted. We both stood up and brushed the grass off our pants. I looked up at his face. I stopped smiling when, up close, I saw his eyes were red.

"Whoa, Johnny, you okay?" I moved closer to him. His eyes widened and he sighed.

"I haven't been able to sleep for three days. I've been having really bad headaches. No amount of coffee can save me." He tripped. I caught him by his arm. "Well, how about we sit and let's stop drinking coffee." I sat him down on a bench and took the Frappuccino from his hands. He didn't protest. "Are you going to see a doctor?"

"We scheduled an appointment in a few weeks. The nurse said to just take Advil or something 'till then." He stretched out his long legs and rested his neck on the back of the bench. I took out my ripped poetry book. Johnny smiled. "Read me something, Prasad." A man passed and gave us, or me, a weird look. I was used to it by now so I didn't really care, but Johnny wasn't. "Hey, wouldn't your company get angry if you were hanging out with me and people started seeing us together or something?" Johnny sat up.

"No, they'd be pleased. Everyone is already speculating that Finn and I together. More attention if there was someone else as well. They tried to get me a faker, but I absolutely refused."

"A faker?"

"Someone to pretend to be my boyfriend." I looked over at him to see his reaction. He bit the inside of his cheek, clearly uncomfortable. But bless his soul, he didn't bring it up.

"Well, in that case," Johnny leaned onto my shoulder, "you were gonna read me something." I smiled and opened to a random page. The smile vanished and my blood turned cold. "Ooh, what's this?" Johnny looked along with me as I read from the poem, *What the Living Do* by Marie Howe. It begins with the words, "*Johnny, the kitchen sink has been clogged for days.*"

"It was written after her brother, Johnny, died," I muttered. I was shaken. This poem had always given me shivers. What scared me even more was that Johnny seemed unaffected. I noticed his foot had stopped shaking. He was breathing

slower. He moved and put his head in my lap and his legs
up on the bench.

"Read me another one." His chocolate eyes reflected the
sky above. I kept reading, moving on to happier love poems.
I guess he was really tired. He fell asleep in my lap. I stroked
his hair. It was true what they said. People do look younger
when they're asleep. Johnny looked like he didn't have a
care in the world with his lips slightly parted, and his soft
breath warming my thighs.

That was how I wanted to remember him.

I had lied to Johnny. Mr. Nelson would not be happy
if he found out about him. He would hate that I was with
someone 'non-famous so non-valuable' to put it in his words.
He was already pissed that I wouldn't allow a faker.

*"I'm trying to help you, sweetheart. Work out a deal with
Winston or let me choose you a faker. Only way you're gonna
get attention is if you give your fans some drama they can
follow."* But, as I stroked Johnny's soft hair, I couldn't help
myself. I didn't want to limit the relationship we had, but
I couldn't let Mr. Nelson know. Right now, no one cared.
Everyone just passed us with a smile like we were any other
normal teenagers. Maybe some frowned as if they'd seen
me somewhere before. But, what would I do when people
did start to care? A truck horn blared, distracting me from
my thoughts and rousing Johnny from his sleep.

"Thanks a lot buddy! My headaches back and I—"
I stopped him by swooping down and kissing him. If our
time was limited, then I will cherish it to its extent. His
brown eyes looked deep into my soul. Like he was taking
a picture so he could remember this moment forever. His
eyes searched my face.

"Now what was that for?"

"Johnny Taylor, promise to never forget me." I guess I was
still wearing a little bit of lipstick from my commercial. His

lips were bright red, not that I was staring at his perfect lips. He ensured me that he wouldn't with our next kiss. His fingers stroked my scalp and entwined themselves in my hair. I fell onto his chest with a dopey smile I couldn't erase.

"Trust me, Prasad, I don't think my mind will ever let me forget you."

Chapter 25

"*And it's in your eyes, your love for me. I see it clearly.*" Finn's voice cracked, making me snort. Ellen, the lady with the company who actually knew music, queued for the music to stop.

"Settle down now. Let's pick it back up in twenty five."

"Maybe I shouldn't have had that Mountain Dew before this," Finn remarked.

"I thought your mom threw away all the soda and ice cream in your house so it wouldn't harm your voice."

"True, but there's this way to cheat the vending mach—" The music started back up and we fell silent again.

The recording room the company used was definitely way smaller than Jamie's. It was shared too so we had to book it for a certain time and the equipment was pretty shabby from all the usage. I could feel my humongous headphones slipping off my head. But they worked nonetheless. The end product was pretty cool. Your voice did sound different with all the technology. It was so clean now without the echo of an auditorium or the distortion of a microphone. It made me smile.

"It's weird to be on the other end of the window," Finn muttered as he tapped the microphone.

"Weirder to hear the lyrics you wrote actually sung the way you wanted." And sung by you, for that matter. They sounded so much more personal and way more impactful when Jamie wasn't mutilating each word.

"About that, my record company works pretty closely with Jamie's company, so I'm there all the time. I saw her listen to that cover you made of her song, and damn was she pissed."

"That was what I was going for." I had done a cover of one of the last songs I had written for Jamie, and it had only gotten a few less views than Jamie's original. "She could do whatever she wants with my words, but my words shall still stay my words."

"That doesn't make sense."

"You don't make sense." I heard something. I moved the blinds of the very narrow window to see a mob of paps standing outside the entrance. "Finn, are we the only people here?" Finn looked behind him, to Ellen, for the answer.

"The only singers, yeah." She nodded her head.

"They're for you, *mon amie*." Mr. Nelson walked in, bringing with him a strong smell of tobacco. He leaned on Finn's shoulder. "Somebody, guess who, tipped them off on your location. Now what I want you to do, Mohana, is to not say a word to the paps and your new faker will drop you off at home. Your parents have already been notified."

"I told you, I don't want a faker."

"My dear, maybe you should have read the small print in the contract. We have full control over you for a month. It's like a trial. In July you can stay or you can leave or we could kick you out. Now meet your new faker." Mr. Nelson motioned to a boy leaning on the door frame. I hadn't noticed him before.

"Ajay Sai." He moved forward and gave me his hand to shake. My mouth opened wide as I looked up into his eyes, then down at his waiting hand. I already knew his name. Ajay Sai was one of the most renowned child actors/dancers of today. Every girl, at least Indian girls, had a picture of him in their bedroom. You can tell why. Perfect jawline, perfect hair combed to the side, damn. He was a world away from Johnny. Johnny was softer, a more lenient jaw, a relaxed face that always showed his emotions clear as day.

"Paycheck." Mr. Nelson took out a check from his pocket. "And, Mr. Winston, I'm gonna keep you here for a little bit so we don't get any paps asking weird questions about you and Mohana." Ajay dropped his hand that was still pointing at me with a smile and took the check. Finn closed my hanging jaw. "You're welcome, *ma jolie*. I can see you like your faker. I spent all night trying to find you a perfect faker that matched your height, looks, and skin tone. The Citizen's Choice Awards are coming too. We can't just send you alone and single, now get out there!"

"Citizen's Choice Awards? I'm invited?"

"They normally invite Wainscott winners and you're publishing an album, so you're guaranteed an invitation." Ajay's clear voice made my heart shudder. He opened the door for me and Finn pushed me out. "See you Tuesday, if you make it." He cast a glance at the hungry paps through the window.

"Mohana? Did I say it right?" He scrunched his beautiful eyebrows. We'd started walking to the doors. I had to jog to keep us with his long legs.

"Mh-hm." *Oh, that was high pitched.* He noticed, but being the gentleman he was he ignored it and kept walking. He stopped outside the main exit.

"Okay, my car's the red one right there. I'm pretty sure your boss told us not to talk to anyone so I think we're just gonna have to push our way there."

"You're the expert," I muttered as loud as I could.

"Oh, and the quicker we sort this out the better. We need a backstory."

"Mr. Nelson told me he'd get a dancer to be my faker, so we could say we met while we were at the Raul concert rehearsing."

"And Mr. Nelson's gonna—"

"Get you a spot as one of the ensemble dancers, yup."
I nodded. He smiled. "Then let's do it." He cracked his
neck like he was going into war or something and put his
arm around me. He opened the door and guided me out
through the sea of paps. And, my, they were animals.

They were the predators and we were the prey.

"Ms. Prasad, is it true you're cheating on Mr. Winston
with Mr. Sai?"

"Anything you can say about your new album Ms. Prasad?"

"Are the rumors true you're pregnant with Mr. Sai's child?"
I gave that reporter a look. I'm not that fat. Ajay just smiled
and tightened his grip around my shoulders. It felt weird.
Johnny normally liked to hold me tighter, like he was stak-
ing a claim. Ajay's grip was soft, not hesitant, just soft. He
didn't need to hold me tight, I'll always be there. I needed
him. We got to his little red car in a heartbeat. That's when
I thought to ask. "Oh, you can drive?"

"I got my license last year." I hesitated, and he picked up
on my concern. "Trust me, I haven't died yet." The words
he spoke wasn't very reassuring, but his actions were. He
opened the door and showed me inside.

The way a person drives says a lot about them. Ajay
always drove ten miles below the speed limit, no matter
how many honks he got. He just flipped them off and
kept driving. And he paid so much attention. His dark eyes
scanning everything. The sidewalk, the road, me.

"You seem a little flustered. You shouldn't mind them.
They'll say a lot of things that you'll have to ignore in
the future."

"Yeah?"

"Of course, just don't give a damn. Listen to me now, don't
learn that the hard way." He started slowing down a mile
from the stoplight. I smiled and took out my phone. I had
to text everyone and let them know the whole me and Ajay

situation was fake. Screw Mr. Nelson! He'd probably prefer the news to be leaked out rather than me being mauled by my friends. There were already one hundred twenty messages in our group chat. I looked up when another driver honked his car horn at Ajay. *"Stupide!"* he muttered under his breath.

"French?" I never understood how French guys always looked so good. Wait—let me restate that—most French guys looked so good. There were mutants like Mr. Nelson. I'll just stick to Italian guys like Johnny.

"I was born in India but I was raised in Québec. I moved here for the shooting of *Maxine* and I just kinda stayed after that. I kept getting offered more roles." *Maxine* was his big screen debut.

"Which do you like better, Québec or America?"

"Definitely Québec." He laughed, "Oh, and uhm you spelled 'promise' wrong. I didn't mean to look it's just, grammar. Your boyfriend is totally your thing." He'd turned red. It made me smile. I fixed my text that I'd been writing to Johnny.

"He's not my boyfriend." I stopped to think. What was Johnny to me? "He's a person who is just really close to me, so my, uh, thingy." He raised his eyebrows.

"If it makes you feel better, I have a 'thingy' as well. Marianne, back in Québec. Now you can trust I won't tell anyone 'cause you know about my girlfriend."

"How long have you two been together?" I asked with a smile.

"One year." His eyes were cloudy. "She's the one who told me first. She looked as if she'd beat me up if I said no. She's got a personality as fiery as her hair, and I love it. I haven't seen her in a while though."

"Why?"

"My managers. It's complicated."

"When was the last time you saw her?" I wouldn't be able to bear not seeing Johnny. It must have been awful for him. He stopped before my house and he turned to me with pained eyes. "The last time I saw her was the day she asked me out, a year ago."

Chapter 26

I took a deep breath of the thick, musty air in the stadium, trying to take in everything. The rows and rows of seats, the strobe lights, the smoke machines. I could imagine the crowd filling the stands, waving their phone flashlights. And it was all going to happen in just six more days.

"Excuse me, doll." I moved to let a short, grubby worker pull wooden planks across the stage. I pulled my hands underneath my sleeves. Everyone was looking at me. The workers, the dancers, the lady who sold that horrid popcorn at the entrance. Some with jealousy, others with awe. I looked around to see if I could find Michelle, the lady who'd told me to wait here.

"Surprise!" Someone hugged me from behind. Ajay handed me some popcorn. "Aww, thank you!"

"*De rien*, can you eat this? Because I can't. It's like bubble gum flavored." I popped one in my mouth.

"It's not too bad. It's just kinda chewy."

"I'm pretty sure that's not supposed to happen." He ate some anyway.

"Did you see Michelle anywhere?"

"I saw her yelling at the costume designer backstage."

"I'm gonna go find her." I couldn't stand everyone looking at me anymore. The dancers, who some I was pretty sure were models, eyed my popcorn with tormented eyes. Looking at their slim bodies, I couldn't tell how long ago they had eaten actual food. Others looked at the popcorn, with amusement, and at my body. At my hips that jutted out weirdly, at my short meaty legs. I sucked my stomach until it hurt and made my way backstage, or tried to at least. A tall bald man stopped me.

"Dancers stay here." He had a gruff voice that made me shrink. With a tiny voice, I tried to respond, "No, sir I'm act—"

"Places!" He roared and every dancer took their spot. Ajay slowly dragged me back by the hand.

"Don't mess with him, he doesn't look all that understanding."

"But—"

"Just follow my lead. The dance itself is pretty easy." He turned me so I was facing him in a position like we were going to waltz.

Ajay had lied to me. It wasn't easy. Maybe for him because he'd danced his whole life and could move his body the way he wanted to, but me, on the other hand, had no control. And don't let a person with no control of their legs dance on a stage full of professionals because it ends in them tripping into a really blonde dancer and crashing into some chairs on the side of the stage, which hurts, like really bad.

"What was that?" I heard the cold voice of the bald man from before right above my head. I shut my eyes tight right on the floor. I heard laughter around me.

"Sir, she's—"

"Quiet, boy!" I heard Ajay exhale sharply.

"Sir, I'm actually the opening singer, Mohana Prasad. I tried to tell you." Even I could hardly hear my voice. But bald-man did. "You can't just waltz in and say you're some singer, or pretend to be a dancer, for that matter! You need talent for that, you need to audit—"

"Excuse me?" Something had flared inside me. "Talent? Buddy, I'm pretty sure I have more than you." The day

I had confronted Jamie after she had left me at the airport, she'd had me removed by security. The guard had said the same thing,

"Sung with Jamie West? You need talent for that." He then threw me out into the street.

"Look, I've been singing since I was six. I have eighteen first places and twenty two seconds, and fifteen participation medals. I know what I am doing. Now let me talk to Michelle so I can do what you guys asked me to do." I brushed off my pants and gave him a glare. The dancers had stopped whispering about me and were looking at Bald-dude to see what he would do. He looked at a few sheets of paper.

"Apologies, Ms. Prasad. I'll show you to Michelle Grace."

"Thank you for understanding," I huffed. Ajay gave me a thumbs up behind bald-dude's head.

After a quick apology I was placed in front of a microphone on the center of the stage. I had gotten a classic big guitar that was dysfunctional.

"The audience is gonna be hype, waiting for Peter so we need the best, energetic performance you can give. We'll save the slow, soft songs for our main event." Michelle, the lady in charge, stood just below the stage. She was a middle-aged lady who looked caffeine-high, which she probably was. She qued the sound person for music. All I had to do was fake strum along with the guitar. The actual music was prerecorded.

"Let me tell you all a story, a story to melt your stone hearts." My voice sounded real echoey. It was to the extent that after I finished my voice still could be heard for about eight seconds.

I only did three songs, and I didn't get any dancers or other music players in the back so I had to move around the stage. I also had to get people hyped, but doing that with a classic vintage-looking guitar that was twice the size of a normal one seemed pretty impossible. I guess if Peter Raul could do it, so could I.

"*We sleep under the same stars, isn't that enough?*" I finished my last song on a soft note that took ages to get down. Working with Jamie had done one good thing, she'd taught me to go softer. It pained me to say she was right about something. Volume wasn't the only thing in music. My soft note echoed through the auditorium. "That'll be fixed when there are people in here. They'll absorb the sound. Plus, the people will be too busy cheering to notice." Michelle hopped on stage with a sheet of paper. "These are the songs Peter is going to perform. Make sure none of yours match the same style. We need a variety." I tried my best to look them over, but we're all human.

"Aww, he's not singing *Pictures?*"

"That one's getting old. No one wants to listen to that one anymore."

"I do," I muttered under my breath.

"Alright dancers! We have rehearsals every day leading up to the concert, same time and duration as today." She turned to me and spoke in a softer voice, "You only need to come to the Saturday rehearsal, that's the one with Peter." My heart thumped in my chest at the mention of his name.

"My parents can pick me up so you don't need to trouble yourself," I told Ajay as we walked out of the auditorium.

"It's not trouble," he started to say, then realizing there were paps waiting he sprang into action, Ajay put his arm around my shoulders as a camera flashed outside the window. They'd increased ever since my album had published. People had started noticing me when I went out. I'd given out autographs.

"Mo?" I looked around to see Johnny, on the verge of laughing. Made sense, Ajay and I were faking conversation, making big gestures and mouthing random words. I raised my eyebrows and made sure he knew to stay there.

"He's gone." Ajay let go of me.

"I didn't know you'd be here, I was visiting my cousin. He's part of—"

"The basketball team." Ajay's clicked his tongue. His eyes widened. "You look exactly like Matthews."

"He's over for dinner all the time." Johnny looked accomplished. He leaned against my shoulder protectively. I smiled, never had I ever imagined I'd see cool, confident Johnny get defensive. I wrapped my arms around his sleeve and shook my head at Ajay so he knew Johnny didn't mean it.

"Alright, see you Mohana." Ajay turned to leave but stopped. Cameraman was back. I quickly let go of Johnny. "I'll walk you out." I ran over to Ajay and took his arm instead.

Every night before I can fall asleep, they haunt me. The mistakes I made. The small ones, like *'remember that one time you were so mean to Josh Marshall'* or *'I can't believe that you thought Kalyani's shirt looked bad,'* but there were big ones like, *'Cause you said that in that little article, now all of Yemen hates you,'* and *'Stupid, I can't believe you wore corduroy in front of paps,'* *'You should have looked back that day,'* Maybe if I'd looked back at Johnny's face that day things would have changed. But I just walked out with Ajay. I didn't see his hurt-stricken face. I didn't hear him whisper my name. I was too busy with myself, 'cause at that time I did something that haunts every singer's worst nightmares. I coughed a single cough.

Chapter 27

"You wanna tell me why you're wearing two scarves and a hat, inside?"

"No." I took a sip of tea. Shaina looked at Kalyani for help. She shrugged.

"Buddy, I don't know about her any more than you do." She emptied out the bunnies' water tray. The local animal shelter always let volunteers like us help. And after we were done, we could play with the bunnies for free! That's why I always looked forward to Fridays.

"Alright, this is Chestnut." The caretaker, a short but fast lady, handed me a small bunny wrapped in a blanket. "He's been having trouble with his hind legs so people have been reluctant to adopt him. I thought maybe a picture with you could—"

"Of course, I'd be happy to help." I took off my hat and cradled the little bunny. It looked like a little burrito with only its head sticking out of the blanket.

"Do you want me to—"

"No, you can stay right there." She took a few quick pics and left with a hasty 'thanks' and the bunny. I coughed again, and put my hat back on with a sigh.

"All singers dread being sick, but it's worse for me. Asthma can make even a little cold seem like you're inhaling ice every time you breathe. Curse my stupid shriveled lungs,"

I muttered with another sip of tea. "I'm not taking any chances. I'm opening for Peter in two days."

"Oh, yeah! And your birthday's tomorrow. My little girl's turning sixteen!" Shaina cradled my head.

"What do you want for your birthday?" Kalyani stroked a fat, gray bunny that was falling asleep.

"Do you know what I really want?" I'd given this a lot of thought. You only get one birthday candle wish a year.

"Peace and quiet?"

"A day to spend with Johnny where you could just be normal teenagers!"

"No, boring!" I laughed. Everyone seemed to think that's what I wanted, to be normal again. Wrong! I've had enough of it, really. Was it weird that I actually liked the attention? True, sometimes it is annoying that I can't even go out to buy gum or something. And, yes, I couldn't casually just stroll out with Johnny anymore. We stayed inside and made sure no one saw us. But, really it wasn't all too bad.

"What I truly want is to win the Uprising Celeb Award at the Citizen's Choice Awards." I checked my phone. "My mom's here, I gotta go. I have another interview." I pet another bunny for the last time and stood up to brush all the bunny hair off my pants.

"Jamie's going against you for Uprising Celeb at the CCA's, right?"

"Yeah, she's also against me for Celeb Pick of the Year. It would be wonderful to shove it in her face that I can do things too. That I'm not some hopeless little girl." I pulled on my boots. "Alright, see you!" I waved to my friends, opened the door and stepped into the warm sunlight. Our silver car sparkled,

"In, in, in, we're gonna be late." My mom took off as soon as I shut the door. "Took you long enough."

"Sorry!" I put on my seatbelt, and gripped my seat. It

was going to be one of those rides where I was going to get close to dying at least eight times. When we stopped at a traffic light, a little kid pointed at me.

"Oh, right, we have a new celebrity in the house." My mom checked her watch.

"Yeah mom, I think your Herniated Disk Presentation really caught fire over the Internet." She gave me a glare and continued driving over the speed limit. "Better that than some useless cat video," she muttered. With my mom at the wheel, the normally twenty minute journey was made in half the time. We hopped out and made our way inside.

"Isn't Wendy gonna be here?" my mom asked.

"No, I apparently have enough experience to do this on my own."

"I disagree." My mom chuckled. We reached a little receptionist. "Mohana Prasad, M-o-h—"

"A-n-a. If you can wait right there, Ms. Prasad, our main interviewer will come get you shortly." Oh, right I was famous now.

It was a side effect from having a weird name. You always spell it before they ask you to because you know it's coming. Guess I didn't have to do that anymore.

"Oh, Sugar, it's great to see you again." I knew that Jersey accent, I whipped around. And there she was. She'd ditched her shorts this time and was wearing a pantsuit. My first hater, Darla Hamilton.

I've had a lot of articles about me now, some good, others critiquing, but the first time is always the worst. Bad articles didn't hurt me anymore, but I remember the feeling I got that day I read Darla's article. "I'll show you to the makeup artists, but I do know for a fact that they won't like the hats, hon, you want a leave 'em with Mama? And speaking of that, parents aren't allowed in so we'd prefer it if you stayed here, Ma'am." My mom knew her as well, she had shielded me the minute she saw Hamilton. She reluctantly moved and I reluctantly removed my hats. She was going to be my interviewer, so I should probably make her like me so she wouldn't ruin me in front of millions.

"Oh, my! This is simply atrocious. I volunteered with bunnies and now I have hair all over me." I pulled a strand of bunny hair off my pants, Darla gave me a weird look. I'll make her like me, some day. I had used my Goody Two-shoes voice on her. It always worked with the teachers. "Do you like bunnies, Ms. Hamilton?"

"Not really, they're too fluffy." She pointed to a room and left without another word. I knew the drill. Two people pulled my hair so hard I had grip the seat arms, then the lady with the sick-smelling powder that made me gag, and there was always that one weird person who didn't do anything, but still called themselves a makeup artist. I was in a not-so-comfy couch in less then a minute. I looked around. "Oh, where are the cue-cards, Ms. Hamilton?"

"I don't work well with cue-cards, dearest, they confuse me. I'm pretty sure you'll do just fine on your own. You've had enough experience to skip the media/screen training." Darla looked over a few papers and fixed her hair.

"Alright, on air in—" The camera person raised his fingers and counted down

"Three, two, one!"

"Hi, hello, and welcome to *Celebrity Night*. I'm your host, Darla Hamilton, but you don't need much info about me." Her Jersey accent was gone. "Tonight, I'm here with one of America's rising stars, Mohana Prasad. So, Ms. Prasad, going to release a new album tomorrow, yes?" I looked at the huge camera, which never seemed that big before. All the crew members were looking at me, oh and I had to watch what I say. Darla had proved how she could spin my words. I'd never noticed any of this, I was always too busy with my cue-cards.

"Just the singles, Darla."

"So you've been planning this for a long time?"

"Watch what you say, Mo." My mind muttered.

"Uhm, I guess I never knew what my true dream was until just recently. All this happening around me has just proved to me that this was, actually, what my true dream was."

"So this was all never planned?"

"Kinda, I mean, I never knew I was this serious about music until recently. Even though I've always loved music it just never seemed like I'd be able to make a career of it."

"So you might consider music as a career, Ms. Prasad?"

"Maybe. I still feel too young to think about my career right now." I gave a laugh that was as genuine as possible. If I never gave a proper answer, then she can't use anything against me. I gave myself a mental pat on the back.

"So let's change topics then. Here at Celebrity Night we expect the full story. But, we never got one for Ajay and you." Mr. Nelson had given us an entire backstory and had made us memorize it word for word.

"I met Ajay when I was rehearsing with him for the upcoming Peter Raul concert, and we hit it off instantly. He told me he liked two weeks after we met, and we decided to start going out."

"And, you kept it a secret because—?"

"We wanted to make sure it was actually a thing before we told everyone, you know? So we decided to make sure we actually liked each other before we told the press."

"Aww, well isn't that the sweetest thing! How did Mr. Winston feel?"

"Oh, Finn, probably just felt a little left out. He was a bit reserved with Ajay for a while, but now they get on like a house on fire."

Wait, oh shit! I realized what I had done a second after I said it. "Actually—"

"Oh, you heard it first here folks. Finn Winston had indeed liked Ms. Prasad, but was terribly heartbroken when she didn't return his feelings."

Chapter 28

"So you're just gonna ditch me on my special day? It's not my sweet sixteen every day!" I pouted.

"And it's not every day my friends from Italy can come visit, besides we'd be really out of place surrounded by famous teenagers." My dad twirled his car keys on his pointer finger.

"Alright, let's go. Have fun Mo. I left some Tylenol in your bag. Take it if you feel a fever coming." I nodded. All the tea I drank was doing some good, the coughs had gone away. Good thing too. I was opening for Peter tomorrow. My mom waved to me as she opened the big doors that led outside. I let out the big gulp of air I'd been holding in once the door slammed. Who'd made sure their boss made them host a birthday party on the day their parents would be busy so they could hang out with a guy close to their heart? This girl!

"Boo!" I felt someone hug me from behind. I smiled at the clock. I'd have an hour with Johnny before people would arrive. I turned around to face him. His hair was slicked to the side more perfectly today, and he was wearing his letterman jacket. "I got something for you." He pulled a little box with a purple bow around it.

"Aww, Johnny, it looks lovely."

"Open it, it's my Mom's. It took a lot of lies and persuasion to get her to give it to me without her knowing why."

He smiled and unwrapped the bow for me. I opened the small box to see a ring, well three rings intertwined with each ring bearing a word.

"*True Love Waits.*" I read out loud.

"My mom's divorced. My dad gave it to her when she turned sixteen. She was apparently his high school sweetheart and everything. She never takes it off." I couldn't say a word. "I'm pretty sure it'll fit on your thumb." He gently rolled the ring onto my left thumb, the silver glinted in the lights. I looked up into his eyes, "I-I understand if you don't like it I just thought—"

"Stop talking!" I engulfed him in a tight hug. "Johnny Taylor, no one can just be that perfect. I love you so much." I felt his chest rise with a breath.

And you haven't even seen me roller skate yet. I'm like Beethoven on wheels." He put on a pair of skates and was on the wooden floor before I could respond or question him. "Come on." His voice echoed through the empty place.

"I never learned."

"Oh, it's easy. I'll teach you." He handed me a pair of skates. As I put them on he skated over behind me and grabbed just above my wrists with his hands. He then put his feet behind my roller skate-laden feet and tilted them in a certain way. He pushed off.

"Wait, Johnny—" I stumbled, and his hands tightened their grip.

"Just relax." I heard his voice somewhere above my head. "Lean against me and just feel the wind against your face. You'll be fine, I promise." I stiffened against his chest with my eyes closed and stayed like that for a good two minutes. Only after we'd completed our second lap did I finally open my eyes. Johnny was going pretty slow. His feet were in rhythm. He'd raise one leg and for a second the sound of the skates lessened, then he'd bring it back down with a *boom* softly nudging my feet forward. Quiet, *boom*, quiet, *boom*. "You ready, Mo?"

"For, what?" Johnny let go of one of my arms and skated up beside me so we were parallel.

"Joh—!" He silenced me with a look so pure and highly contagious. It calmed me and I quickly fell into his beat: quiet, *boom*, quiet, *boom*. That's when a loud crash distracted our moment. Johnny stopped me by skating in front of me and letting me skate into his chest. We both turned around to see Finn on the floor by the snacks. His hair appeared to have a whole bag of chips tangled in it.

"Oh, am I disturbing something? Oops, it's this slippery wooden floor." His grin didn't leave as he started pulling all the chips from his hair.

"You fuckin' idiot!" Lavender's petite form had blended into the black walls with her black dress. Her iconic line had brought a smile to my face. Then I realized I was still hugging Johnny. In my rush to get away from him I forgot I was wearing skates. I slipped and fell straight on my back.

"Oh, don't do that. You guys were already becoming my OTP and everything." She walked forward to help, but Johnny had it covered. His arms tried to lift me.

"Oh, wow! Since I'm closer to you now I think I have the perfect liberty to say you've gained weight," he muttered as he heaved and brought me up. I looked over to Lavender.

"It would really ruin the whole Ajay and me situation if you were to say anything. So, Lavender, can you please not—"

"Tell? Love, I got you. Why would I ruin such a beautiful relationship? Now you ought to get cleaned up 'cause I just saw Jamie West's little limo out the window."

"Oh, I guess I should leave then." Johnny began to turn, but I stopped him.

"No, stay. You can keep me from going insane." He looked

grateful. The moment was ruined though by Finn gagging on a chip.

"Sweetie you're a mess." As Lavender went to pull chips out of Finn's hair, and made sure he didn't eat them, Jamie sashayed in.

"Oh, I guess I'm early. None the matter! I see you got interesting company." Jamie's eyes swept across Lavender cursing and tugging chips out of a seriously red faced and stuttering Finn, and Johnny, who was bending down, removing his skates. Her eyes lingered on Johnny as he got upright again, and I couldn't do a thing about it. It burned my heart.

"Let's take a picture, Jamie, Johnny?" He turned around as soon as his name had come out of my lips. "My dear cameraman, take a few pictures, will you?" I handed him my phone, trying to touch as much of his hand as possible, and made sure she noticed when he got confused about being a cameraman.

"Of course." He took two quick shots, and I took a few selfies, trying to smile as genuinely as I could. More people started to arrive and boy did it soon get crowded. Mr. Nelson had invited a lot of people: child actors, YouTubers, dancers, models, etc. I didn't get to meet them, though, I was too busy with the pictures.

"You okay?" I asked Johnny who was massaging his arm from all the pictures.

"Yeah, I'm fine. Tense party though, huh?" We looked around, and for once I was happy that I was too busy to party. Everyone was in their tight knit groups giving their competitors looks. Occasionally someone would go talk to someone else, but it would only be about their careers, never anything else. So, people left pretty early and the party was over in an hour.

"Do we have to clean up?" As everyone milled out of the doors, Finn popped up behind me.

"Nope." I sighed, "Popcorn this time?" I muttered as I dusted little bits of popcorn out of his hair.

"You don't expect to put me on skates and not spill anything." He looked at me expectantly. I closed my eyes. I'd been avoiding it all day, yet it had to be said. "Finn, I'm so sorry."

"No, it's fine, really. What's done is done, we just have to figure it out," He sighed. Finn had been chased by paps asking him about me after Darla's interview. I really hated that woman.

"Finn, it'll probably go away in a few weeks."

"I don't think so, It'll go on as long as I am seen with you." He looked at me and I knew exactly what he was thinking.

"Finn, no."

"Mohana, yes. It's really the only way." He pulled out his gray hat from his pocket and put it on. "Never really told anyone this but I used to have a younger sister." Oh, he only ever mentions his older brother. "She died of cancer when she was like six. I haven't been the same ever since." He looked at me with such a pained expression, it made my eyes watery. "You've always reminded me of her, same looks and the same personality. And after you cut your hair, it took a while to even look you in the face. Mohana, you don't know how much I hate that people are shipping us together. You don't know how much it hurts and disgusts and weirds me out." He looked at me for a response. But what was I supposed to say?

"So you're just gonna leave me?" my voice cracked.

"Mo." He didn't have to explain anything to me. I understood. I nodded. I blinked my tears away. He sighed and attempted a weak smile. He turned to walk away but stopped just in front of the door. He looked back. "I'll keep my ears out for you. I know I'll hear great things." I took a raspy breath. "Same to you, Finn Winston."

Chapter 29

"Johnny, is it worth it?" I sat on a table and started playing with the table cloth. Johnny was massaging his scalp.

"Mohana, what's wrong?" He rushed to my side when he saw the mascara down my face.

"Was it worth it Johnny? To be famous, but to hide your true personality, or to lose all your friends so people would know your name?" It all came out, all my tears. All of the stress and anxiety I had been facing this past week, it all came out like a boulder rolling down a steep hill.

"I'm here for you." Johnny hugged me as I cried into his shoulder. "I'm here for you." He repeated it over and over again, it was pretty calming.

"And, do you know what the worst part is? There's a part of me that's okay with it, Johnny. There's a part of me willing to sacrifice my friends and family for fame. A part of me that's ready to do anything. How does that make me different from Jamie?"

"J.K. Rowling said, *'It does not do to dwell on dreams and forget to live.'* This is the place you are in so let's figure out a way to solve the problem, not mourn and destroy yourself over it."

"You read Harry Potter?"

"I started reading them for you. I'm on the fifth book,

but it's humongous. It's like the size of a fridge." I snorted into his sleeve.

"Oh, I got makeup all over your jacket. I'm so sorry." I attempted to brush it off. "No it's fine, let it be. I-I'll keep it as a reminder of you." He smiled, "Oh, you're rubbing off on me Prasad! I'm full of fluff like you now." His smile made me shiver like the old days. "You're welcome."

"You look cold." He draped his letterman jacket over me. "Thanks."

"How does Ajay do it? De-Du-"

"*De rien.* It's French."

"I can speak in other languages too. *Sei il benvenuto mia cara.*" His voice sounded even better in Italian.

"Mhmm, can you make pasta too?"

"I can try. Doubt you'll be able to eat it though." Something shiny caught my eye. "Jamie left her purse," I muttered and went to pick it up. "We should throw it away, that'd be fun." Johnny took it out of my hands and placed it on the table.

"No, that would be bad Mohana. She is annoying though. I see why you don't like her. Pretty, but really annoying," he said nonchalantly. I whipped my head around.

For the next part, none of you can judge me. I like to think it was the emotional distress that made me go haywire or maybe all the questions and doubts I'd kept inside and ignored, it's the only way I can cope with what happened next.

"If she's so pretty then why don't you go kiss her?" It came out in a yell that made Johnny jump. I think it surprised me too. I flinched. "Besides, she's way better than me. She'd make you popular."

"What does that mean?"

"Shruthi told me. I just didn't want to believe it. I guess I always knew deep down though, I know you only like me because I'm famous."

"Lies!"

"So you could go brag to your friends you kissed Mohana Prasad, so you could—"

"*Mohana Devi Prasad*," Johnny made me stop, he took a deep breath, "You're one to talk."

"Excuse me?"

"You're one to talk." Johnny's deep voice had the habit of breaking whenever he got excited. Like when he talked about a baseball game, or when he talked to me. But, now, his voice didn't break once. "You don't want to be seen in public with me. You ditched me for pretty-boy Ajay. You're one to talk."

"You know Mr. Nelson made me do that!"

"Do I? And if he did, why did you agree? Don't talk to me about a contract." I had opened my mouth. "If someone told me to stop seeing the girl I liked-*loved,* the girl I loved, for something important to me, like basketball, I would never agree. I would drop it immediately. I would never play basketball again."

"This isn't about basketball!"

"It doesn't have to always be about you either." He regretted that one as soon as he'd said it. He closed his eyes. Now that caught me by surprise.

"What?"

"Think about it, everything's based on you and your fame, Mo. It's getting kinda one sided now." His headache seemed to have come back. He squinted and rubbed his forehead. "You never notice anything I need. You never cared for my feelings. You're too busy with Ajay."

"So this is about Ajay? Admit it, Johnny, you're jealous." He didn't hesitate for one second with his response. "Yes, Mo, I am jealous. Jealous of the guy who is hugging my girl, jealous of the guy I took a picture of today holding her. I'm jealous like any other guy'd be." He seemed totally calm, unlike me.

"If you're spending your time being jelly then maybe we should stop!" I didn't like where this was going. I wanted to take it back, but I couldn't

"Cause you changed, Johnny, and that's the truth. You aren't the same person you were in seventh grade. The shy, quiet reader that I liked? You aren't him!"

"And you aren't the same driven, hardworking, doesn't-care-what-others think-of-them Mohana I liked. Maybe this is better. I'm gonna leave." He didn't grab the jacket that was still around my shoulders. He turned and started walking away.

"Fine, Johnny, leave. But don't come to me for a poem. Don't come to me because any other girl wouldn't take you, just never come back!" I collapsed on the floor in a heap. "Just never come back." I sobbed, "Don't ever, ever come back!" My cries echoed through the empty roller park. All I needed at that moment was someone to hug me, tell me it was okay, someone like Johnny. Did he hear my cries? I didn't know. He didn't come back.

"Oh, honey!" I turned to see Lavender rushing toward me. "What happened?" I couldn't talk, I couldn't breathe really. I pointed to a bag in the corner with my inhaler. She got it for me. "Good thing I forgot my purse, love, who do I need to kill?" She rubbed my back in a compassionate way as I took my two puffs out of the inhaler. I gave her one look and it was all she needed. "Bitch what the fuck did he do?"

"He's gone." That's all I could get out of my mouth. *He's gone.* "Guess your OTP isn't canon after all."

"This isn't about me, it's about you."

"And it was all my fault."

"What?"

"All my fault, Lavender. I was the one who got angry, it was all the stre—"

"The tension. All celebrities face it, trust me. Now crying

isn't gonna solve your problems, it it? No, you are gonna apologize or talk to him or whatever tomorrow. Now, let's get you home."

"Thanks, I really mean it. Sorry, I—"

"No, the only apologizing you are gonna do is to your guy. Up, up, up!" I smile when I think of it now. Lavender didn't know. No one knew. Maybe I could have known if I'd paid attention. But, I didn't, 'cause of the dumb thing I was. Again, my mistake, *'You should have looked back that day.'*

Chapter 30

"*Smile, nod, wave. Repeat, smile, nod, wave.*"

"You're getting good at this."

"I know." I finally got a break to stretch my back. I had been bent over for at least thirty minutes over my table. Another fan came up in a Peter Raul tour sweatshirt. "Hi!" I said as enthusiastically as possible.

"*Smile, nod, wave.*" That's what the coach had said about crowds. Yes, Mr. Nelson had paid for a teacher to come and train me on interacting with fans.

My pen ran out of ink. I'd signed at least one hundred fifty autographs. Guess who spent all of last night signing, and resigning their name so they could do it in a mere second?

"Here." Shruthi handed me another one. It was my third pen this evening. The outstretched pen wobbled in her hand. She was jittery. Well, she was going to meet her future husband after all.

"Only two more hours 'till you see your Peter." I told her with a smile. It made my heart beat too. I was going to see Peter Raul!

"Oh, but you already saw him," she said. True, I had seen him in rehearsal yesterday right before my birthday party. But only from afar though.

I got a headache thinking of yesterday. I hadn't checked my phone all day. I didn't know how I'd react if I got a

message from him, or if I didn't for that matter. I rolled
the ring on my thumb.

"True Love Waits" True love waited indeed. I sighed.
I would have to apologize to him tomorrow. Maybe take
him out somewhere for a change. My thoughts were distracted by Shruthi's strangled shriek.

"Look, look, look!" She pointed to my phone as it buzzed
with a text.

"That's my cue, let's go." I grabbed Shruthi's arm and
headed backstage. She seemed too shocked to function.

"I'm gonna see him sing, from backstage! I'm going to
be closer to him than ever. Oh, and see you too of course."
I smiled at her as I pulled on Johnny's letterman jacket. It
was cold backstage. I rubbed the spot on the jacket just
above my heart, his last name. I couldn't just leave it in my
closet where it had rested all day, neglected and sad-looking.
I winced as its warmth settled into my skin.

It was like a cage I had built to trap myself.

"Mohana!" I looked back to see Ajay rushing toward me
with his phone, "We need—"

"—a picture," Right. I handed Shruthi my phone. "You
wanna move over a little bit?" I muttered to Ajay who had
taken his natural position with his arm around my shoulders. He raised his eyebrows. I gave him a pleading look in
response. He moved so we weren't touching. I didn't even
need to see the picture to know we looked awkward. "Oh,
come on, Shruthi I thought we were over this!" I clapped
loud twice to wake her from her stupor. She'd been staring
at Ajay.

"You wanna take off Johnny's—?"

"Nope."

"You okay, Mohana?" Ajay looked at me concerned.
I thought for a bit.

"Nope, let's hurry up I gotta go in a bit." Shruthi took

two quick pictures just as Michelle, the organizer, rushed around the corner.

"Good, in your place all makeuped and ready to go?" she asked while checking her sheets of paper. I nodded and grabbed the huge guitar.

"Bro, are you gonna wear the jacket?" Shruthi asked me.

"Yes." I wasn't taking it off.

"The paps are gonna freak, Mohana," Ajay told me.

"Then let them." If they did, maybe Johnny would realize how much he meant to me. Johnny. *My* Johnny. Something in me snapped, "Shruthi, my phone please." My heart thumped loudly as I heard the phone ring. What was I even going to say? He didn't pick up so I called again. I struck luck the third time. "Johnny, look, about yesterday—"

"Mohana?" A confused voice interrupted me.

"Melody?" My throat froze up. " Uhm, where's Johnny?" I flinched and looked up at the clock. This was gonna get real awkward and real weird real quick.

"Johnny? He-uhm," I heard a sniff, "W-why are you asking?"

"I just wanted to—" I paused, "Wait, Melody is he alright?" I heard another sniff. "Melody?" I felt my voice go dangerously quiet. My mind quickly remembered his red eyes, his habit of tripping too much, his lack of sleep.

My mind remembered the eerie poem I'd read him.

I forced my brain to not think of any of that. He probably just sprained his ankle from basketball or something.

"Mohana," her voice sounded so, so tired. That's why her voice cracked, right? "Johnny, h-he's—" That's when I heard her cry. "My boy is in a coma, Mohana, from Meningitis."

It's nothing like the movies. There's no fading of sound and light. There's no dramatic and loud slow-motion drop of the phone. There's just that uncomfortable jolt of painful nervousness and fear that jogs up your stomach. Like when you figured out you got an F on an important test, just twenty times more powerful and worse.

"Wait, what?" I wanted to cry. I wanted to scream. I wanted to somehow get the emotion out, but I couldn't. I couldn't put it together.

"Johnny? My Johnny? In a coma?"

"Doctors don't know anything. He came home yesterday and went right to his room but—" She took a harsh breath. "I heard him fall and ran upstairs to check on him and saw him having a seizure—" I cut the call. I really didn't want to hear more.

Wait, what was I doing here? I needed to go see him. I moved, but I was blocked instantly. "Whoa, whoa, whoa." Michelle furrowed her eyebrows, "What are you doing?"

What was I doing? Distortion hit me like a brick. I stumbled. Ajay caught me. "Mohana!"

"Johnny—" I trailed off.

"What happened to Johnny?" Shruthi gave me some water but with the lump in my throat I couldn't swallow anything.

"It doesn't matter, Ms. Prasad. Since I am partnered with the record company you are signed to, I have the right to make you stay."

"Then I quit," I shot back without a second's worth of hesitation. Like Johnny said yesterday: *"If someone told me to stop seeing the girl I liked for something important to me, like basketball, I would never agree. I would drop it immediately, I would never play basketball again."*

"As Nelson probably told you, we have total control over you until July, which is tomorrow. I won't hesitate to sue you. Now you're on in five, catch your breath." She talked into her walkie-talkie.

"Mo, sit." Shruthi somehow had gotten a cup of hot tea out of nowhere that she gave me after Ajay had pushed me down onto the top of a box. "Now what happened to

Johnny?" The tea felt good. It chased away the confusion and I was left feeling *hollow.*

"H-he went into a coma, doctors say 'cause of Meningitis." I drew the jacket tighter around me. It still even smelled like him.

"Can't you see? She won't be able to sing even if she wanted to." Ajay had risen to face Michelle. "The only thing that's gonna happen is the audience getting angry."

"She wouldn't do that. It would really only affect her. Nothing would hit us, but you will have many people unfollow you. We just need you on stage for even just a second so people know we did our part. Now get up." She practically dragged me to the side of the stage and shoved the guitar into my hands. "Now just like we practiced, yes?" She glared at me, daring me to say anything but yes.

"Michelle, would you do one favor for me?" She had to, I mean, if the industry hadn't already robbed her of humanity. I gave my phone to Shruthi and told her to call Melody. Michelle, after a lot of debate, finally agreed to my idea so I finally walked out into the light.

If everything had been normal, then I would have noticed that the stadium was absolutely humongous. If everything had been normal, it would've taken my breath away. If everything had been normal, I would've noticed the air was already kinda misty. If everything had been normal, I would have noticed all the small details. Like the way everyone seemed to be teenage girls, how I was greeted by thousands of fans wearing Peter Raul merch, how my dream was finally being achieved. But, nothing mattered like before. Far, far, far off I saw Michelle in the sound booth. Guess she had super-speed. She gave me a thumbs up to show everything was ready.

"Hey guys!" The fans gave a cheer at my words. "So new plan, I'm actually gonna start this evening with a slower number by Peter himself." Do people do that? Sing the main celebrity's song to open for that same celebrity? I didn't care.

"A really close friend of mine just got hurt recently, and he's hospitalized." I looked out and I imagined I was talking directly to Johnny. I had told Shruthi to tell Melody that she should make sure Johnny could hear this. I'm pretty sure people can still hear in comas. That's how it was in the movies. "This song has always been one of his favorites, and I just need to let him know one thing, I'll never forget him. He'll always have his *Pictures*." The music started and I fake strummed along on my dysfunctional guitar.

"When I look over my shoulder, I feel as if a kiss is overdue." The familiar lyrics never sounded as relatable as now. I closed my eyes and imagined his warm hug.

"Oh, I see it all, I see it all my dear. The idea I have for me and you."

I imagined his grin, his warm hugs, his deep rumble of a voice saying the lines over and over again like he used to. I stopped singing to hear the crowd sing the words.

"So spin the globe. Let's go wherever you want to go."

His favorite line. I remembered our first kiss.

He let go of my lips for a well needed breath. Not for him, for me. He was perfectly cool and stared at me with those deep curious eyes while I gasped for breath.

My first kiss. It took awhile for it to sink in. He let go of me, looking kinda worried about what would happen next.

"I-I'm sorry, I-." No, I wouldn't let him. I surged forward and kissed him again, my hands on his collar, holding him close. I was pretty sure I did it wrong. He didn't mind, he still kissed me back.

"Don't be sorry," I muttered, a sudden bout of shyness came over me and I couldn't meet his eyes. I looked around the empty bookshop. He led me over to an old beat-up sofa. After we had made that kind of contact we suddenly couldn't let go of each other. Johnny gripped my hand tight, giving me a warmth that surged through my entire body starting from my hand.

"I still haven't told you something. My first crush—" I raised my eyebrows. I knew I was inexperienced in matters such as these, but I was still pretty sure you didn't talk about your past crushes to the girl you just kissed. "Let me finish! I was in the library at our middle school finishing my history paper in sixth grade, before I met you. Mrs. M's class were in there too, reciting poetry. That's when I heard a girl read the prettiest song in the prettiest way." Johnny looked at the ground for a second. I remembered that day. Song lyrics counted as poetry so I read Peter Raul's *Pictures* for a grade.

"You inspired me to start reading poetry, Mohana, the thing that makes me happy the most. I remembered you after that. I couldn't stop thinking about you."

He looked at me with a smile. I had imagined this a million times. But I had never thought about how I would feel. I don't even remember how I felt at that moment. All I remember was his face, his smile.

"You're different, Mohana. You've always been different to me. Not just cause you're pretty, cause you are, you have a way of making all my troubles vanish when I'm with you. You will always be different to me, Prasad, you have and always will be the one."

"Let me hold your hand so we'll never have to part."

That was the line that broke me. I felt a tear slid down my cheek. I heard my voice waver. But I kept singing. I didn't ever want to stop.

"I'll save all those pictures of you looking so fair. They're only pictures my dear, only pictures."

Pictures by Peter Raul
Sung by Mohana Prasad

When I look over my shoulder
I feel as if a kiss is overdue
Oh, I see it all, I see it all my dear
The idea I have for me and you

Oh yes, a perfect roadmap
Filled with our wishes and dreams
An outline, a plan
And we'll make the perfect team

So let's conquer the world
Place by place
Let me hold your hand
So we'll never have to part

So let me get my camera
And we'll run through the streets of Alberta
Or safari in Uganda

So spin the globe
Let's go wherever you want to go
I'll save all those pictures
All those occasions
With you looking to fair
They're only pictures, after all, my dear

Pictures my dear

Only pictures

Pictures I know look at
To remind me of the past
Oh, it never did last

Oh
I love you,
Did you know that?
But that's only our past

Because we spun our globe
And we went wherever we wanted to go
I saved all those occasions
When you looked so fair
Are our only pictures, my dear

Chapter 31

"*Comatose— Meningitis—* "

"*Beep, Beep, Beep.*"

"*Drugs? My boy never—*" I heard Melody next to me whimper again. I fiddled with the ring he gave me and looked up at Johnny. He looked peaceful with his eyes closed and his rhythmic breathing as he lay in his hospital bed. His chest went up and down with the beeping of the machines. All the beeping machinery around him kinda ruined the whole 'calm' effect though.

"Mohana?" Melody shook me awake. I looked over to her and the doctor.

"You go to school with him, yes?" This was the first time the old doctor acknowledged my presence. I nodded. "Has there been anything off about him?" I nodded again. "Like?" I took a deep breath.

"He'd been tripping a lot in school, recently, and he mentioned that he hadn't slept in a while 'cause of his headaches."

"Was he stressed, recently? School, finals or something?"

"Not that I know of." That was a fib. He had been stressed the night of the seizure, because of me.

"You really should have brought him in when he said he was having headaches. We would have seen the Meningitis with the blood draw or the spinal tap." He addressed Melody. She scrunched her eyes and softly laughed. It made my heart break, her laugh.

"He was supposed to attend an appointment today."

The doctor sighed,

"We'll do our best, Ms. Taylor, but the real answer is we don't know. Comas aren't very well researched so we don't know everything. He could awake this instant, two years from now, or never. We just don't know. For now just keep talking to him."

"So he can hear us?" I stood up and walked to his bedside.

"Again, we don't know. But we're going to assume he can." He left with a reassuring nod.

"Mohana? I'm gonna go handle some insurance things. Can you stay with Johnny for a while?" Melody got up, her voice a mere whisper. I nodded. She left and the door shut with a slam.

"*Beep, Beep, Beep.*" The sun was starting to set outside. The golden rays from the window illuminated his neck and his jaw.

Man, he could even pull off a hospital gown.

I took his warm, left hand and held it between both of mine and just looked at him, building up the courage to say something.

"It's Mo," I said in the most awkward, high pitched voice. "Y-you're probably mad at me. I shouldn't even be touching you, but, I can't help it Johnny. It's all because of me, isn't it? I made you like this." The last few tears that remained leaked out of my eyes. "I didn't mean any of it, anything I said on Saturday. I'm so sorry, sorry for the past few weeks. You gave your heart to me, but I was too busy to take it. I was so wrapped up with my music and the paps and Ajay, oh Johnny I'm so sorry you thought you had to compete with him. I'm so sorry I made you think like that 'cause you never did. Ajay can never come close to you. He can never near you! Johnny Taylor, no one can ever near you."

I remembered the words he said to me that fateful evening

in the book shop. "You have and always will be the one," I whispered. I looked for anything that would maybe change. Did I imagine his eyes flutter, maybe his breathing was faster? I checked the screen that showed his vitals. Nothing had changed. So I just stayed there, kneeling on the floor next to his bed, watching the sun slowly illuminate his whole face.

"Johnny, please wake up, please." I gripped his hand tighter. "Please!" My phone rang, disturbing my plea. I gave it a dirty look. It was Nelson. My dirty look intensified. "Johnny, listen to this." I picked up the phone. "Yes?"

"My dear, good news. It's that time in July where we get to decide whether to keep you or not! We decided to save you. Sure, you're gonna need some training and we're gonna have to change some things about your behavior. We can't have something like yesterday happen again, but I think you have some potential, my dear." His raspy voice made me scowl. I looked at Johnny as I said my next words.

"I quit."

"Excuse me?"

"I'm pretty sure the contract lets me do that after a month. And I don't think this is gonna workout, Mr. Nelson, so I quit."

"So you're just gonna leave your fame, fortune, everything? Honey, we were just getting started. After your performance yesterday we were gonna take over. You were gonna become rich. Are you really gonna throw it away for your freedom or whatever?"

"I don't care! If I ever do want to continue music then I certainly won't do it signed with you guys." I cut the phone and checked Johnny's vitals again. Nothing. I sighed just as Melody opened the door.

"Nothing?" she asked. I shook my head. She walked over and knelt down next to me. She kissed his head. "There was this one time when he was four, he fell off a slide and got a concussion. The hospital freaked him out. He's like his father. He doesn't like to be contained too long. The machinery scared him. After that he'd always be careful to never hurt himself again." She sighed contently. "That's when he started reading. Thought it was the only way he couldn't hurt himself."

"At the age of four?"

"Oh yeah, and the books he couldn't read, I'd read them to him. He finished Percy Jackson when he was six. He was a strange child." She ran her fingers through his hair.

"How's the whole insurance thing? Is everything okay?"

"Let's not talk about it," she laughed. "They're stealing my money right in front of my eyes, but it's fine. I just need you to wake up." She talked to Johnny.

I stayed for a while helping Melody with her paperwork. Laboring through the math that Johnny could do in five minutes. If only he was awake.

"Do you have a ride home?" Melody asked me after we finally finished a decent amount of work.

"Yeah, my parents will pick me up in an hour if it's no trouble for you."

"Trust me Mohana, I'd have gone nuts without you. Can I see what you got?" I had taken out my emergency writing notepad that I'd been hunched over. There was nothing to see though.

Never in my life had I ever been wordless. No matter how sad, worried, or awful I felt I could always write. It was something I was good at. When you had deadlines, you just kinda threw away your emotions and got to work. But now I couldn't write a word. It didn't matter, Johnny was lying unconscious before my eyes, nothing mattered anymore. It didn't matter if I slept, or ate. Speaking of, I hadn't eaten dinner yet. My stomach rumbled. I told it to shut up. I remembered rehearsals for Peter's concert, and how all the girls mockingly looked at my waist and walked a bit more proudly, jutting out their own slim stomach. In fact, I haven't seen one famous person as heavy as me, so it didn't matter if I ate. Why should I be getting good food when Johnny was getting nutrients through a tube?

"Oh, Melody I have to go." My phone dinged.

"Okay, I'll see you later then."

"Of course." I tried to stand but something jerked me down. That's when I realized I was still holding Johnny's hand. Melody smiled. "He won't go anywhere, I promise." She softly pried my hand away from his. "I could always tell he had something for you. He didn't shut up about you at home. I'm also pretty sure he had your page marked in the yearbook." A glimmer caught her eye, my, well *her*, ring that Johnny gave me. I heard my heart thump. She smiled and pushed it down further on my thumb. "It suits you."

Chapter 32

"*Are our only pictures, my dear.*" A loud cheer from the kids made smile as I strummed the last notes out of my guitar. A little girl hugged my legs. She had a breathing tube.

"Another one, please?"

"Sorry, sweetie. I have to go now. I'll see you next week." Lavender had appeared in the doorway to the child's nursery in the hospital.

"If I make it." She rubbed her bald head. It broke my heart that her little head was thinking such things. "Archie said I looked like a boy. Is it true?"

"Of course not sweetie. You look like a brave, bold girl. Now, I'll see you later." I softly broke away from her with a wave and walked to Lavender

"Hey, I bought you something." She bought out two bars of chocolate.

"Oh, thank you, you shouldn't have!" I took them with a hug. I'd give them to my sister, food somehow made me queasy now. I hadn't eaten in a while. I knew it wasn't serious or anything. I could still drink liquids.

"Yeah, I should! You poor thing." She gave me a sideways hug. "Now, where is he?" I opened the door to Johnny's hospital room, Melody wasn't there.

"It's been two day since he—" It seemed like forever though. Lavender nodded thoughtfully.

"He can hear us right?" She looked down at calm, peaceful Johnny. I nodded. She bent close to him.

"Wake up!" she said loudly. I smiled.

"Aww, it didn't work." She sat down in the chair next to his bed. "Is it true you're quitting?" She didn't have to specify the question. I knew what she was talking about.

"Yeah." I nodded and sat down on the ground next to Johnny's bed. "I guess I don't have what it takes, I mean, look at how it ended up. My crush is in a coma."

"You just got signed to a really bad company. It wasn't right for you. You're still going to Citizen's Choice, right?"

"Is it in two weeks? How can I?" I didn't even release my whole album. But it still sent an excitement wave through my stomach. Getting an award, dressing up. I hated myself for it. Why should I feel any emotion when Johnny couldn't feel a thing?

"What do you mean? They don't take back invitations for the awards, and I'll be there. You gotta come."

"I only have five songs out."

"I have none! Look, Ryan and I got famous over song covers. We put out videos on YouTube. No record companies. I think this is the thing that would suit you."

"Song covers?"

"No, being a YouTube star. Many people get introduced like that. It would be no problem getting views since you're already that famous and everything."

"I don't know Lavender, it's just, fame has destroyed a lot of things. It destroyed friendships, it destroyed him—" I gulped.

The doctors had said he probably would never be the same again. He probably won't be able to speak as usual, read as usual, he for sure couldn't play basketball anymore. That unpleasant feeling came over me again. The water I had drunk didn't feel so good in my stomach.

"You gained so much, too. The day I saw you at trials, I knew you weren't just meant to be a normal person." She paused, trying to figure out what to say. " Some people," she started, "are like that. They need attention. Not in a bad way! They're just born like that. They aren't supposed to be forgotten. Just try again, for me. There's a little talent show downtown tomorrow. It's only for cover artists. There'll be some important judges there. I'll be there too. You should join me."

"But I haven't done a cover before. The tune of the song is more of Finn's thing than mine."

"Nonethematter, let's do a cover." She took out her bag and her computer. I frowned. "You carry a notepad, I carry a laptop. I'm in college. I need any time I can get." She opened it up and got my guitar that I had propped against the door for me.

"We're just gonna do it here, now?"

"Oh, yeah! Different backgrounds are cool. And the whole dim lights thing looks good." She sat on the floor next to me. "Don't think too much, just let the music guide you. You like Raul, right? Pick one of your favs and just adjust a few things. I'll join you when it feels right." I didn't need to think about what I'd sing, and she didn't need to ask what I was going to sing. She pressed the red record button.

"Hi, this is Mohana."

"I'm Lavender again."

"And, we'll sing *Pictures*." With a small breath, I started.

The first time I was asked to write poetry was in second grade, and it was something I couldn't forget. The small amount of letters that could create thousands of words which could in different patterns create numerous sentences containing infinite ideas. I could do anything with my letters. It excited me. I couldn't sleep all night. That was how I felt. it was different. I had listened to that song over a hundred times at the minimum, but this was different. I had so much power. I could twist and change the song to my will. I made some notes longer, I made some staccato. I closed my eyes and I let my voice guide me, I let my ideas flow in a different medium that wasn't paper and pen. I ended the song with a soft note.

"*Ding-Ding.*" The heart rate monitor on Johnny's left beeped.

His heart rate was higher then usual.

I sprinted over and grabbed his hand.

"Johnny?" It was the first time I saw him move in a while. He took a big breath. His chest heaved and went back to its normal position.

The machines went ballistic.

"Get Melody!" I shouted at Lavender over the wild beeping.

"Uhm, Mrs. Taylor!" Lavender went to go get Melody. I laid on his chest and listened to his heartbeat. It seemed normal to me.

"I miss you, Johnny, come back." Melody came in with a few nurse. They checked the machines and thankfully made them quiet down.

"It's normal again." One of them muttered to what I guessed was the Head Nurse. She was wearing a different color uniform than the others.

"There was definitely a spike in his heart rate, but it's normal again. We don't know what caused it, but we'll let the doctor know. Try doing the same thing you were doing when it happened. I guess it had reached his ears. He was close to waking up. We might have to keep him here for one or two more days." The nurse didn't even look at me or Lavender. It angered me. I was important to him too. Melody turned to me after the nurses had left with a questioning glance.

"We were singing. She said he almost woke up, he-I—"

I needed to try harder. I picked up my guitar from the ground and started strumming. I don't know how long, but I kept going. Lavender had left with a shoulder pat and Melody had went to call Johnny's dad, again.

My fingers ached, but I didn't stop. Why should I be able to feel comfortable when Johnny couldn't feel anything? The sun was setting, it was getting darker. I finally stopped when my phone started buzzing. My parents were here. I tried to pick up my phone but it slipped and fell out of my wet hands. Wet? I looked down at my hands to see the tips of my fingers had been cut by the guitar strings and were bleeding. My guitar was dripping with blood too.

Chapter 33

"This is good. We need to get you out and about. We need to get your mind off things."

My mom rambled on as usual. I opened the window. It did feel good. I hadn't been anywhere else except the hospital and our house for the past few days. I closed my eyes to the wind blowing on my face. "I really do like this, the whole YouTube thing. You can be yourself and still be famous, no contracts. That Nelson man scared me. Weird little specimen."

"Agreed." I smiled as the big buildings of the Minneapolis Downtown started to appear. We broke off the highway and drove deeper downtown. I checked the address Lavender had sent me. "This is the place," I told my mom as we neared a brown building. It looked ancient with its deep cracks and coarse, brick wall. We entered through a little door on the side of the building. Lavender was sitting in what looked like a lobby.

"Glad you guys came. We'll be singing in a conference room over there. We have to get you signed in first though." Lavender nodded to my mom and led us deeper into the old building. We stopped in a room where people were lining up.

"I need to use the restroom. I'll be back. Don't move." My mom left me after we were in line.

"What are we waiting in line for?" I asked Lavender. I leaned to see the front. We were waiting in front of a weight machine and a few people holding clipboards. Nervousness prickled my stomach.

"Oh, it's just that some record companies like to know your weight sometimes. But it doesn't matter for you since you're not looking to get signed to one anyway."

"Mr. Nelson never did that to me."

"Believe it or not there are people worse than him out there. Some back-of-the-alley record companies who prefer their singers beautiful and skinny. You're lucky you weren't signed to one of those," she muttered, checking her phone. I looked around at everyone's slim bodies and long straightened hair. I sucked my stomach in and crossed my arms in front of it. I'd washed my hair today, but it wasn't as long or shiny as the others. People noticed. They smiled mockingly at my clothing, my shorter height, my jutting hips.

"First rodeo, love?" a girl in front of me mockingly asked after one look at my leggings. She was wearing a very airy-looking dress that hurt my eyes.

"If you knew who she was, you would definitely know it's not her first competition." Lavender had put her phone away instantly. Her stance had changed.

"Of course I know who she is. Everyone knows little Ms. Mohana Prasad, who only won fame because she was at the right place at the right time."

"Beg your pardon? She won the Wainscott."

"Only because she was lucky enough to be with one of the best voice coaches of all time, and she wasn't even spotted. She paid her way in!"

"Sorry, I think you misunderstood. We didn't pay for Melody. She selected me," I butted in.

"Keep telling yourself that sweetheart." Another girl further up the line responded to me. "I was there for a beauty pageant. I saw it all happen. I saw your mom chase the coach down. *'Oh, please. My daughter can sing I promise.*

She's hurt right now cause of that stupid judge. Listen, I'll pay you this much for just one day, just one lesson,'" she mocked openly. "Your little coach lady only agreed after she saw the big bucks your mom took out." She burst out laughing,

"Bitch, you little liar!" Lavender gripped my wrists to keep herself from lunging at the girl. It was painful, but I was too shocked to care.

It couldn't be true, could it?

"You didn't think *Melody Taylor* kept you for free, did you?" The girl in front of me kept talking. "She doesn't have time to just 'select' people, hon. She has like forty girls she's training. I'd sell my grandma for just five minutes with her." Please tell me it wasn't true. It couldn't be. Melody was such a nice person. She didn't just choose me because my mom paid her.

She had supported me.

"Oh, you guys. You've got it all wrong. She got in with her talent." I looked gratefully at a girl behind me.

"With her talent to move that ass of hers. She dated Melody's son, Jonathon or something like that, while she was with pretty-boy Ajay and everything. She was wearing the son's jacket when she performed at that one concert. He was probably the one who got her a spot."

"What did you do to get him to date you? I've heard he's a true snack." The girl in front of me looked down leeringly. I was on the verge of tears. Lavender suddenly pushed me out of the way and was holding the neck of the girl's dress.

"You jealous little thing, one more word!"

"And what short Ms. Sin—"

"Next." One of the ladies holding clipboards interrupted their fight. The girl in front of me stepped onto the scale.

It read sixty-eight.

Oh fudge. She smiled and got off the scale.

"You got in easy, Prasad. I haven't ate sugar in two years.

Not all of us have rich mommies who can pay for our fame. Some of us gotta work for it." Someone behind me pushed me to the scale. Everyone was paying attention now. Even the people in charge had mean little smiles. I gulped and shut my eyes. I climbed onto the scale.

"One-hundred thirteen," the lady holding a clipboard muttered. I heard the giggles, the laughs. I didn't open my eyes. I tried to cover my hips with my hands.

"Have fun getting another company with that body." I heard a voice next to my left ear. I gripped my eyes.

"Mohana?" a voice called out. I opened my eyes.

"Oh, look, it's the rich mamma."

"Shut up, Rachel!" Lavender radiated anger, even I got scared. I motioned with my hands to tell her to calm down. I needed to know. "You remember the Carnatic contest with the mean guru, where we met Melody?" I faced my mom.

"What about it?"

"Mom, did you pay for Melody's lessons?" I interrupted her.

"Why on earth would y—"

"Answer the question, Mom."

"Of course not. She liked your voice."

"Promise?" I looked at her hands. My mom's a good actor, but her hands will always give it away. She was a surgeon, and if her hands were still she was confident, but they were shaking,

"Yes." She looked dead into my eyes.

"Then why did she ask for your signatures?"

"What? Voice coaches like Melody always ask for consent forms if they want to take on a student for free and they're younger than eighteen."

"Well, I—" I was about to ask another question, but it was too late. There were titters and laughs around us. My mom's hands shook harder. "You paid for Melody. She never wanted to take me." I felt the room spin. "You paid her then asked her to never tell me. You made me think I could actually do something."

"Sweetie, I——" And that's when everything went blank.

I woke, standing in a field of wheat that looked like it was out of the picture that hung in Johnny's hospital room. The same barn in the background, the same bright sun. It confused me because today was cloudy, but I wasn't complaining. The sun was at the perfect intensity where it was really bright, but just slightly warmed you as it penetrated through your clothes and didn't burn the back of your neck. Kinda like stage lights. A fierce, warm wind swept my hair to my side. I turned to face against it when I saw it; a figure in the distance.

A boy.

I couldn't see his face even though he was turned toward me. It was him though, that much was obvious. The same height, the same stance, and his last name on the right arm of his sweatshirt. I felt my feet fly toward him, the wheat brushing against my thighs. I laughed out loud and spread my arms as I ran downhill. I ran into his chest, which was as soft as a bed, and enfolded him in a tight embrace.

And he hugged me back.

"Ding-Ding." The heart-rate monitor interrupted our hug. That stupid thing in Johnny's room that kept beeping every five seconds. The scene started fading, including Johnny.

"No, stay." My voice was rough and dry as the disappearing wheat.

"I never left." I must have still been delirious, I still heard his voice. His chest turned out to be the bed. I was on my stomach. Someone was rubbing my right hand. It made my left hand feel cold and I felt unbalanced. I blinked hard trying to focus my eyes on the person.

"I'm gone for three days and you're in the hospital room across me. How am I supposed to trust you alone with our kids?" A deep rumble of a voice. It didn't leave. The whole farm scene had left, why didn't he? Was he—

Don't expect it, cause when you don't get it, it won't hurt as much.

But I had to check, I blinked harder and turned onto my back.

I was still dreaming.

He slowly came into focus.

"You?" I hoarsely whispered. He winked at me. "Didn't expect me to leave you that easy, now did you?" He moved a few strands of hair off my forehead, and that's all I saw before everything went blank again.

Chapter 34

Johnny was still in his hospital gown, but other than that he looked perfectly normal. The same grin, the same smile, the weird jokes. He'd suppressed them now because the doctor was in the room.

"She's very malnourished. I'm very surprised you didn't see it being you are a pediatrician after all." She turned to my dad, who had turned very red through his brown skin.

"She seemed perfectly normal until she fainted. We couldn't tell a thing. The dosage seems pretty high, you sure it's right?" My mom was checking my intravenous fluid.

"We got your daughter in the most practiced hands, Madam. She'll be fine, but we need to discuss what happened, Mohana." She sat next to my bed and gave Johnny a look.

"I'll see you then." He walked out with his normal gait. I couldn't understand. The doctors said he'd never be normal again. That it would be a miracle if he could even stand up again.

"Now, Mohana, we think you experienced a bit of depression over the past week. You haven't been eating, correct? And your mother said you were stressed when you fainted, so the lack of nutrients probably kicked in with you being emotionally imbalanced." As the doctor kept talking my mom had taken a position gripping my arm. They both looked awful. My dad was just plain confused, but I could never explain what my mom looked like. She just looked lost.

"Has she lost any weight?" my mom asked.

"She has lost ten pounds. She hasn't eaten a single meal in three days and she hasn't been taking proper fluids."

"And I never noticed," my mom whispered.

"She can be unplugged from the I.V. later on today, but I do recommend that she stay here until at least the end of the day tomorrow. I'll send one of our counselors in after a little bit." She left after checking my vitals again. My mom was over me in a quarter of a second. She was checking my fingers that were still wounded from my guitar.

"Depression," she whispered as if she just wanted to feel the word in her mouth. "Never would I have thought—" That was the first time I saw my rock-hearted mom cry. My dad hugged her and me.

"We'll get through this. It'll be fine. We're lucky, really. We figured out the problem at the start. Now let's get your mind off things. Your awards festival is—"

"No," My mom didn't shout, she whispered. But that whisper was as powerful as the loudest shout in the world, "Never again. I've been patient, Mohana, but it's obvious. This fame thing isn't gonna work out. It has only brought trouble so far."

"Hey—"

"No, she's not getting hurt on my watch ever again. I'm not devil enough to take away your music. Do what you love by all means. I just don't think our family can handle any more fame. We won't do anything for a while and we'll just let her name die." My mom gave the stare she's known for and my dad backed down.

"Okay, alright. But we'll give her space for now. Mo, do you need anything?" My dad automatically switched into the clear voice he used on patients. And I didn't have the strength to get mad over it. So I sent them out to buy apple juice since I was put on a liquid diet so my stomach could get used to food again.

"Knock, knock," Johnny peeped in. "Everyone gone?"

"Johnny could you get your mom?" I asked him in a whisper. I was still thinking about downtown and what had happened.

"She ran home. I don't think she combed her hair the whole three days. Why do you want to see her? Pay attention to me. I just crawled out of a coma for you." He sat next to my bed, his eyes looking clearly hurt. He was still in his hospital gown.

"Johnny—"

I wanted to ask, Did your mom actually want me around or did she only accept me because of the money involved? I didn't ask him that, as he had said, "It doesn't have to always be about you."

"Could you hear me when you were in the coma?" I asked him instead.

"Oh I heard a lot of voices, and a lot of sad guitar music." He paused with a faint smile. A smile I had thought I would never see again. "Then I heard a voice singled out. I think it was my mom's. I think she was talking about how you'd collapsed. Next thing, I could actually open my eyes again." I pulled his arm so he was laying next to me.

"Johnny, I'm sorry. It's 'cause of me y-you're here. It's over now though, all of it. No more Mr. Nelson, no more Ajay."

"What happened to Ajay?" Johnny butted in.

"He's gone, no one cares about him anymore, old news. No more of him."

"Shame, he was starting to grow on me."

"It's only cause he asked about your basketball player cousin, isn't it?"

"Maybe, but I can't let you take all the blame. It was my fault too, I should have told you how I felt. We could have worked out a solution, but I didn't. So—"

He turned to face me, our noses touching. He stretched

out his pinkie. "Promise me no more secrets." I did with a smile. We both stared up at the white ceiling together, my head tucked under his, pinkies still crossed. "It was a struggle," Johnny interrupted our brief silence, "I wanted to open my eyes so badly. I just wanted to see something one more time."

"Well, I was a mess without you." I laced my fingers with his.

"I can tell." He examined my cut and bruised fingers. And then he brought his eyes up to examine me. "You don't seem too happy about it, quitting music." It was a statement more than a question. I didn't ask him how he knew. I bit my lip.

"I'm not quitting music. I'll still sing, just not on stage anymore." I sat up and looked back at him. He was laying on his side with his head in his hand, the classic ready-for-the-tea pose. It made me snort. I felt like I was in some demented sleepover with our hospital gowns and the wires attached to me. "It doesn't matter. My mom doesn't want me to continue either. And I get it, I mean, it only caused trouble."

"You don't seem so sure."

"But Johnny," I wanted to deny it, but I couldn't. "It gave me something though. Something I never felt before, a sense of happiness and belonging. A joy I can never bring myself to explain. I close my eyes and see the lights catching the dust scattered around a musty, thick-smelling stage. It makes me a bad person, doesn't it? I like something that causes so much pain to others." I sighed.

"No," Johnny paused and laid down again and stared up at the ceiling, "You have to give up something for anything you do really. For basketball I give up my free time. You just kinda have to decide which is more important, the thing you're giving up or the thing you want to do." He looked over at me, dead serious.

I pondered, the good-girl answer would be to give up

music and focus on my friends and family. The safe route, where no one gets hurt and everyone's always safe. If I did that, though, I'd never feel like I belong. I'd always be an outcast and a person who never feels like they fit in with the normal crowd. I'd never be fully happy. But did I really want people to get hurt because of me? Should people pay for me to be happy?

"Huh." I scrunched my eyebrows.

"There'll always be two sides, your heart and your brain. On matters outside of school, it's normally best to listen to your heart." I crisscrossed my legs on the bed.

"How do you know?"

"What?"

"How do you know to trust your heart?"

"You."

"Pardon?" I rested my head on my hand, ready for a story.

"Well, a while after I actually met you my heart told me you were the one to chase. My brain, though, told me to like Melissa."

"Melissa? Oh I remember her." I wrinkled my nose. I remembered that dark spot in time in eighth grade. The day after I realized he liked me and came out of the denial stage, then he started going out with her. I remember it wrenching my heart. That's when I truly realized how much I liked him.

"We had a thing for like two months. I never told anyone about it, I don't think she did either. It wasn't all that good. After a while it kinda became like my job or duty to go ask how she's doing. I realized how she and I would never work out at a basketball game. I was playing and got a ball to the face, blood everywhere. Melissa was talking to her friends, but you, Mohana, had a look of pure terror. You flinched more than I did."

"Me? At a basketball game?" That wasn't possible.

"You were with the band."

"Oh, I remember that. You had like a fountain rushing down your nose."

"I broke it up the next day. She didn't even care. She was with Levi Jones in like two days after that. I realized then and there it has always has been you, Mo."

"Then what about Sage?"

"The only reason I agreed to go out with her was to make you jealous, Mo. Yes, maybe after a bit I did kinda start trusting her but she could never compare to you."

"Wha-ugh, Johnny! Don't toy with a girl's emotions like that. No girl deserves that sort of thing."

"She's not exactly the nicest person is she? And did it work?" He raised his eyebrows at my hesitation. Of course it bloody worked. The mood suddenly changed as he got closer. His eyes flicked to my lips which I bet were chapped and horrid-looking. I still closed my eyes though. The door opened with a bang and we jerked apart,

"Mo, Mo, Mo guess what! I-ooh, who's that?" I gave the death glare to my sister.

"Oh, I'm just a friend." Johnny smiled at her. She tilted her head.

"With a face like that? I'm pretty sure that's not true."

Chapter 35

"**O**ur little secret, remember?" I gave my dad another glare. He pulled up to the temporary outdoor stage.

"Yes, yes," he muttered. While he got my guitar from the trunk, I fished in my bag for a long lost friend. Yes! They were still there.

My sugar cubes. I snarfed three to make up for the ones I hadn't used the past few months.

"Ms. Prasad, right on time!" I looked over surprised. A man rushed forward in a suit that was normal enough. You were probably used to it now, an authoritative figure who presided over me. But, never once have they come out to meet me.

"Mohana!" I shook his outstretched hand.

"I'm thrilled you could make it. Everyone here's so excited." He parted some tarp hanging from a sloppily made tent to form backstage. "It's not as fancy as you're used to, I'm sure, but it's all we can do for now. We've been running low on funds for a while now, but you showing up will definitely help." Two people were carrying a poster of a teen cradling her head. The words on the poster said, *"Let us help. You are not alone."*

"Of course, it's my duty," I muttered. How could I refuse to play at a fundraiser for a charity that helps people out of depression? No one should go through what happened to me. As I thought back on it, it scared me more and more. My lack of appetite, my wish to just disappear, how I'd just stare at the ceiling wondering *'why?'* when I was supposed to be asleep. To think, what I'd experienced was just minor, for other people it was worse.

"—and after your songs if you could make your way down to that table over there, the fans would love getting some signatures. Also, if you could mention how it would help if at least every person donated five dollars, it would help a lot." I nodded and picked at my guitar. "And, sir. If you could wait down there." The guy in the suit pointed out into the audience. My dad hesitated. Both my parents were scared these days to leave me alone.

"He stays here," I said harshly. I didn't even look up, but I felt suit-guy frown.

"If you insist, Ms. Prasad." He left shortly. I heard him outside introducing me. From the crowd's cheer, I could tell it was pretty large. It surprised me. It had seemed like a smaller space since it was a parking lot.

The crowd gave another cheer and the familiar rush of adrenaline jogged up my spine.

I had tried to be smart. Ever since my mom forbade me from my fame I had been posting online. Like Lavender had said, YouTube had no managers. See, that way I could also ignore Johnny's advice.

"You just kinda have to decide which is more important, the thing you're giving up or the thing you want to do." I wasn't making public appearances to boost my popularity so I wasn't technically doing what I loved. But this fundraiser had ruined it. It made me automatically choose my fame over family and friends. It made me a monster, didn't it? I couldn't help it though. I wanted it so bad. The happiness, the joy of performing. I moved the tarp that served as a curtain and the people packed into the small parking lot

cheered. I wanted that automatic smile that comes to your lips, that eagerness, that feeling.

"Stop lying to yourself, you know you want to win Citizen's Choice," My mind was telling the truth. And I was so close.

"Let me tell you all a story, a story to melt your stone hearts," I sang. People's minds worked weird. I sang the same music, just from a different setting now. Suddenly my Instagram followers almost tripled and I got comments about how a hospital couldn't part me from my music and how suddenly my music was better and more heartfelt. Maybe it was, I didn't know. "Thank you all so much, really you all are too kind. Make sure to donate at the entrance, it really does help any at-risk person." With a final wave I walked around the edge of the lot to the table set up for me, complete with postcards and a pen.

"Sorry to steal you away but we have one of your doctor appointments in like an hour." My dad had somehow managed to sneak up behind me.

"In like thirty minutes, please?" The people there had somehow managed to get the fans all in a line. I signed a note card and gave it out with a smile.

"Fine," my dad muttered, but stayed behind me.

Smile, nod, wave. It was instinct now. So was my signature.

"My my, you've grown a lot since your last visit, hm?" A quiet voice stopped me in the middle of my signature. I looked up to see a brown-haired lady with tired looking eyes. I swear I'd seen her before. "Brianna." she answered my confused look. "I'm a friend of Melody's, the fashion designer. I gave you your outfit for Wainscott."

"Oh! Brianna, of course I remember. Your leather jacket looked astounding on stage."

"Not as outstanding as your performance." A few people shouted in the back for her to get out of the way. "I guess I better get to it, then. I've always been interested in a study abroad program thing. It's six months at a fashion school in Milan, with world class tutors and everything. They're considering me now after they saw the jacket you were wearing at Wainscott and—" I motioned for a few volunteers to go sort out the fuss in the back.

"Keep going."

"It's just I was wondering whether I could make your dress for the Citizen's Choice Awards. If they saw that, it would really lock in my spot on that plane to Milan."

"Oh! Uhm—" My neck burned as I felt my dad raise his head from his phone, waiting to see what my answer would be.

"It's okay if you got someone else to already make it. Maybe some big company. I just thought maybe if you haven't found anyone yet that I could really make you shine."

"Uhm, Miss? If you could please." A volunteer motioned for her to get out of the line, but I grabbed her arm and made her stay.

"No, Brianna, I haven't gotten anyone to do my dress yet. And if I wanted someone, it would definitely be you, but—" How was I supposed to explain that I had to miss a lifetime opportunity because my mom grounded me.

"But, what?"

"My parents want me to lay low for a while."

"They want you to miss the Citizen's Choice Awards?" she asked with a frown. I nodded painfully at Brianna, signed a card and gave it to the next person in line with a smile. "It's your first award show and everything." She asked even more confused. But how was I supposed to explain an Indian parent's mind. I couldn't, so I didn't even try.

"I know," I painfully responded.

"Well, let me know if they change their mind. I'll always be there, at the building." With an awkward bow of the head she left, taking my opportunities with her.

Chapter 36

"And always know that you are safe to share anything with me."

"Mh-hm!"

"And if you are feeling dizzy or unstable take those medications I prescribed."

"Medications! Of course!" I gave him a thumbs-up.

"Uhm, Ms. Prasad? Is everything alright?" My therapist looked concerned.

"Oh everything is divine. I feel perfectly chipper this evening actually." I gave a big smile, surely he'd let me go now.

"Alright—"

Yes! I nearly dragged my dad's arm out of its socket. "Dad we gotta go. Johnny's getting discharged today and I gotta speak to Melody."

"Johnny? Getting discharged?" He nodded with a faint smile and walked with me. Of course he did. Parents think they're so smart. "I'm gonna wait in the lobby, you hurry on down." We parted ways and I started walking faster.

I abruptly stopped halfway there, causing an angry-looking lady to run into my back. With a quick apology, I ran into the closest bathroom.

Man, I felt bad for the mirror. Half my hair was sticking up with all the static electricity, giving me a deranged-scientist look. I ran my fingers through it, trying to make it pass for at least decent. It didn't work. Sighing, I walked back to the heavy wooden door of the bathroom. Johnny and I must look like fools to everyone else. A six-foot, very good-looking giant next to a short five foot three inch girl with hair that defied gravity. A large thump on the door ignored the rant in my head. Someone was leaning against the door. With an exaggerated eye-roll I raised a hand to knock, but stopped when I heard the familiar voice.

"Doctor?"

"*Melody?*" I put my ear against the door.

"What's wrong?" She whimpered. It's one of the scariest things, hearing an adult whimper or seeing them cry. It defies what you have thought your entire life, that adults are fearless. That they know what they're doing. My heart lurched as I heard Melody whimper again. My fists clenched on the door.

"Miss, I hate to inform you of this, really, we tried our absolute best. But—"

"But what?" My stomach gave a really painful tug. I blamed it on indigestion.

"But what, Doctor? You said he was getting better, that he could go home now." I heard her take a sharp inhale. "What's wrong with my boy?" It was my heart now that hurt. Could my heart have indigestion?

Yes, yes it could.

"I always had doubt. I mean, no one recovers from Meningitis that quickly. It takes a few weeks."

"So? He's special," Melody cut off the doctor. But I could tell from her whisper she already knew what was going to happen next.

But so did I.

"Mrs. Taylor—" I shut my eyes. Hadn't I suffered enough? Please don't say it, please! "From his heart rate and the tests we took today we have concluded—" Everything was silent. I couldn't hear anything else except my heartbeat. I sweat cold sweat. My Mom has told me enough horror stories. I knew exactly what he was going to say. It didn't stop me from praying though. I shut my eyes harder until it hurt, and then some more, "Your son, Miss—" My prayers weren't answered. Those little words still came. Those small words that shook the foundation of my world, my everything.

"He isn't gonna last much longer."

I let out the pent-up air softly as it sank in.

He's going to die.

It was ages before Melody could respond. I could feel her pain radiate through the heavy wooden door.

"When?"

"Again, Mrs. Taylor, he doesn't have long. I've estimated this evening or, if he's lucky, sometime tomorrow." I heard her sliding down the door. I slid down with her.

"I-I've unplugged him from the I.V., so he's perfectly comfortable. He hasn't been informed. I decided to leave it to you. So uhm, until later?" I felt the doctor's hesitant footsteps leave as I sank onto the tiled floor. I felt Melody thud onto the floor outside the door with me.

Every semester after classes ended, I got scared. That might have been the last time I could see Johnny. The feeling I got when I saw him, it might fade. And I didn't want it to fade, no. Luckily, it never happened.

I thought it was fate.

I'd come back to school and he'd be there, fiddling with his shoes or something, and the tension would leave me as I sank down in a seat behind him and stared at the back of his pristine head. This was different. He was actually going to leave now. There wasn't that little chance that he might show his face in a new class next semester. I might never—never see him again.

What was I going to do? The warm feelings that had latched on to my heart after Johnny had brought them to me painfully withdrew. I still felt its claw marks engraved in my heart. I had a feeling they wouldn't heal anytime soon. Now I just felt, alone. I heard a scratch on the door as Melody raised. I heard her footsteps sprint in a direction opposite of Johnny's hospital room. I gathered up my strength, and rose as well. I didn't wait for the room to stop spinning before I opened the door and was out. I shaded the sun out of my face as I walked the normal hallway. It was too bright, way too bright. I wiped the tears off with the back of my hand and softly opened Johnny's door, and there he was. Looking perfectly healthy. He was sitting on his bed as he watched the sun sink beneath the rural scenery.

"Mo!" He grinned. "I was thinking—" I walked forward and sat next to him, admiring his face in a way I never had before. Trying to memorize every line on his soft face, the warm red that colored his cheeks, his full red lips. I clenched my fist and smiled back. "What a feat."

"Cats or dogs?"

"Pardon?"

"Do you like cats or dogs? I've always wanted a dog, but if you want a cat then I don't know if we can afford something like that."

Holy shit.

He was talking about our future. It took a while for me to understand. I choked back a sob as he turned away from me to stare at the dying sun.

"'You must live in the present, launch yourself on every wave, find your eternity in each moment.' That's Henry David Thoreau," I muttered.

"You could have just told me to live in the moment."

"Ah, but that, my dear ignorant lass, does not adhere to my poetic spirit. Thus, it makes me strive to speak in this manner."

"P-pardon?" He made me smile as usual.

"I'm a poetic person so I'm gonna speak like that, alright?"

"Alright." His smile was disrupted by a single cough. He grasped his throat and quickly motioned to the sink in the little bathroom. I put my arm around him and we painfully made our way there. He wouldn't stop coughing and when he did he spat something out into the sink. I felt myself go lightheaded. "You seem so small but you have the grip of a—" He gasped. I tightened my grip around him as he coughed out more blood. A groan escaped his mouth as he rested his head on the faucet. I took the time to let a few more tears leak out. Johnny was too good though. Even in his weakened state his hands found mine and gripped them reassuringly, "I-I—"

"Ssh, it's fine. It's okay. Everything is just fine, I promise." My words were directed more to me than him. With a grimace, he rose back up.

"Mohana." His whisper had already reduced my world to ashes, but what he said next blew those ashes away as if they were nothing. Three little words that crumbled everything, that are still etched in my memory and probably will be until the end of my days. "I'm so tired. Mohana, I'm so tired."

Chapter 37

After a while his nose started bleeding too, and it wouldn't stop. It was as if his body wanted to drain him of all blood.

I led him back to his hospital bed where we sat in companionable silence. Companionable, not comfortable.

He wasn't stupid. He knew something was wrong, but he didn't ask what. Good thing too. I don't think my response would have been all too good if he had. So we just sat there, fingers intertwined. A creak from the door interrupted us, uneven footsteps slowly entered. Melody met my eyes, and I met hers back. A silent understanding passed between us. She knew what I knew and I knew what she knew.

"And what happened to you?" Johnny cut our silent conversation by eyeing his mom's pants. I squinted. Was it Hot Cheetos Powder? The red stuff definitely looked like it.

"I raided the vending machine," she said simply, as if it answered all our questions. She sat down in a chair on the other side of the bed and slowly caressed the palm of the hand I wasn't holding. "You," she muttered, running her fingers through his hair, "look just like your father, you know? Exactly like him." If Johnny had a slight doubt about what was to happen to him, it was probably cleared up by now. Melody didn't even try to hide it. I don't think she could even if she wanted to. She looked up at me and we silently agreed. She unplugged the thing on his finger, which was the only thing that attached him to the machines now. Everything else was already taken out of him.

"Where are we going?" he asked as we both grabbed an arm and hoisted him up. Frail, that summed him up. All of his muscles that he had built up with years of basketball didn't seem to be working at all. It tore my heart more than it was already torn.

"Johnny?" I widened my stance so I wouldn't fall as he leaned against me. He'd changed out of the hospital gown now and was in a red sweatshirt. It was the same one he wore when we were at the theater.

"I have an idea. You wanna go on an adventure?"

* * *

Too beautiful, the stars were too beautiful that night. The sun had already left as we had staggered up the steps to the roof. It was a cruel imitation of that night at the theater. Except for the fact that I was the one holding him this time.

"Is my dear Mother not coming?" His legs gave a dangerous wobble, but regained strength before he would have collapsed on top of me.

"No, she, uhm, she had to make a phone call." A phone call to all of his relatives to explain why he wouldn't be coming to this year's Thanksgiving dinner. We stood there, side by side, gazing up at the stars.

"Mo, why do you do it?" Johnny broke our silence. I was grateful. The silence had begun to be unbearable.

"Do what?"

"Sing? I know you like it and all that but there's more to it than that, isn't there?" Leave it to Johnny to know me more than I knew myself. "You're absolutely right. Ever since I was little, no one really paid attention to me. I was always the shy kid, the one in the corner that no one knew the name of," I rambled, " but one thing was always different with me than other shy kids. I ached to prove myself. I hated it that no one knew my name, that I was always in the shadows. That was around the time my parents signed me up with my music teacher and I dived into Carnatic, and it was great. Why? For once I didn't feel like a disappointment. I was never as good at school as my famous and perfect doctor parents. People always looked at me weird when I told them who my parents were. But one thing my parents can't do is sing. Then I met Jamie and the ache to prove myself and the whole 'I'm-not-a-disappointment-when-I-sing' thing combined and you know the rest."

I looked both ways, oh yes! There was a bench to my right. I slowly walked Johnny to it. His legs worked less and less effectively as we hobbled on. We both sank onto the bench, exhausted. I looked up at his face. I've never seen him out of breath, ever.

"K-Keep talking."

"About what?"

"Anything just, just don't let my mind start thinking." He pinched his own leg, hard. "Completely numb," he whispered. He broke me once again. I yanked down on his collar and claimed his mouth before he couldn't move his tongue anymore.

"Distracting enough for you?" I whispered against his lips. He kissed me again, his lips perfectly melting to match mine.

"Exceeding expectations as always Prasad," he whispered, and rested his forehead against mine. How long we stayed like that? I don't remember. It was just him, me, and the way-too-pretty stars. "Mo?" He interrupted the silence again and moved so the side of his head rested against mine. So the corners of our lips touched. "I just wanna hear it. I-I'm not gonna last long am I?" How he managed to keep voice cool and steady even now? Again, I don't know. "And remember," he took my pinkie with his own, "no secrets." I choked out a silent sob, hoping he didn't notice. I was just glad I couldn't see his face. He took my silence for an answer. "Huh, that's good in a way. I don't have to take my ACTs."

He was joking, at a time like this.

He leaned against me casually, as if he meant to do it, but I could tell. I could tell he was starting to lose control of his body. "And to th-thi to th—" I silenced his failing tongue with a finger on his lips.

His body was losing the war.

"Stay with me." My grip on his arm tightened. Not yet, I thought to myself, just not yet. Just a little longer.

"A white picket fence," I muttered as I snuggled closer against him. "A white picket fence surrounding a modest, not-to-big-or-small house. A beautiful house in a lovely neighborhood with a flower garden in front that I tend to.

I'm a Pediatrician, just like my father. I come home a little early that day to bake a big pecan pie, your favorite. Laden with shopping bags, I step in and start baking with my handy-dandy cookbook, putting every ingredient in, knowing it would enter your mouth so it had to be amazing.

As I make the crust I get a little something on my ring, *the ring*. I brush off the flour tenderly.

You come home an hour or so later, sweaty and tired from basketball or baseball or whatever you are playing then. The sweet smell greets you as soon as you enter the door. I rush forward, give you a little hug and ask about your day.

And, you tell me.

I take out the pie and only give you a little bit before you have to go and wash up. But before you do, I give you a hug and breathe in your scent, your perfect scent that's familiar and safe. I lean forward and say, 'Happy first anniversary, Johnny Taylor,' and you say, 'Happy first anniversary, Mohana Taylor.'"

Somewhere through that I'd started crying. I wiped my eyes with the back of my hand. "How does that sound, huh, do you like that?" I asked, trying to keep my voice under control. I had to stay strong, for him, I had to stay strong.

"P-phf—" It took him a couple tries, but he finally got it. "Perfect."

"We just have to get there Johnny, just stay with me, please?" He grunted in response and grabbed my hand with his. Being the poet he was, he had a pen in his pocket. I let him scribble on my hand. I closed my eyes and prayed. Prayed and prayed.

But my prayers weren't answered.

If you've never seen someone die before, it's certainly not like in the movies. There's no dramatic fall, or a gasp before they leave.

They just do.

And when you realize it, it's already over. That was how it was. One moment he was there, the next moment he was sagging into me a bit more forcefully. I gripped his hand to confirm. It didn't grip me back. That's when my hand caught my eye. It was laden with a message, his last message. The tears and the strangled sobs I had managed to save roared out as I deciphered his messy last thoughts.

"*All our occasions, when you looked so fair, are our only pictures, my dear.*"

Biting my lip, I looked up at his face that was resting on my shoulder. At his perfect, beautiful face that will now haunt me forever. Those blushed cheeks, those red lips, those glassy eyes that reflected the stars' light above us, all the light he couldn't see. I stared at the face of the first boy I loved, the boy that ripped and mauled me up for good. I stared at the prone face of Johnny Taylor.

Chapter 38

"But it was all you wanted, wasn't it Mohana?" Wendy questioned me.

"All I wanted?" My reply was dangerously low. I didn't even know if she heard, "All I wanted was to stay with the boy I loved but was that too much to ask? All I wanted was to do the thing I liked to do, but do you know where it has led me? Huh?" I was pretty sure she could hear me now, so could the whole hospital. "I'm sitting in a hospital with a blanket wrapped around my shoulders, throat hoarse from crying over the dead body of a boy that I'm pretty sure died because of me. And you want me to attend an awards show in bloody Hollywood? Because what was it? Because it was all I wanted? Trust me Wendy, it definitely isn't, it definitely isn't anymore." I started crying again. At this rate I wondered how there was still fluid left in me.

"Mohana—" Wendy was silent for a while, "Mohana, especially now, you-you need something to distract yourself. It's not healthy, I-I'm not saying it for my gain either. Don't let him die in vain. Do what you love." I shut my mouth, which was going to send her another string of abuse, and sighed.

"Even if I wanted to, I can't. My mom doesn't want me being there. How am I supposed to get to Cali?"

"I wonder, a sixteen-year-old girl on a plane. Never heard

of a phenomenon like that. End of discussion, you're coming to Cali."

"Wait, no. I'm not—" She cut me off, and I was too tired to call back. A glint caught my eye as I lowered my hand that was laden with my phone. The ring Johnny gave me. I twisted it to see the words,

"True Love Waits." That unexplainable pain ripped through me again.

"Uhm, Miss?" I looked up to see the tentative secretary. "I-I believe they're for you." She pointed out the big glass doors to a mob I hadn't seen yet.

Leave it to the paps to know where you are even if you hadn't told anyone. But I guess it was part of the job description. With a nod of thanks at the secretary I hobbled over to the door, and they pounced in their own unique way. They all quieted and a more professional looking man spoke up. "Miss Prasad, may we know what it is you are doing at a hospital at this hour?"

"Me?" I cleared my hoarse throat. "Someone close to me was recently hospitalized and now—" I teared up but I couldn't get it out.

"Would this perhaps be the boy whose jacket you were wearing at the Raul Concert?"

"Yes, he is." *Was* I mentally corrected myself.

"The son of your former vocal coach?"

"Yes."

"The one you were dating?" I hesitated. I thought of saying yes for just a second, but no. I couldn't, I couldn't ruin Ajay's reputation like that.

"No, he and I were just very close." *Very, very close, but he slipped from my grasp.* They all nodded their disbelieving nod. I couldn't care less.

"Changing topics here, what are your plans for Citizen's Choice? Have you figured out your attire?" I gave the lady next to the man an incredulous look. Had they no heart? Of course not. They probably ran on bottles of celeb tears.

"I haven't thought of it."

"Why not?"

Strangulation is against the law. Strangulation is against the law. Strangulation is against the law. Strangulation is against the law!

"I've been *preoccupied.*"

"So you are definitely going? There was a bit of confusion for the past few weeks with you quitting music."

"Again, preoccupied. I haven't thought of it." *Get the hint lady.*

"Y'all better clear out now!" The security guard had arrived! I gratefully turned toward him. There was only one, strange! They usually came in trios or quartets. "I mean it, my boss will be severely displeased if y'all stay without his say-so."

The paps didn't want any trouble, so they cleared out. As they filed out of the hospital lobby, I squinted to read the swirly letters on the guard's uniform and smiled.

"'Madame Tilks Shoppe for the Actor. Schools rent out stuff for musicals and such all the time from there. And I gotta say Madame Tilk has grown quite fond of me so I get stuff for free, beats getting ogled at by a forty-year-old any day." *It couldn't be.*

"So you're as good as they say then. You even got the whole Minnesotan accent down and everything." Ajay gave a bow.

"Happy to please." He straightened back up and raised his arms toward me. Without a second thought I walked two strides and was engulfed by his soft touch with my head buried in his neck. It was a world different from Johnny's embrace, which was more tight and demanding. As if he said *'I need you.'*

Ajay's hug was more *'True, I need you, but you need me too.'* I could use that word to describe both of them perfectly, different. While Johnny possesed, Ajay held. While I was burned by the intensity, curiosity and the fire of Johnny's eyes, I drowned in the deep, cool, calculating eyes of Ajay. But never once did I have to choose which one was better. Contrary to popular belief, there was never a choice to be made. Ajay was amazing, which was certainly true. You couldn't guess how close one grows to another when one's faking a relationship. But he couldn't even be equal to a millimeter of Johnny. He was-*is* what I need, and I was what he needed. "Due to the fact I was your faker, I believe I have perfect liberty to say you look absolutely dreadful."

"Thanks for letting me know," I dryly remarked.

"Madame Tilk would be displeased. She once made me wear blush, bah! Apparently it complimented my cheekbones."

"She's not wrong," He softly broke the hug and led me back indoors where we sat in a secluded section in the lobby. His tilted head and deep eyes staring into my bruised soul.

"When did it happen?"

"You can say it out loud. It's not gonna revive him or anything. Johnny died like two hours ago." Sooner I got used to the fact, the better.

"The coma?"

"About a week ago, Meningitis." He took his eyes off me and I felt like a fish thrown back into the water. He stretched out in his chair with his hands in his pockets, his eyes mapping out what to say next.

"It-it gets better. It definitely does. Life seeps back in a little," he muttered softly. It brought a smile to my face.

"How do—" I stopped when I saw his eyes flash. I mentally slapped myself.

"Oh, I know, trust me I know." I wisely kept my mouth shut. He kept his eyes fixed on a spot just above the door. "Marianne, remember her?"

"Your girlfriend from Quebec? Yeah."

"I-we-you see, I lied. I saw that you didn't want me to know about Johnny so I thought if I told you it would make you feel better. Anyway, the day she asked me out we went on a drive. I'd just gotten my license and I was speeding, and I was an idiot Mohana. I took my eyes off the road for one second and the next thing I know we flipped." He raised the sleeve of his right arm and turned it to show me a white scar on his underarm extending from his wrist to his elbow. "I woke to see her bloody face, Mohana, laying next to me in my upturned car. She was very much dead. That was the real reason I moved here, it was after that I attended that interview and the rest followed suit." I reached out for his hands.

"You didn't have to tell me that."

"Oh but I did." He sat back up and was now turned to face me. "And I'll let you know it definitely gets easier, especially if you have someone who supports you." He put his warm thumb on the corner of my lips, inviting me to lean in to him.

Whoa there buddy.

"Thanks Ajay, really." I took his hand off my cheek and gave a squeeze. "I gotta go check on Melody, and my parents told me to be back like fifteen minutes ago." I gave a smile and turned on my heels to walk out. I never felt his eyes leave the back of my head.

Chapter 39

"*You have to.*"

No I don't. I could just sit and pretend to watch the clouds but really just wallow in self pity.

"*But you're Mohana Prasad, a writer! This is what you do on a daily basis!*"

But I was also considered a rising and happy celebrity, which I definitely am not now.

"*For Johnny, do it for Johnny.*" I cursed the voice in my head and looked back down at the empty notepad. Like everyday I went through the process. Number one: how was I feeling? Number two: what words could be used to describe that? And number three: what rhymes with those words?

But what if you didn't feel anything? What if you couldn't even get past the first step? I let my pen clatter to the floor with a heavy sigh. A shout came from outside the window. Ria's friends were playing with a jump-rope as if everything was okay. In the window diagonal to mine, I could hear Morni playing her flute, as if everything was okay. The lady on our right was cleaning out her garage, as if everything was okay, when it wasn't. Nothing was okay. Johnny's *gone*, never to be seen again. I was wordless for the second time in my life and I didn't know if I could recover from this one.

"Mohana?" My mom entered with a knock. She held a black dress on a hanger. "All washed and ironed."

"When is it?"

"Melody couldn't get a spot at the Funeral Home until this Friday night." The night of the Citizen's Choice.

"You just kinda have to decide which is more important, the thing you're giving up or the thing you want to do." Johnny's question, friends/family or fame? And I thought I even had a choice.

"You still do," a quiet voice in my head whispered. I killed it immediately.

"Well, I'll leave you and your words then." My mom hung the dress on the handle of my closet and left with a purse of her lips. A buzz came from my notepad, my phone, Brianna, the dress. The dress for the Citizen's Choice. I opened the text reluctantly.

"There, look at that. Isn't that just stunning?" The little voice still hadn't died. It was right though. The top was a shimmery gold and off the shoulder. At about the midriff a beautiful, rich, velvety maroon fabric flew to the ground. Simple yet elegant, vintage yet modern and trendy. Wind from the open window made something click in my room. I looked up to see the hanger, still laden with my funeral dress, hitting the closet door.

"Classic, two dresses." The voice in my mind rolled its eyes.

What was I? A book character in some cheesy novel?

Recently, it seemed more and more like it. I couldn't take it anymore. With a heavy thud, I jumped off my window ledge, grabbing my notepad and pen off the floor. My legs weak from lack of use, I hobbled downstairs and let the front door slam behind me. I grabbed my bike.

The true first time I wrote poetry was in the woods behind our house. It was a beautiful place where sun filtered through the trees and birds chirped happily, and maybe I'd taken Johnny there a few times, but it was my place, unique just for me. I pedaled through the flowers and stopped in front of my favorite rock. When I was younger I'd named her Jessica. She was my best friend with a happy personality as bright as a rock could be.

"Jessica, best friend! How are you?" I muttered, pressing my forehead into her. I probably looked nuts. Did I care? Nope! "I couldn't bring Johnny today, I'm sorry. He did have a fascination with you, I know. But I don't think he can make it anymore." I looked farther down, where she was a bit weaker because of all the erosion. Where dozens of initials were engraved into her,

"YS+SM, GP+WC, SV+ER." The newest one being, "JT+MP."

"Oh no, am I hurting her?" Johnny finished writing my initials with his stick and threw it back into the mud. The faint smile that had appeared when I introduced him to Jessica still hadn't left.

"Jessica's eternal. She doesn't need mere mortal feelings." I stepped behind him to inspect our initials. I picked up the stick again and added a line underneath. There, final. Well, until it eroded away. It didn't matter. Even if his initials disappeared, he'd still be here.

How utterly wrong I was.

"No, she's not eternal. She's gonna erode and turn into sand one day." Johnny stood up, brushing his legs.

"That doesn't mean she disappears. She's still there, just in a different form." Like my love for you. It would always be there, eternal. I didn't dare say it out loud. I kept it in my head. Maybe I could use it for a song later. I climbed up onto her, still thinking about words that rhyme with 'eternal' when I felt a gasp escape me. Johnny had climbed up behind me, and I was now pressed into his muscular front. He rested his chin on my head, occasionally shifting it into another position to take in another part of the woods. And just like that we became one with the eternal woods, my eternal Jessica, that was the key word to describe that evening, that was what we were supposed to be, we were supposed to be.

"Eternal, we were supposed to be eternal Jessica."

"Uhm, Ms. Prasad?"

"Yes?" I snapped looking back. Who would dare to interrupt my conversation with Jessica? A flabbergasted older-looking couple looking as if they were on a walk, that's who.

"O-Our daughter is quite a fan of yours and I was wondering if I could get an autograph. Well, if you're not too busy that is." The lady added with a look at Jessica. With a quick signature on a clean piece of paper from the notepad, I sent them off. The birds chirped in the sudden absence of noise. That was my first poem. It was about the music birds made. I still had it somewhere. Even though there were grammar and spelling mistakes, it was still important. Just like this was my space, writing was my thing.

"*And it always will be.*" The notepad, still clutched in my hand, called out to me. I stared down at it. The war didn't last long, it won. I pressed the notepad to Jessica and raised the pen. I let the cogs in my brain spin for a minute and wrote on, stopping occasionally to scratch something out.

"You really are lucky, huh Jessica? Now what would rhyme with 'past' and mean something along the lines of being lonely?" Now, I wasn't one of those cheaters who used the Internet. My lyrics were one-hundred percent genuine and were delivered straight from the heart. Except for that one time in ninth grade, but hey, I had pneumonia. What's your excuse? A bug landed on the notepad where there was supposed to be a title. I still didn't have one. Another bug landed on my work. I brushed it away. It was that time in the evening. Before I could be ambushed by the army of the little devils, I packed up my notes and waved a final wave to Jessica.

I felt it immediately, as soon as Jessica had disappeared from my sight. It had come back. The weight, the stress on my heart. If felt heavier now since it had left for just a little longer. My foot slipped off the pedal. I never was going to escape this was I? I could postpone the pain for just a little bit by writing, and I guess that's exactly what I was going to do. It popped into my head at that exact moment. I knew what I was going to title it.

"*Now what would rhyme with 'past' and mean something along the lines of being lonely?*"

"Outcast." I braked, hard, scaring some children. "Ha! Outcast!"

Chapter 40

"*And now you're part of my past, you've left me an, an outcast.*" Four sets of eyes turned to me, none of them blinking. The fifth set kept their eyes on the road, since they belonged to my Mom and she really didn't want to pay to fix a crushed car.

"*That was Mohana Prasad's* Outcast. *The song has recently caught fire online as an Internet sensation!*" An explosion covered up the sound of the radio. No, not the explosion that included fire and mass destruction, although it was just as effective.

"On the radio!"

"Not just that. It's on SVKF, the most heard station in the Twin Cities!"

"During commercial free hour. Meaning—"

"Thousands and thousands of people will have heard it. Shush!" Shruthi was sitting in front, she motioned to the radio.

"*—boosting her chances for Uprising Celeb at the Citizen's Choice that is indeed this Friday. She might even have a chance now of beating Jamie West, the awards favorite. Reminder that the polls are indeed open and first ten voters get a free—*" My mom's eyes drilled into my soul from the rearview mirror.

"Here we are girls. Have fun! Mohana, just one second. Help me get something out of the car." My friends walked into the mall happily, unaware of the storm brewing.

I followed my mom to the back of the car with my head down. "This goes against our agreement, doesn't it?" she muttered at me. I looked up in surprise. She looked more worried than mad.

"You said writing was fine."

"On the radio, though? They probably asked permission first."

"Well, they asked Wendy," I muttered as she pulled open the back trunk door to cover us from view and faced me, putting mere centimeters before our faces. But before she could speak, I butted in. "Mom, it's the radio! It's such a big opp——"

"So you're not going to the award show?" She cut right to the chase, her eyes pleading.

"I—"

"Mohana, look at what it has cost." She held up my nearly-healed fingers. "I just don't want you to get hurt anymore. Please, just attend your friend's, Johnny's funeral. We can live like it was in the past, the good old times," she huffed. How could I explain to her that it would never be like the 'good old times' if you could call them that? After all that I'd experienced, how could I just sit at home and submit my songs when my managers asked like a good little girl? How could I just go about, avoiding Jamie when I was just a hair away from beating her? How could I just be Mohana Prasad, the dumbest girl in her friend group, the one who could never be considered an equal to her friends? I couldn't explain that to her so I just nodded, took the guitar out of the trunk, and left for my friends.

"So, we were thinking. Since it's the first time your music got played on the radio, you buy us ice cream as a treat?" I dismissed Shaina's idea with a wave of my hand.

"I'm busy, now help me set up."

"What's the magic word?"

"Now." We got ourselves a cozy corner in the mall, and I got out a big banner.

"Let us help, you are not alone." The only reason my Mom let me do this was because it was for such a good cause. I jumped up onto a bench as a crowd began to form.

"Depression. It's a word that send chills down your body, doesn't it? As someone who has just come out of it, I promise one thing. It's definitely not incurable. Every penny donated helps, so please do." The crowd cheered. I frowned. I wrote the speech in the car on the way here. I wasn't expecting all that big of a response.

"Mohana is right. Truly every penny does help." A voice made me turn around. Of course, Ajay with his big entrances. He walked forward and extended a hand that I used to jump back down. As always, perfect timing.

"Thank you for coming," I said, solemnly.

"Of course. Mohana I—" *Nope*, pretending I couldn't hear him over the crowd, I whirled around for my guitar. Yes, I had been ignoring him recently. Yes, I didn't open his texts. Yes, it might have been because he painfully reminded me of someone else who'd held my heart. Finally yes, I did know it was a vile thing to do, but I didn't have any choice.

His eyes caught me from the bench he was sitting on. He was just brimming with questions, but polite enough not to ask.

Just as I predicted, we filled up the box he was handling in about ten minutes. I smiled as the song ended. Ajay and his six-pack, reliable since 2002.

"What are you wearing to Citizen's Choice?" Ajay had sneaked up behind me.

"What's it to you? I'm probably not going anyway." I took the donation box from him with a nod of gratitude.

"Not going to Citizen's Choice? Why, got a tea party with your friends that's too important?" He chuckled. "I worked for two years to go walk that red carpet. And, you, got it in like six months. You can't just skip it!"

"My Mom—"

"—Doesn't want you to get hurt. Maybe she doesn't realize the thing that caused the pain is your only way of bliss? Look, you're smiling. When was the last time you smiled?" His eyes bore into me. The last smile was a fake one, the one made to cover all the sadness and fear inside me. Last time I smiled was on the night Johnny died. "Besides, first reason Mr. Nelson hired me to be your faker was so we could go to Citizen's Choice together. Come on, don't make me feel guilty of accepting all those paychecks for nothing," he added in a lighter tone.

"Give me some time."

"So you could avoid me again? No, I don't think so." He raised his hand as if to brush my cheek, but then torturously pulled his hand back to lace it in his hair. "For me. Go for me," he added so low it barely reached my ears. My mouth opened and before I knew it, I had said the word he wanted to hear. "Yes."

"Huh?"

"Yes, fine. I'll go to the Citizen's Choice. Only for you though." I frowned. There was something wrong with that sentence. "Wait, stop, Ajay! Why are you so invested in me going anyway?"

"I just wanna see you happy, Mo. I am your 'boyfriend' after all." He smiled his content little smile.

"*Were.* You *were* my boyfriend. We're old news now, aren't we? Mr. Nelson didn't even have to stage a breakup. " Did I imagine it, or did his face loose a little color? That's always a problem with brown people. You don't ever know if they're blushing or pale or just fine.

"Okay, so Wednesday evening, 5:30 to be exact, we're leaving for Citizen's Choice. I will pick you up from your house."

"Ajay, I—"

"You think too much. Stop doing that. It's so much more fun when you just do things and don't think about them so much."

"I-I've never traveled alone without my parents. Hell, I've never even packed by myself. My Mom always helped!" What was I doing? I couldn't. I'd never-oh. His hand gripped my shoulder. Anyone passing probably thought it was friendly, but only I could tell it was something else, something else entirely.

"On what circumstances do you think I'm leaving you alone? People on airplanes are sketchy."

"Why are you using a public plane? Don't you have a private jet and like eighty servants bringing you virgin margaritas?"

"I do, but the jet broke down, so first class shall suffice." Suddenly serious, he turned and faced me with his deep eyes. "For every thing you try, you miss out on something else. For example, I get a private jet and cases of virgin margaritas, but then I miss my hometown and all my relatives." I exhaled sharply. Johnny Taylor never left me, did he?

"You have to give up something for anything you do really. For basketball I give up my free time. You just kinda have to decide which is more important, the thing you're giving up or the thing you want to do."

"I'm taking your silence for an answer. Wednesday, 5:30, be ready."

"Ajay—"

"Shush, just trust me. I'll keep you safe, always."

Chapter 41

How I managed to survive an entire day and a half was a mystery to me. With the looming threat inching closer and closer by every clock-tick.

"Mom, Ajay's gonna pick me up in a while. Shruthi and Neela wanted to meet him so we're going to Starbucks with Ajay's two bodyguards."

"Okay."

I kept my suitcase under the bed, but I was pretty sure I was forgetting something, making me go back and check it at every spare minute I got. Finally the time had come, 3:15. Like clockwork, Ajay was waiting outside in his little red car. I'd already hid the suitcase in the bushes. With about enough scratches to lose quite a lot of blood, the suitcase was loaded and we were driving down the highway.

"Your Mom's a doctor, she'll understand. Anyone who is anyone, really, would understand. There's always one choice you will make that will determine everything. And I believe you just made it." Ajay was actually going the speed limit rather than his normal ten miles below. I guess he was feeling the excitement too.

"I didn't make the decision. You did."

"Yeah? Why'd you follow through with it then?" He stumped me there so I shut up and continued working on my text to my family. How are you supposed to explain to your Indian parents that you left them, with a boy, and you're going to be on a plane together for approximately three whole hours?

When we arrived at the airport, Ajay parked the car, then with the kind of strength that I didn't expect his pampered self to have, he hauled me and both of our bags inside with surprising speed. "They're never on time, never. And we can't afford to miss this flight. We gotta do this on our own."

"Huh?" To help matters, it was raining without mercy. I hung onto the umbrella like it was a Grammy.

"My bodyguards, we're not waiting for them. Come." With our bags in tow, he set off at a brisk pace to the entrance. Jogging, I tried to keep up.

"I-*huf*-am not a-*huf*-little girl. Give me my suitcase." He looked kinda surprised. As if observing a science experiment, he gave me the suitcase with his head tilted in. Distracted, I didn't notice the little bump on the floor of the entrance. The wheel caught, and with a heavy *thud* I was suddenly sideways on the floor. I looked up to see Ajay open his mouth. He shut it after the glare I gave him. Without accepting his hand, I clambered up myself, and grabbed my little purple suitcase.

That's when I noticed it. Something was wrong. It wasn't something, it was an absence, an absence of noise. The whole gloomy airport had its eyes on us, well on Ajay. But hey, I was still working on it.

"Eyes down, keep walking. Before sense hits them, go!" He walked as fast as you could without running. I saw what he meant once we got to security.

The worst part of dealing with an airport is going through security. Grumpy old men and strict women in tight buns shouting at you to go faster. Not my type of fun. It angered them even more that Ajay brought with him a whole mob of people, who had finally come out of their paralysis and were swarming us.

"*Merde*, Americans are vicious." He pulled me out of the crowd and shoved me into the metal detector. He jumped in after me, barely missing the pointy pens and papers. It got better, kinda, after Ajay's bodyguards arrived. All of them were wearing identical tight black shirts that showed all their muscles. They all had the same intimidating stare. They kept the people at bay. So the mob started assaulting us verbally instead of physically. And wow, question after question. So many questions! My head was buzzing as the security guards pushed us out of security, happy for us to be gone.

"Jason, that's about the fourth—" The bulkiest looking security guard interrupted him by leaning and whispering something into Ajay's ear. The rest glared at me as if I would suddenly sprout out a knife and stab their precious celebrity. "No!" Ajay hissed. "Fix it, now!"

He even stomped his foot. And he accuses me of being a baby. He looked ready to throw himself on the ground and throw a complete tantrum.

"Sir, we can't."

"Then you're fired!" I tried to get closer to listen, but Ajay pushed me away. Pissed, I shoved back and stepped up to the guard, trying to look as brave as I could.

"What's wrong?"

"I can't—"

"What's wrong?" He looked helplessly over to Ajay who made a little 'harumph.'

"We have to ride in *economy* instead of first class. Apparently someone's more important than me. Horrendous, I'm suing the airlines."

"Is that all?" At that moment, I dawned on a realization. It changed everything, my entire view on the world. Ajay, without the muscles and the bodyguards, was just an overgrown, petty toddler.

"No, wrong. I'm Ajay Sai. I don't ride in economy like some caffeine-high, middle-aged man with a gut. I—" I grabbed his arm to shut him up and we made our way to the gate. When I turned around and looked over at him, his eyes were suddenly misty. Gone was the emotion. He tilted his head playfully and said, "How about you try?"

I shook my head and handed the lady at the gate our tickets. She smiled and scanned them, then we made our way through the gate. Once we had found our assigned seats, I collapsed in the window seat, my legs screaming for a break.

"I can't believe it. She didn't even say good evening. Like I don't matter." Ajay whimpered.

"Welcome to Economy," I muttered, still worn out from the adventure.

"And I swear that is a blood stain. What gory things happen here? Someone murdered over a twenty-dollar bill? " I yanked him down into the seat. "Just sit Ajay. Sit and be quiet." I heard a chuckle.

"Well, well, your majesty is tired? Perhaps your majesty should lean against me to rest his poor head?" His chuckle shut off when I actually followed through.

It wasn't long before I felt myself starting to relax. Right now, the only thing I needed was a comfy spot to fall asleep against, and Ajay's arm exceeded expectations. Just as I was about to drift off to sleep, he said, "What happened to my strong, independent girl?" His voice was a mere whisper. It was hoarse and weirdly comforting and *satisfying*? I felt a tingle of delicious pleasure fly down my spine.

"I'm very strong and independent. Just not when I'm tired and sore." I moved my head away from him to lean it against the back seat, but he didn't let me. I felt him move. I felt his arm snake up and around my shoulders. Grabbing me, he pulled me into him, creating a spot of warmth and comfort just for me. I obliged without thought, sliding sideways. It reminded me of another familiar chest. It made me draw closer, snuggling into his warm figure. His chest was oh-so warm. I felt him rest his hard chin on my head protectively and stare out the little window of the plane. It was in that position my eyes closed and my mind drifted off.

Chapter 42

*H*e looked even better in a tuxedo than I imagined. He offered me his elbow like we were in the Victorian Era. I took it without hesitation and we walked down the red carpet, camera flashes illuminating our happy smiles. A sudden shove took me by surprise. I regained balance and looked up at Ajay, but it wasn't him anymore. It was Johnny. I reached out for him but he smacked my hand away. He opened his mouth and his low voice gave me a feeling I realized I desperately needed. The words he said though, I didn't need: "Traitor."

I awoke with a start, but instead of the backs of the small cramped airplane seats greeting me, a smooth ceiling enfolded above. I sat up in the soft mattress, still clothed in the shirt and leggings I'd been wearing on the plane. The glass chandelier above me illuminated the rich red carpet and the mirror opposite me. I looked as disheveled as a girl who spent about an hour wandering around an airport. Regretful, I rose out of the comfy bed and went to open the lush curtains that kept the light out.

"Took you long enough." I jumped. I turned around to see the illuminating rays from the opened window hit Ajay, who was leaning against the frame of the door that connected our rooms. And, *oh*.

"*Look away right now. Mohana Devi Prasad take your filthy little eyes off that six-pack.*" He was dressed in sweats, *only* in sweats, leaving his top undeniably exposed. I could see those bulging muscles in his crossed arms. I could see that foretold six-pack in its full exposed glory.

"Like what you see?" Ajay even had the nerve to wink. Red faced, I hastily turned to stare out the window at the tall buildings and people in suits walking in a hurry.

"How'd you get me here?"

"You must have really been tired. You slept the entire ride and was still knocked out when we landed. I had Jason, my head security guard, carry you out." He was right, I was tired. For the first time in days, I'd actually fallen asleep without Johnny nightmares waking me up at night. But that wasn't on my mind right now."

"Your main security guard carried me in front of the entire crowd of LAX? Including the paps?" I turned to him, mortified. Ajay shrugged.

"You were out cold. I couldn't bring myself to wake you." He stepped up to me and we fell into silence, staring at the busy city. I found myself suddenly thinking about Johnny.

"*Everyone's too busy these days. Always running to drop their kids off or getting to work on time. If only the world would slow down, don't you think? If only the world would slow down there would be so many new relationships among people, more friendships. Don't you think, Mo?*" He turned his passionate eyes on me. "*Suicide rates would go down because people would be more aware of one another. So would depression rates and anxiety and—*" I silenced him with a finger on his lips.

"*Okay, okay we get it. That man should have said sorry when he bumped into you. Let's not get down to stats.*"

"*Aw, why not? I had a few charts and data at hand.*" His hot breath tickled my finger, I moved my hand to cup his chin.

"*Johnny Taylor,*" I muttered as I stared into his eyes. I could never, never get tired of those eyes. Those sparkling, curious, chocolate warm eyes that made you want to smile and laugh forever and forever. "*You are such a nerd.*"

"An abominably cute one, don't you agree?"

When I snapped out of it and returned to reality I said, "Ajay? Do you feel as if everyone's always in a hurry these days? Do you think they need to slow down?"

"Hm." He stroked his chin in silent contemplation. "No, in a growing world and a growing economy, if people slow down then they'll be behind. Our world would stop advancing. Speaking of that, we need to go. I need to get my tux and you need your dress."

I'd already texted Brianna. She had shipped the dress to the same big warehouse where Ajay's Armani Tuxedo was stored. When we got to the warehouse, we were led to a nice big room complete with a stage mirror and everything where we could try on our clothes for the awards ceremony.

Ajay and I emerged from our changing rooms at about the same time. "Oh look, we're matching," said Ajay. We stood together in front of the mirror. He straightened his red bow tie that matched the bottom half of my dress.

The dress fit like a glove. It reminded me of the blue, leather jacket I'd worn with Finn at Wainscott. Nostalgia hit me like a train. My first fitting in a warehouse full of Adidas clothing where I had to change in a weird smelling bathroom. Now, I was wearing a personal-made dress and standing next to Ajay Sai. And yet, I preferred it back then when I was surrounded by the people I liked and loved: Melody, my Mom, and Johnny.

"I have to go make a phone call," I muttered.

"No pictures of the dress though." Ajay let me through the door to the connecting corridor. I hadn't picked up my phone since we'd left the airport. There were no texts from my friends or family. Ouch! Next time someone gets lost in the mall, I'm not hunting for them.

"Hello? Mohana!" *What the heck? Why does she sound happy?*

"Mom? Hey—"

"How's California. Boiling?"

"Mom, I ran away from home," I tried to clarify. This wasn't what I was expecting, not at all.

"What do you mean, sweetheart? It doesn't count as running away if I already know about it. Ajay told me the entire situation and said you were just scared I wouldn't let you go. That is true, I probably wouldn't have, but man that boy is a debater."

"Wait, Ajay told you?"

"Oh yes, apparently you guys were on the plane and you were asleep?"

"And you weren't mad?"

"Oh no, I was seething. He said something about music soothing you, or something. But my doubts were cleared. If he can win an argument against me, the boy can survive the world. I'm glad you're with him."

"Oh not for long." He won't be with me much longer indeed.

"Wha—?" I cut on her. *Oh-ho-ho* he is dead. Sending me into a nervous frenzy by making me think I was betraying my mother, but telling her right from the start? My eyes fell on a needle set that was placed on top of a sewing machine that was left outside for repair.

"I don't like that glimmer in your eyes, not at all." He'd appeared, leaning on the doorframe of my dressing room. He'd listened to the whole conversation.

"You shouldn't. If I were you, I'd be damn terrified." My hand twitched toward the needles. Wanting to stab each one of them into some portion of his body. I wasn't really too fussy where. "Why?" I asked. There weren't any more words necessary.

"You didn't think I'd encourage rule breaking, did you? I was just curious."

"Just curious to see how far I'd go before cracking?"

"No, to see how far you'd go for music." Forget his face. My eyes fell on his suit.

"*Now, how much would that have cost?*" Ajay saw my eyes wander back to the needles and to his precious Armani suit. In two quick strides he had swiped them. "I'm going to keep these, and you try to keep your temper under control. You should be thanking me really you know."

"Know what?"

"Know why, why you're destined on this path, Mohana? Destined to be famous and walk red carpets every weekend? It's in your blood, and nothing can deter you. Even the death of your boyfriend."

Silence. He'd crossed the line.

"And is that supposed to be a good thing?" My anger was replaced with something else entirely. A feeling no word has been made for yet, at least none that I knew of.

"Yes actually. It shows that you were meant for this, and that isn't a bad thing. You will always remember him. Your heart will always have a place for him. It's just you'll be off doing other things. You don't have to quit your path because of him."

Ajay wasn't as tall as Johnny, but he was still tall enough to look down into my eyes. The difference being while Johnny's eyes made my insides catch on fire, Ajay's made me shiver. I didn't know which one I preferred. "I also wanted to know something else." In trying to get the needles, he was closer now. I tried to take a step back, but the other side of the corridor stopped me.

I was trapped.

Mustering all my strength, as if I was heading to battle, I met his cool gaze. In seconds I realized this battle already had a winner, and it wasn't me.

I'd surrendered a long time ago.

I found a hurricane, a storm of emotions in those dark eyes.

"I—" For just a second I forget entirely about Johnny. For a second he wasn't in the back on my head, nagging at me. For just a second I wanted to let go and just be a normal girl.

"I wanted to see how far you'd go with me." He put his arm on the wall next to me, letting the wall hold him. His breath tickled my face. So close. Johnny's face suddenly whipped in front of my eyes.

"*Traitor.*" The nightmare I had came back to me with full force. As Ajay lowered down to close the little gap between us, I ducked away leaving him to headbutt the wall.

"I-I should probably get the dress off. M-meet you at the entrance in five minutes."

Chapter 43

"Her highness won't even take a little bit?"

"No."

"Oh, come on! Look at how prettily garnished it is, magnificent. Don't you agree?"

"No."

"Okay, uhm, the décor—"

"No."

Ajay chuckled and ate a little more of his burger. "Well, someone's grumpy. Or is it nerves? Are you nervous?"

"No—" I hesitated, "Y-yes, very." So nervous I couldn't pick up my sandwich without it dismantling. "Jason? What's the time?" I asked the burly guy sitting next to Ajay.

It definitely was an experience, eating at a fast-food joint with Ajay Sai and his main bodyguard. Because according to Ajay, greasy food was the only thing that could stop your nervous heartbeat, literally too. The people around us definitely thought it was weird that a celebrity with a net worth of $6 million was eating a measly burger. They gaped at us with their mouths in a perfect 'o'. Ajay seemed used to it. He stretched out in his seat across from me, black leather jacket elegantly stretching with him. His legs brushed mine under our booth. He quickly moved them.

After our little episode in the corridor, he's been very cautious. He made sure not to touch me, locking himself in his room as soon as we came back. He didn't bring it up either for the whole of the day.

"3:28." The guard grunted at me, as if in the two seconds he would spend answering my question, someone could attack his precious boss.

"Perfect, we have to be back at our rooms by four, the makeup artists will meet us there, change and be ready 6:30, and get there around 7:15."

Ah 7:15, the time when I'll walk my first red carpet and pose next to the Ajay Sai. Tell me this a few months ago, and I would have smacked you. A whole shudder passed through my form. Ajay noticed, his eyes scrunching. I shuddered again, but this time it wasn't nerves.

"Okay, that's it." Ajay left his half-eaten burger and stood up suddenly. "Jason clean up and come, time to leave." He jerked his head to our trays. "There's a hot server and I don't want her mad at me." Jason picked up the trays and headed for the trash cans as if this was something he did everyday. How would I know? Ajay could literally tell him to rob a bank and Jason would have to comply.

"You're Ajay Sai. I don't think she's gonna get mad over throwing away your tray. I'm pretty sure she'd save your burger. Try to clone you with your saliva or something," I muttered.

"Clone? Is this what girls do in their free time? Try to clone celebrities?" He was still looking over at Jason, who was struggling through a group of teenagers.

"It's what I'd do if I got Peter's DNA." I smiled in happiness.

"I'll pass the message along when we see him tonight." Jason finally got to the trash cans and dumped everything out. "And now we go." Suddenly, I was jerked sideways by the arm and dragged out of the door.

"Ajay?" He dragged me a bit farther, and we stopped at the entrance to some fancy looking building. Men and women in professional clothing were entering and exiting busily, not noticing us. Out of breath, we both leaned against the cement wall of the building. "Wouldn't Jason get lost trying to find us?"

"No, he just kinda stays where I leave him, staring at people until they get too uncomfortable and leave."

"You've done this before?"

"'Coarse I have. Jason never wants me out of his sight and you my dear aren't the only one who has nerves."

"Oh, so the famous Ajay Sai, who doesn't ride in Economy, likes to sully his feet with road dust?"

"I was normal once too. I really didn't like it, filled with pain and regret. You don't have time for that here, no time for the past. You gotta keep rushing, keep practicing for that next audition or interview. " With a chuckle, he walked out into the middle of the sidewalk, getting annoyed glares and shoves from the people passing by. "Why am I so concerned with you?" He shouted over the noise of clicking heels and footsteps. "Because you remind me of myself, born for attention. But it gets to me too, the people. I like to come to places like this when it happens. Where the paps can't find me and no one notices me at all. They're a dime a dozen in big cities like Hollywood." He had his hands in his pockets, looking down as his shoes. "Makes me slow down, seeing others in a hurry. Makes me feel a little more normal and a bit insignificant. It's needed in everyone's life though. Being famous all the time isn't amazing for the soul." I saw what he meant. For once I didn't feel as if I needed to hide myself because the paps were watching. My brain finally clicked.

I didn't need to hide anything.

My eyes caught Ajay's lean figure, a figure I could get, just for me. I got off the wall I was leaning against and took a step toward him. I was torn with indecision. What would he do?

"He'd kiss you back, he wanted to yesterday. You saw," a voice in my head told me. *"Maybe he was just gonna butt heads with you. That's it, that makes more sense. You really have a big head, Mo, Ajay Sai wanting to kiss you? Psh!"* another voice argued.

"But you saw his eyes, those emotions. Those weren't fake."

"You already missed the funeral of the guy you loved for an awards ceremony. You are not gonna get even more selfish and hurt him more than you've already."

That point was strong enough to freeze me in my tracks. It always had been. This time though, there was another voice in the back of my head that spoke, a voice I never knew I had. My foot had other plans. Ajay saw my foot take another step towards him. He didn't look up to meet my eyes. He just staring at my—.

"No paps. Right now we're just normal teenagers," I said softly. He met my eyes swiftly.

"That's the theory," he whispered and looked up.

"I missed this Ajay, thank you." Another step, he was in touching distance now.

"My honor, your majesty, my queen." He gave a mock bow. Did my eyes deceive me or did he just make another step towards me? My heart beat like a drum against my rib cage, as if it wanted to rip out. The tension was thick, thick enough even oblivious me could sense it. His eyes analyzing, my eyes wanting. He suddenly cut off our eye contact by looking the other way.

"Mohana, the mystery I never could solve."

"Pardon?" I didn't like it, I wanted to scream, to yell, to shout *'look at me, look at me just one more time. I-I need you. I need you!'* My aggravated feet took two steps this time. Directly underneath that pristine sharp face of his.

"Clearly talented, ready to use your voice, yet you won't. Clearly kind and inviting, yet you shut me out. What is that you truly want Mohana?" Craning his neck, he looked down at me.

"What do I want?" *You, I want you.* "Does it matter?"

"Definitely, so I can help you get it."

"And why do you want to help little me?" I asked with a stupid grin on my face. What was wrong with me? I was *flirting?* Was this how you do it? Was I even doing it right? I was taking serious advantage of this whole normal-teenager moment, doing things I didn't do even when I wasn't famous. Putting a finger on his chest, I stared at those captivating eyes. He stared back at mine.

"To please your majesty, my queen of course." He was whispering again. Hoarse and gentle. Like waves.

"Well, then. Do you know what your majesty truly wants?" On my tippy toes, I whispered into his ear. "Her deepest desire? She wants—" Pausing for effect, I licked my lips and said, "You." And that was all he needed to hear. He dove down and our lips crashed like the sea on the shore.

Welcome to the Mohanaian Shore. It was a mix of need, want, and rich enjoyment.

As if he'd held back for a very long time.

I reached up and cupped his cheeks and he simply melted under my touch. Again, different. Different entirely. While Johnny's lips perfectly melted to match mine, Ajay's clashed with my lips. Imperfect, but he made it work with pure will and precision.

"Likewise, my queen," he muttered. "All I want is you."

Chapter 44

"*I'm a monster.*" That was the only thought that ran through my mind. Not that I was standing on my first ever red carpet, not that the whole country was watching my every move, not that this was the moment it all changed, it was just, "*I'm a monster.*" Over and over again on repeat. Hand on my hip, I gave them a smile as fake as Jamie in an interview. For inside I was sobbing, wracked with guilt.

It was something I'd never felt before, regret. I never had time for it. I lost a competition? Work harder and win next time. I won a trophy? Work harder and win a bigger one. But this? Regret, guilt, I absolutely hated it.

"*He could have done so much better before all this. When you were just some nerdy little girl hiding behind some fat book. Yet, he liked you. Not some blonde, pretty, tall, slim girl, you. And what did you do? You didn't even stay loyal to him for a whole two weeks!*" I felt my smile wave. I fixed it immediately. But that didn't stop my brain. Its thoughts just got louder.

"*Your thumb, look at your left thumb. See, that's his ring, his mother's ring, a ring that he gave you. I mean, how do you even get your mother's most prized possession without telling her why? But he did it for you, and you succumbed for a minute's wanting. He was so out of your league. You never deserved him!*"

"You alright? You look a bit flustered." Ajay was next to me in a heartbeat. I choked, but played it off as a dainty cough. "It takes some getting used to," he said, motioning with his head to the paps, "but it definitely gets better. First one is always the hardest one."

When I looked up at Ajay, the bright lights made his chocolate, hazel eyes glow. I could see his pupils dilate, and that was all it took for the guilt to withdraw for just a second. I hated myself for it.

"Time?" I asked in a mere whisper. He glanced down at his Rolex watch.

"7:30."

"That means I gotta go." With a bow of my head, I parted. The paps shouting their final questions.

When I wasn't kissing an actor with a net worth of $6 million yesterday, I was rehearsing. A partner and I were scheduled to perform second in the show. In other words, they wanted us out of the way so they could put the people's favorite celebs last so they'd stay. I walked into a dressing room in the back of the gigantic stage where there was my trusty guitar leaning on the wall and my other dress already placed on the chair with my sugar cubes on top. I popped a few into my mouth quickly. I zipped into the dress quick, but I guess it wasn't quick enough.

"Hurry up! I'm more famous and I finished before you!" The voice of my beloved stage partner was accompanied by a series of violent knocks. Grabbing my guitar with an eye-roll, I opened the door to a fuming Jamie. "If I get a pimple from the stress you've caused me, you better start running." Laden in the same dress as I, she whirled around and stalked off. I followed her with a smile, remembering the long nights in her recording studio bent over piles and piles of papers.

And now, we were gonna share a stage together.

"Ugh, disgusting," Jamie uttered to herself at the first pair performing.

"The Salinas Brothers? They've won two Grammy's," I reminded her, curious to see her reaction.

"Of course you'd think they're great. That's why I'm Uprising Celeb's favorite."

"*Used* to be." She turned to face me at my reminder. She raised her eyebrows.

"You think I'm gonna let my little writer beat me?" she hissed. "No, Mo. You can't just waltz in here and get an award in like six months. It takes patience, dedication, and raw sweat."

"Oh, but it's been done before," I whispered, taking a step forward. "*Talented* singers do it all the time. Singers who don't rely on their songwriters. Singers who stay loyal—"

"Really? Gonna talk about loyalty to me?" she chuckled. We were at the foot of the stairs that led to the top of the stage.

"Yes I am! It's not a normal thing, leaving your friend behind at the airport so you can perform at a big show and get spotted by an agent."

"I just did what I had to do." She's stepped close enough that I could smell her strong perfume. "No one would've heard me over that donkey's yell of yours. No one would've been able to see the little altercations, the minor and gentle fixations I make to the music over your blare. It was an opportunity I took."

"Are you even listening to yourself?" I stepped closer, my face in vehement disgust. "Took an opportunity? Janaki, I cried myself to sleep for months. No opportunity is worth that!"

"That's where you're wrong," she said, her eyes narrowed. "You know that I wouldn't give this up for anything. You know I wouldn't exchange this life even for fucking Peter Raul's. I *need* this Mo."

"At the cost of your loyalty, your dignity?" I searched deep within her eyes, looking for a small smidgeon of my Jamie. All I found was a cold emptiness, an icy desire. She giggled.

"Now, now, Mohana Prasad's talking to me about dignity! When she herself moved on from high school jock Johnny to pretty-boy Ajay in a heartbeat. Johnny was the popular one, talk of the whole school. You used him to go up the ladder and when he was too little you jumped right on to the next one." She looked content at my lack of speech. "You're just as bad as me." And with that, she whirled around. With a shaky breath, I followed her. Recovering quickly, I flashed a smile as bright as the sun as the lights hit me and the cameras turned to face us when in reality my eyes wanted to leak like a roof on a stormy day.

"Let me tell you all a story, a story to melt your stone hearts." I internally winced as she sang my lyrics. She finished her part and stepped back, making way for me. She gave me a glance.

"Give it all you got." And I did. I sang with the usual gusto, but my mind was far, far away. I ran off stage as soon as the song ended, Jamie's smile chasing me.

Where was it? I looked around, oh where was it hiding? Yes! There is was! The bathroom. Man as I ran into those horrible, but oh-so inviting stalls, I felt a part of me I never knew I missed rejoin me. It had been way too long since I'd cried in a horribly smelling bathroom. I snapped up from my hunched position, a pair of footsteps had joined me. Now who was dumb enough to spend the CCA's in a dirty bathroom?

"Psst, Mohana! Please tell me you're in here. The last few ladies in the bathrooms were kinda mean."

I unlocked the stall door. It couldn't be, but there he was in his full glory. He exhaled once he saw me. "Oh, good. If I'd heard one more scream I'm pretty sure something important would have shattered in my ear."

I had him by the scruff of the neck in no time; ramming him against the wall. I shook him as hard as I could.

"Don't you ever—listen to me, *ever*—leave me again!"

Chapter 45

"Finn! You can't just walk into a girl's—" Lavender froze in the doorframe once she saw me yelling a torrent of abuse at Finn. She stumbled as another figure burst into the bathroom.

"Mohana's in trouble, I—" Ajay stopped as well when he saw me still clutching Finn's collar.

"Oh no she's fine," Finn reassured him with a smile. "Maybe just a bit peachy." With another glare, I reluctantly let go of his collar.

"How'd you find me?" I directed the question at all of them.

"Well, I followed Finn. We're not as important as you so we sit in the back. Even then, he somehow knows you're in trouble." Lavender walked toward Finn and intertwined their hands. Finn's face flushed.

"Oh, I'm telepathic. I always know when you're in trouble and where you go." I raised my eyebrows at Ajay's answer. "Okay fine, West looked way too happy once she had taken her place and you still hadn't come back. I know the places to go on a stage for some peace and quiet. It took a lot of rooms but I found you eventually, and that's all that matters." Walking forward, he immersed me in a vice-like hug that numbed the pain. As if he knew it would numb the pain. A voice distracted us.

"How long?" Finn pointed at us, at our intertwined hands. I looked up and saw Ajay tilt his head as he thought for a bit.

"About three hours and fifty eight minutes."

"You?" I asked.

"About a month, Finn didn't want to tell anyone for a while. But that's not why we're here." It was Lavender who answered. "Why are you here, Mohana, crying in a bathroom during your first award show?"

"The question is why am I here at an awards show instead of at Johnny's funeral?" I broke apart from Ajay and crossed my arms. "It was the last time I could have seen him, and I missed it for something as stupid as a performance."

"Missed it for something as stupid as me?" Ajay looked, *hurt*. The strong, bold, Ajay Sai was capable of feelings? "Mo, he will live on in your heart forever, but he isn't coming back. I'm here though. To stay or to leave is your choice, but I love you." The last three words made me choke. "I wouldn't dare ask you to get over him, cause I know I'm still not over Marianne, but why won't you let me help you?" I held his gaze as I thought about it. What was I to do? The normal two voices in my head suddenly merged into one.

"You will always stay loyal to Johnny, always in your heart. Right now, though, how about you stay loyal to Ajay?" I nodded to myself and without a word walked over and hugged him. And that was all he needed. He, in turn, tried to squeeze the life out of me. Our moment was interrupted by someone else walking in to try to use the bathroom.

"I think she's in shock." Lavender remarked at the frozen girl whose eyes blinked rapidly at Ajay. He smiled and bowed his head politely.

"Hello there, this bathroom's currently occupied but I'm pretty sure the others are free." She smiled and nodded eagerly as if her whole life ambition was to be told where to use the bathroom by the legendary Ajay Sai. She dashed off.

"Unfair, they see a pretty face and they're under a spell. All I get is a scream and verbal abuse. You're not even that good," Finn scoffed at Ajay and kept muttering about girls and bathrooms.

"Pardon? I have a net worth of $6 million. How about you?" That shut Finn up. "And Mohana, it's time we were off. An uprising celeb is gonna be revealed in a bit." An idea suddenly came to me. I smiled and cracked the door a bit so we could hear everything.

"Everything started in a bathroom, so let's end it in a bathroom." I smiled. "Besides, it's never this easy. I mean, it never happens the way it's supposed to. At the Wainscott auditions, Wainscott itself, this whole path to fame is twisted and turned and ends up totally different. So I'm just gonna sit here, and see how this unfolds." I sat on the countertop next to Lavender.

"She always like this?" she asked Finn.

"Oh, she's normally worse. I think she's toning it down for pretty-boy." He tilted his head toward Ajay, who also took a seat next to me. "And if you hurt her, I'll hurt you." He directed it to Ajay. I snorted at Finn. Ajay just politely blinked and eyed his twig form.

"With the $6 million, I also have a six pack."

"So?"

"Just letting you know. Wouldn't want you to get hurt."

"*—and the nominees for this year's Uprising Celeb Awards are—*" We immediately quieted down. All flinching when we heard Jamie's and my name. As the person who was gonna announce the award walked up the stage. I quickly jumped off and started pacing. *Don't expect it, 'cause when you don't get it, it won't hurt as much.*

"*Aww, screw you!*" A voice in my head responded. Something was definitely wrong with the voices in my head.

"This year's Uprising Celeb is…"

BaBoom, baBoom. My heart was trying to jump right out of my ribcage.

"The very young but talented—"

BaBoom, baBoom. This was everything that I'd worked for. This was how I was to beat Jamie.

"Came to the top with raw talent and sheer will—"

"BaBoom, BaBoom." This was the end of the long and hard journey. I looked at everyone else, at all I'd gained. A better relationship with Finn Winston, a new friend in Lavender Sink, and Ajay Sai.

"And that person is—"

BaBoom, baBoom. True, I'd lost many things. I'd lost my three-year crush-but-really-obsession. I'd lost liberty and privacy, but I wouldn't do a thing different would I? I smiled. I'd never felt like this before.

BaBoom, baBoom. Life had always been a competition. I had to compete against all the other girls to get the Johnny Taylor, I was forced to compete against my friends to get better test scores because I was Indian, I had to compete against my friends for just something that was unique for me. But I've always had it, didn't I?

It was music, music will always be unique to me.

BaBoom, baBoom.

"The writer of the record breaking song, quickest to get on the Billboard chart, *Outcast* by Mohana Prasad."

Epilogue

Her face contorted, my Mom forced the last button of the petticoat of my half-saree into place. The same half-saree I wore on *the* day.

"I don't remember it being this tight."

"It wasn't. It means you're getting fat," my Mom responded with a smile and reached for her phone.

"Pictures? You're still taking pictures?" I asked with a smile.

"As long as you live under our roof we're taking pictures." My dad walked in with a big SLR camera. I sighed and posed, only to be shoved to the side by Ria.

"Oh and make sure you get this to me. I can get playground credit." She was growing strong enough to push me now. Grabbing her around the shoulders, I posed.

We made it two hours early as usual. My paranoid doctor parents always needed to be early, even though everything only started when they arrived. The Raga Carnatic competition hadn't changed a bit. The same organized chaos with little kids mouthing words into the microphones trying to be funny and devilish, and Auntys bragging about their kids. Everyone hushed as I entered the little auditorium. It made me smile. I took the exact same seat in the front row that Jamie had taken. I didn't have the bodyguards though. I looked to my right at the same old humongous guru. He looked even more sour than usual.

"Mohana, long time no see," a voice called out behind me.

"How about we keep it that way?"

"Hi, Shreya!" I stood up with a genuine fake smile that only working with the paps could bring. I glanced behind her where, without a doubt, there were popular girls standing. Even now, I was only a tool to her.

"I've listened to a few of your newer songs. I think they're all so amazing."

"Really? Which ones?"

"Uhm, all of them! Listen, I'm fourth in line to sing. You'll listen right?"

"'Of course." With that, she left me in peace and the first girl came up. She nervously glanced at the guru, me, and somewhere in the back. Curious, I peeked back, and there she was. In the exact same crisp, white blouse and with the exact same clipboard. Melody gave me a little nod and a smile. A smile so familiar to another I knew. I looked next to her. The spot was empty without restless Johnny and his basketball.

I occasionally visited his grave. I'd lean against it and read *Harry Potter*. Poor thing never got to finish it. I even occasionally took Ajay, who always knew where to get the best flowers. But this wasn't the time to mourn. I looked back up at the girl who finished her song. The guru picked up the mike and from what I could tell, it wasn't good news. So I flashed her a bright supportive smile and gave her a nod that said, *"Good Luck."*

"Dreadful, keep singing and you will become an outcast in your society," he said.

She inhaled sharply at the words and I saw her eyes water. But the guru couldn't have chosen better words. She looked at me ashamed. I gave her a wink and mouthed the words, *"But what's wrong with being an Outcast?"*

SIGMA'S BOOKSHELF

Sigma's Bookshelf (www.SigmasBookshelf.com) is an independent book publishing company that exclusively publishes the work of teenage authors, who are between the ages of 13 and 19. The company was founded in 2016 by Minnesota teenager Justin M. Anderson, whose first book, *Saving Stripes: A Kitty's Story*, was published when he was 14, and has since sold hundreds of copies.

"I know there are a lot of other teenagers out there who are good writers and deserve to have their work published, but don't have access to the kinds of resources I do. I wanted to help them," he said.

Sigma's Bookshelf is a sponsored project of Springboard for the Arts, a nonprofit arts service organization. Contributions on behalf of Sigma's Bookshelf may be made payable to Springboard for the Arts and are tax deductible to the extent permitted by law. Donations can be made online at www.SigmasBookshelf.com/donate.

CPSIA information can be obtained
at www.ICGtesting.com
Printed in the USA
LVHW041904300320
651613LV00005B/272